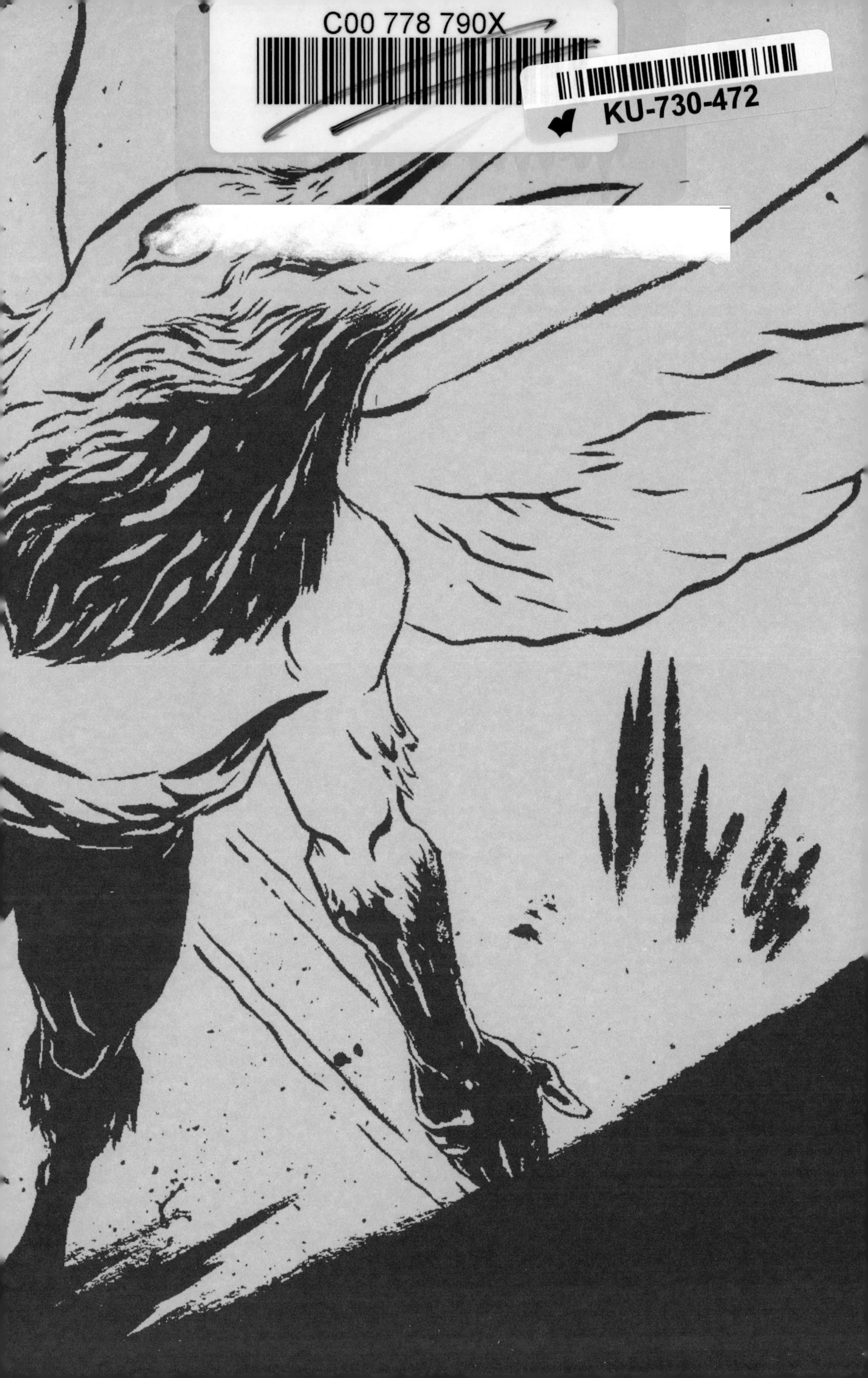

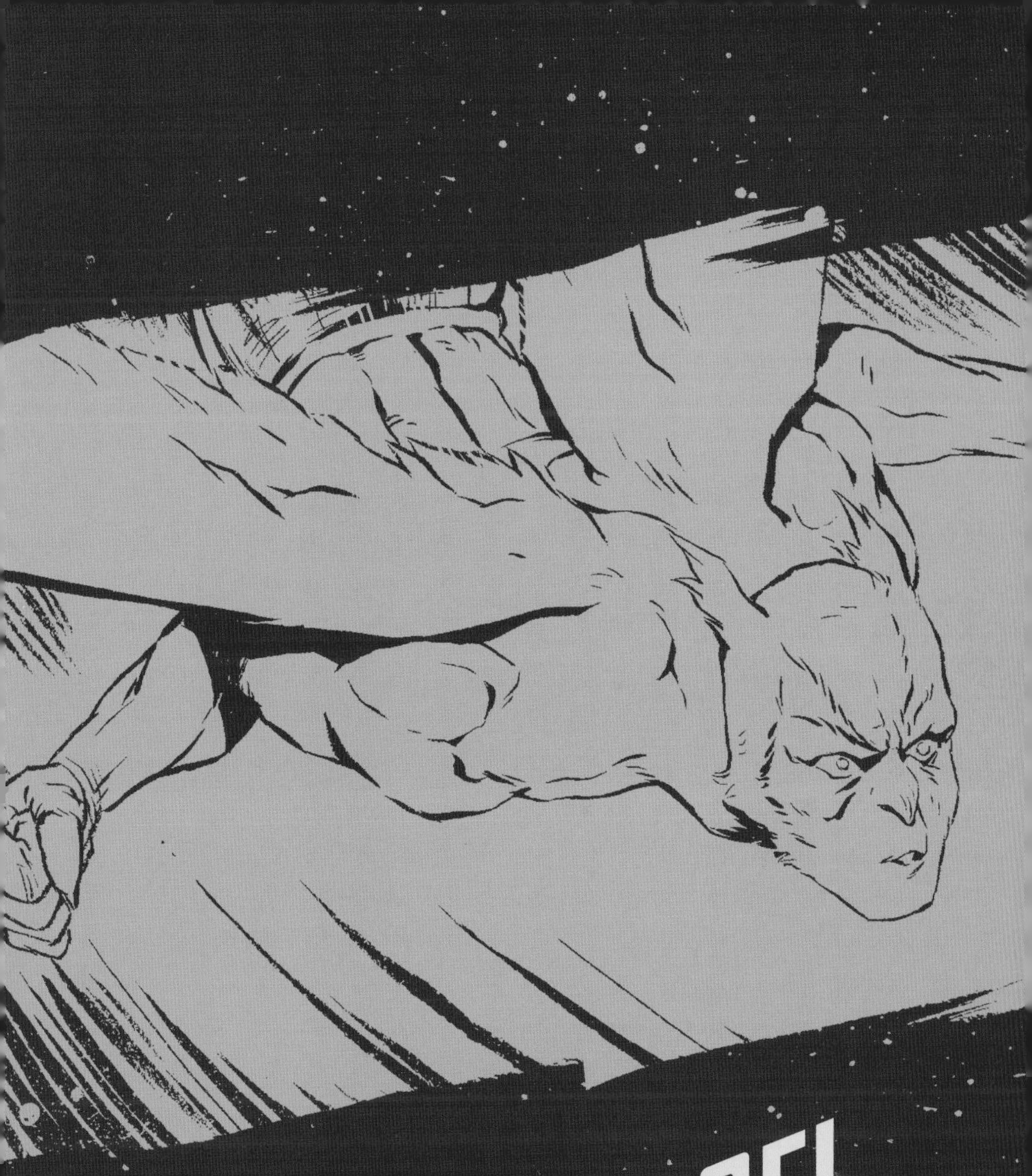

ANGEL CATBIRD™

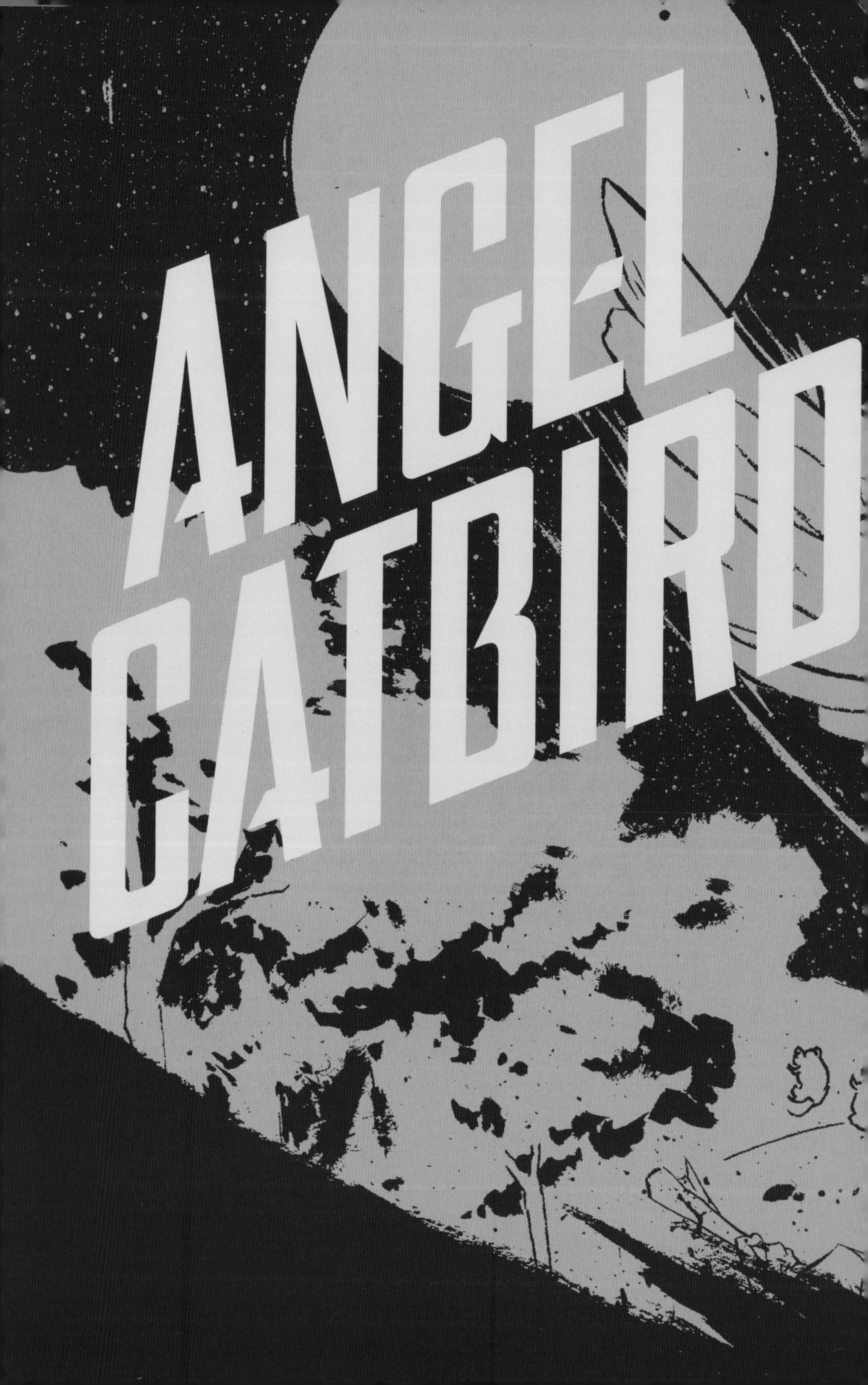
ANGEL
CATBIRD

Story by
MARGARET ATWOOD

Illustrations by
JOHNNIE CHRISTMAS

Colors by
TAMRA BONVILLAIN

Letters by
NATE PIEKOS OF BLAMBOT®

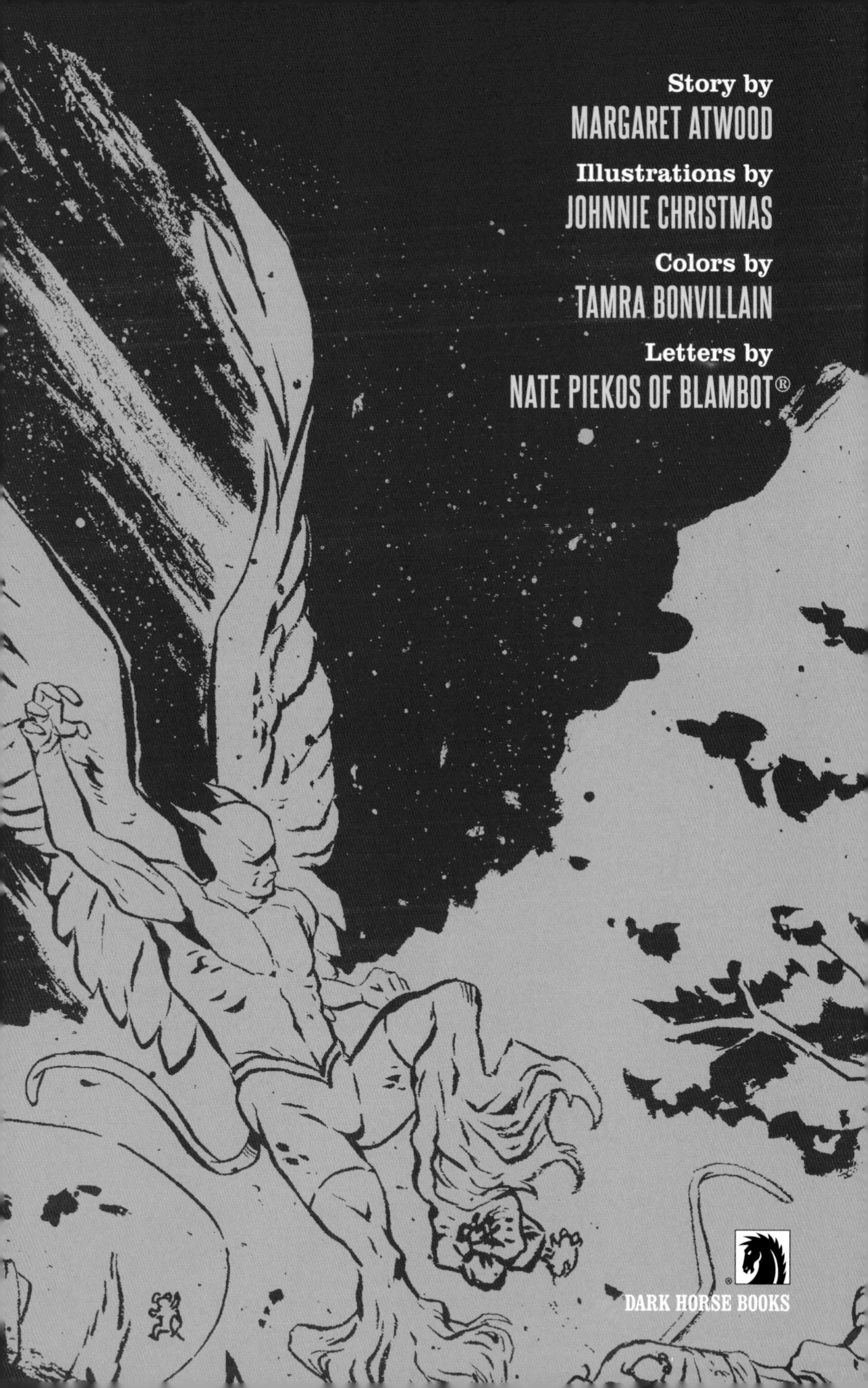

DARK HORSE BOOKS

President and Publisher MIKE RICHARDSON

Editor DANIEL CHABON

Assistant Editors GARDNER CLARK AND RACHEL ROBERTS

Project Adviser HOPE NICHOLSON

Designer BRENNAN THOME

Digital Art Technician CONLEY SMITH

NEIL HANKERSON Executive Vice President • TOM WEDDLE Chief Financial Officer
RANDY STRADLEY Vice President of Publishing • MICHAEL MARTENS Vice President of
Book Trade Sales • MATT PARKINSON Vice President of Marketing • DAVID SCROGGY
Vice President of Product Development • DALE LaFOUNTAIN Vice President of Information
Technology • CARA NIECE Vice President of Production and Scheduling • NICK McWHORTER
Vice President of Media Licensing • KEN LIZZI General Counsel • DAVE MARSHALL Editor
in Chief • DAVEY ESTRADA Editorial Director • SCOTT ALLIE Executive Senior Editor •
CHRIS WARNER Senior Books Editor • CARY GRAZZINI Director of Print and Development
LIA RIBACCHI Art Director • MARK BERNARDI Director of Digital Publishing • MICHAEL
GOMBOS Director of International Publishing and Licensing

Published by Dark Horse Books
A division of Dark Horse Comics, Inc.
10956 SE Main Street
Milwaukie, OR 97222

First edition: February 2017
ISBN 978-1-50670-127-1

10 9 8 7 6 5 4 3 2 1
Printed in China

International Licensing: (503) 905-2377 | Comic Shop Locator Service: (888) 266-4226

ANGEL CATBIRD VOLUME 2: TO CASTLE CATULA

Library of Congress Cataloging-in-Publication Data

Names: Atwood, Margaret. | Christmas, Johnnie, illustrator.
Title: Angel Catbird. Volume 2 / story by Margaret Atwood ; illustrations by
    Johnnie Christmas ; colors by Tamra Bonvillain ; Letters by Nate Piekos of
    Blambot.
Description: First edition. | Milwaukie, OR : Dark Horse Books, 2017. |
    Summary: "On a dark night, young genetic engineer Strig Feleedus is
    accidentally mutated by his own experiment when his DNA is merged with
    that of a cat and an owl"-- Provided by publisher.
Identifiers: LCCN 2016010286 | ISBN 9781506701271 (hardback)
Subjects: LCSH: Graphic novels. | CYAC: Graphic novels. |
    Superheroes--Fiction. | Genetic engineering--Fiction. | Adventure and
    adventurers--Fiction. | BISAC: COMICS & GRAPHIC NOVELS / Superheroes. |
    COMICS & GRAPHIC NOVELS / General. | FICTION / Action & Adventure.
Classification: LCC PZ7.7.A896 Ang 2016 | DDC 741.5/973--dc23
LC record available at https://lccn.loc.gov/2016010286

G. WILLOW WILSON

FOREWORD

Like all true Chimeras, the work of Margaret Atwood defies easy categorization. From the bleak dystopia of *The Handmaid's Tale*, which seems more relevant than ever in our era of newly restricted reproductive rights; to the sly surrealism of the *Oryx and Crake* trilogy, in which humankind reaps the whirlwind of hypercapitalism and ecological destruction; to the lush psychological drama of *Cat's Eye*, which throws the lessons of adolescence into painful relief, Atwood moves nimbly from subject to subject and from genre to genre. And like a Chimera, she seems to be fueled by some secret fire, one that makes her as dryly, mirthfully witty on Twitter as she is in the pages of the *Michigan Quarterly Review* or *Harper's Magazine*.

Most fiction writers alive today have been influenced by Atwood's work, whether they know it or not: by tackling the most pressing issues of each unfolding decade, she has achieved a kind of cultural ubiquity. I first picked up *The Handmaid's Tale* in the mid-1990s, when I was twelve or thirteen, which in retrospect is probably a bit too young to tackle that book. In the awkward grip of puberty, it read like a kind of body horror, a warning that there was no part of womanhood which could not be commodified. To encounter a novel like that in the banal, apolitical atmosphere of the nineties, when sexism and racism were "over" and strong viewpoints were seen as impolite, was an electric experience; it showed me that you could, in fact, address real-world issues in a meaningful way within the realm of fantasy and science fiction. Speculative fiction wasn't simply an escape; it was also an arrival.

Do Atwood's disparate creations have a unifying message? If they do, I think it might be tidily summed up as a simple directive: resist complacency. Resist it with whatever tools you have on hand—with wit, with humor, with irony, or with anger, but *resist* it, and do not apologize.

In *Angel Catbird*, we see that message at its most jubilantly pulpy. It is an unselfconscious romp through a world instantly recognizable both to fans of Silver Age comics and to the furriest corners of the Internet, a world in which the boundaries between human and animal blur and our most primitive instincts come into play. Like all great superheroes, Strig, the titular protagonist, is only momentarily alarmed by the onset of his strange powers: when you are given the ability to transform into a half-cat, half-owl, half-man (that's three halves), you must carpe that diem, and he does. *Angel Catbird* represents a side of Margaret Atwood we don't get to see very often: an unabashedly geeky side, one conversant in the tangled continuities of superhero comics and at home in fandom. The story is pure, distilled nerd catharsis, delivered by a literary legend.

Atwood's story is well served by coconspirator Johnnie Christmas, whose gleeful, kinetic art style pays homage to the era of Jack Kirby and Russ Manning, masters who peaked before the age of irony and to whom pulp was a kind of religion. If there is a joke, Christmas and Atwood are in on it together, and it makes for one heck of a read. There are puns, and then there are cat puns, and then there are Dracula cat puns, and then there are *visual* Dracula cat puns, and if you hung around for the end of that list, this is the kind of graphic novel you need on your bookshelf.

Meow.

Our Story So Far...

STRIG FELEEDUS WAS A BRILLIANT GENETIC ENGINEER, A PROUD CAT OWNER, AND ON THE CUSP OF SOLVING A TOP-SECRET D.N.A. SUPER-SPLICER FORMULA.

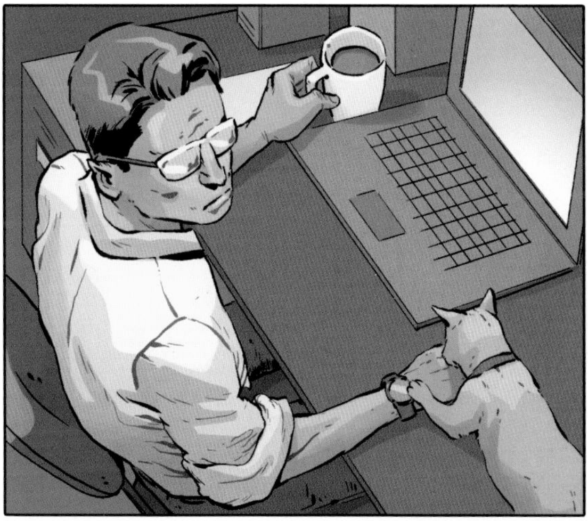

THEN FATE TOOK A TURN FOR THE **WORSE!**

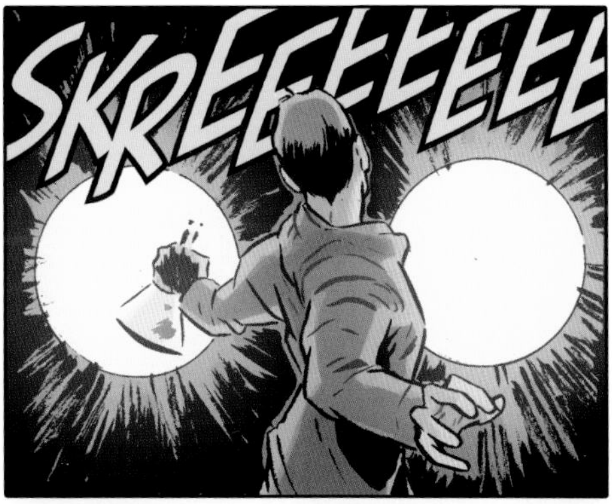
SKREEEEEEE

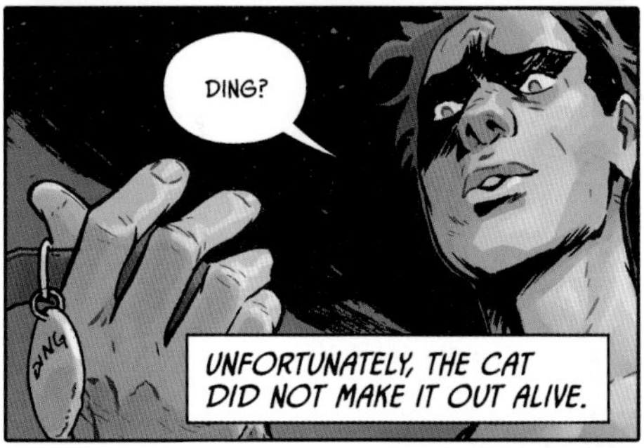
DING?
DING
UNFORTUNATELY, THE CAT DID NOT MAKE IT OUT ALIVE.

AFTER A MYSTERIOUS CAR ACCIDENT, HIS D.N.A. GOT MIXED WITH THAT OF AN OWL AND HIS PET CAT.

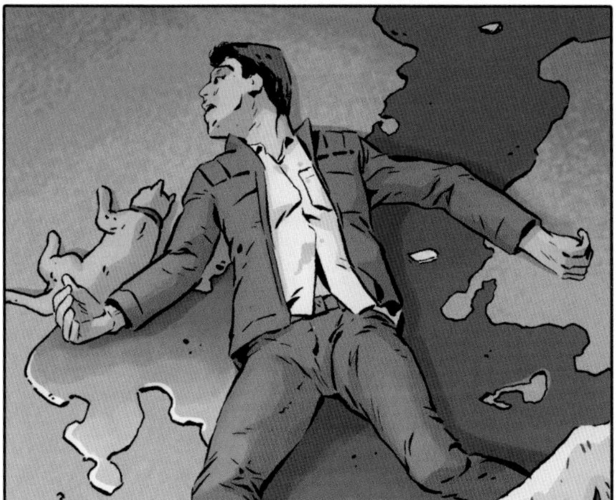

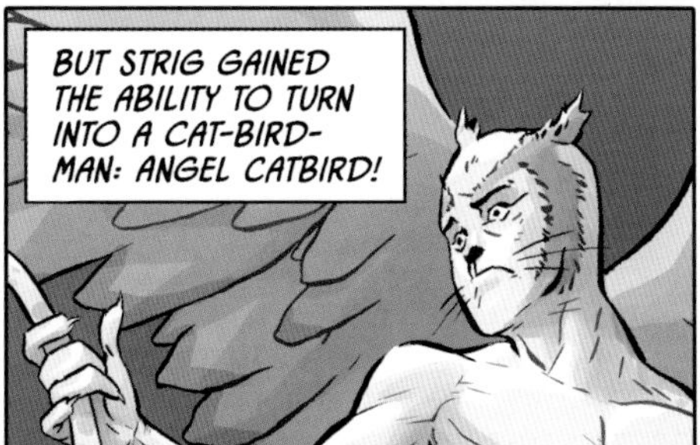
BUT STRIG GAINED THE ABILITY TO TURN INTO A CAT-BIRD-MAN: ANGEL CATBIRD!

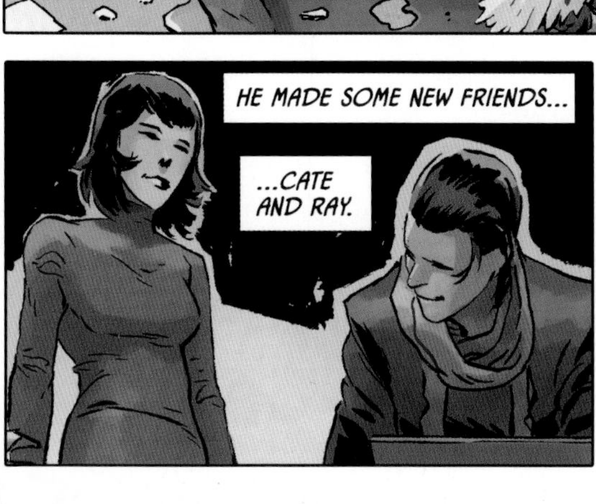
HE MADE SOME NEW FRIENDS...
...CATE AND RAY.

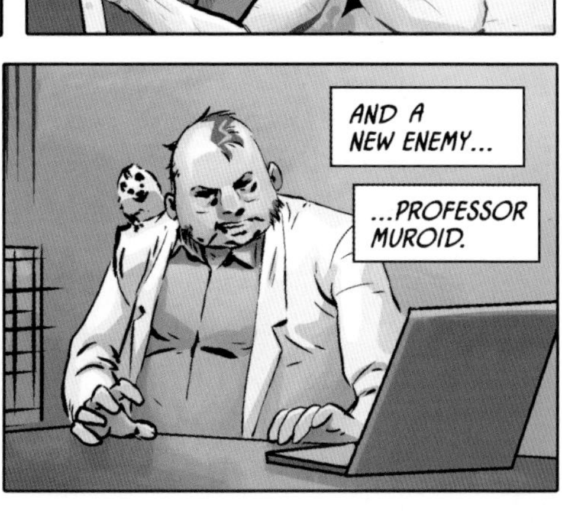
AND A NEW ENEMY...
...PROFESSOR MUROID.

STRIG STUMBLED UPON AN ENTIRE UNDERGROUND HALF-CAT CULTURE! HUMANS WITH THE ABILITY TO TURN INTO CAT FORM, CATS WITH THE ABILITY TO TURN INTO HUMAN FORM, AND EVERYTHING IN BETWEEN.

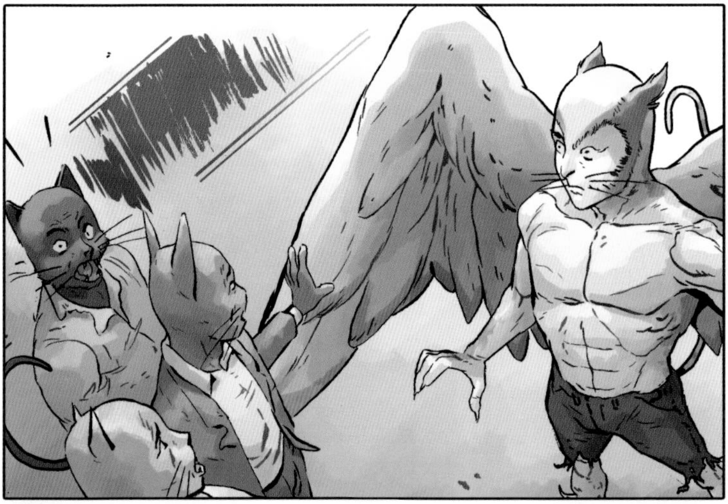

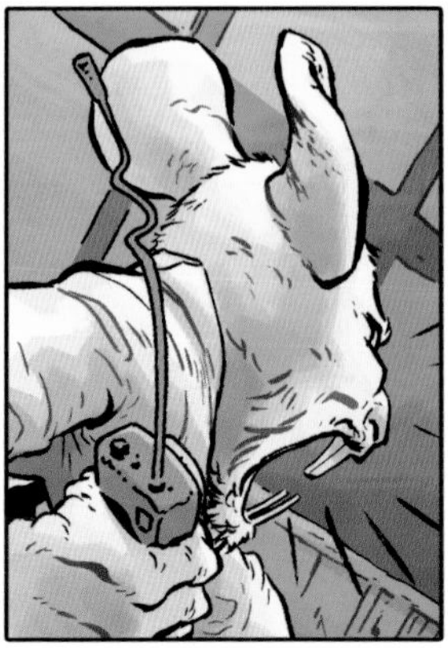

HE DISCOVERED THAT HIS BOSS, PROFESSOR MUROID, WAS A HALF-RAT INTENT ON WORLD DOMINATION AND THE EXTERMINATION OF ALL CATS AND BIRDS! SO STRIG'S HALF-CAT COMRADES ASSEMBLED TO PUT AN END TO MUROID'S EVIL PLOT!

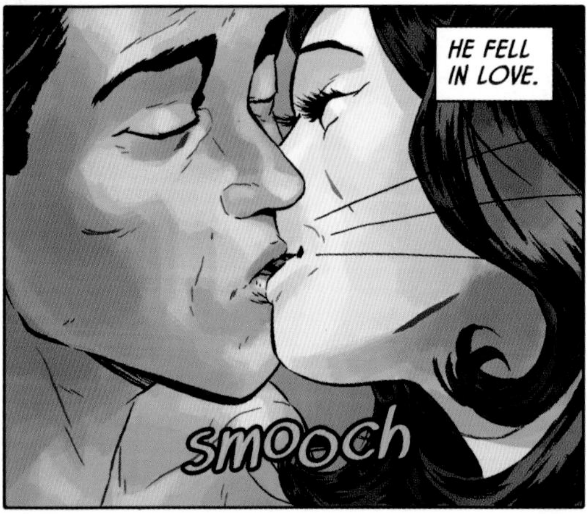
HE FELL IN LOVE.
smooch

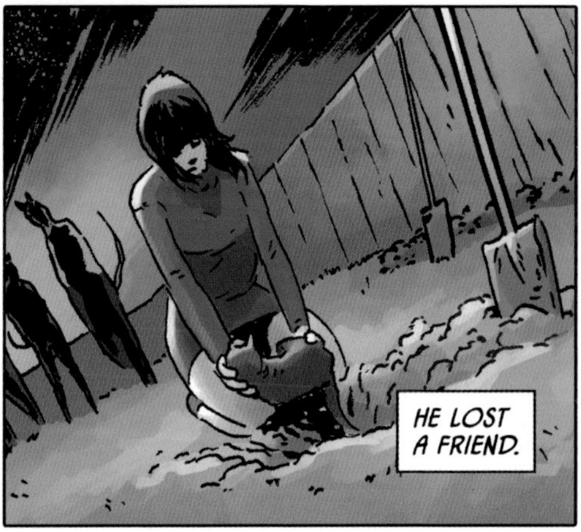
HE LOST A FRIEND.

AND THE HALF-CATS DISCOVERED MUROID'S EVIL PLANS VIA U.S.B., COURTESY OF COUNT CATULA, PART BAT, PART CAT, PART VAMPIRE!

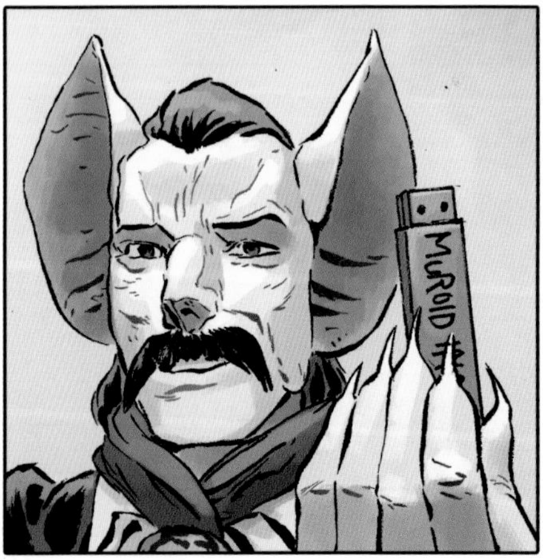
MUROID

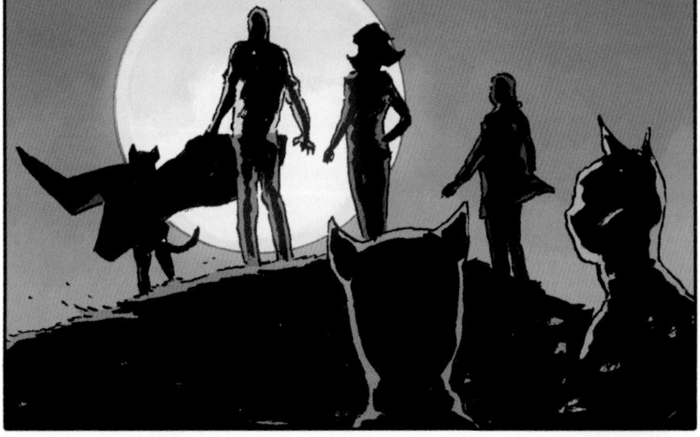

AFTER THEIR HALF-CAT CLUB WAS BLOWN UP BY MUROID, TEAM CATBIRD SET OUT FOR CASTLE CATULA, WHERE THEY HOPE TO SET UP A BASE OF OPERATIONS--AND WHERE POWERFUL FORCES WILL BE CALLED INTO PLAY.

And Now...

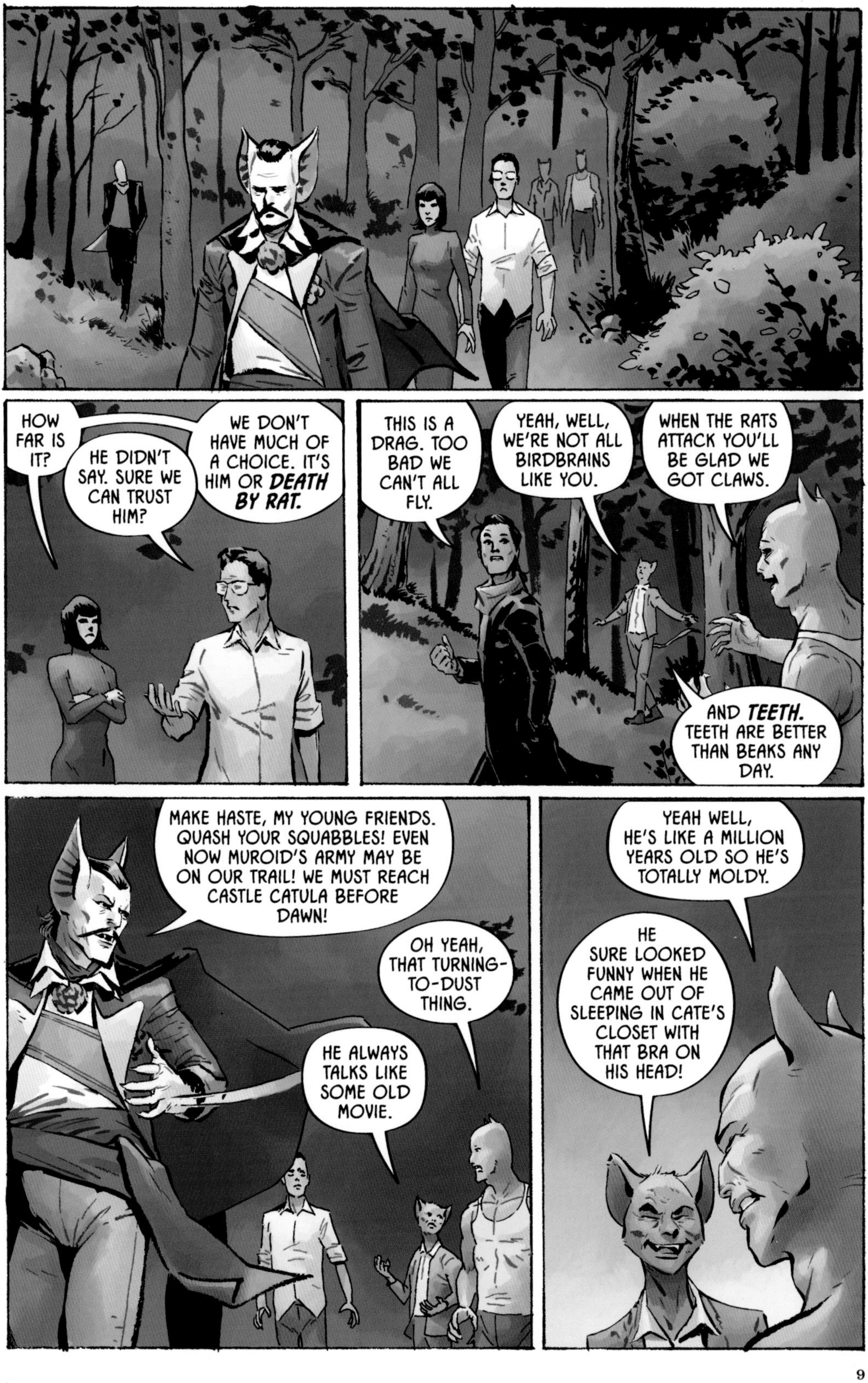
HOW FAR IS IT?
HE DIDN'T SAY. SURE WE CAN TRUST HIM?
WE DON'T HAVE MUCH OF A CHOICE. IT'S HIM OR DEATH BY RAT.
THIS IS A DRAG. TOO BAD WE CAN'T ALL FLY.
YEAH, WELL, WE'RE NOT ALL BIRDBRAINS LIKE YOU.
WHEN THE RATS ATTACK YOU'LL BE GLAD WE GOT CLAWS.
AND TEETH. TEETH ARE BETTER THAN BEAKS ANY DAY.
MAKE HASTE, MY YOUNG FRIENDS. QUASH YOUR SQUABBLES! EVEN NOW MUROID'S ARMY MAY BE ON OUR TRAIL! WE MUST REACH CASTLE CATULA BEFORE DAWN!
OH YEAH, THAT TURNING-TO-DUST THING.
HE ALWAYS TALKS LIKE SOME OLD MOVIE.
YEAH WELL, HE'S LIKE A MILLION YEARS OLD SO HE'S TOTALLY MOLDY.
HE SURE LOOKED FUNNY WHEN HE CAME OUT OF SLEEPING IN CATE'S CLOSET WITH THAT BRA ON HIS HEAD!

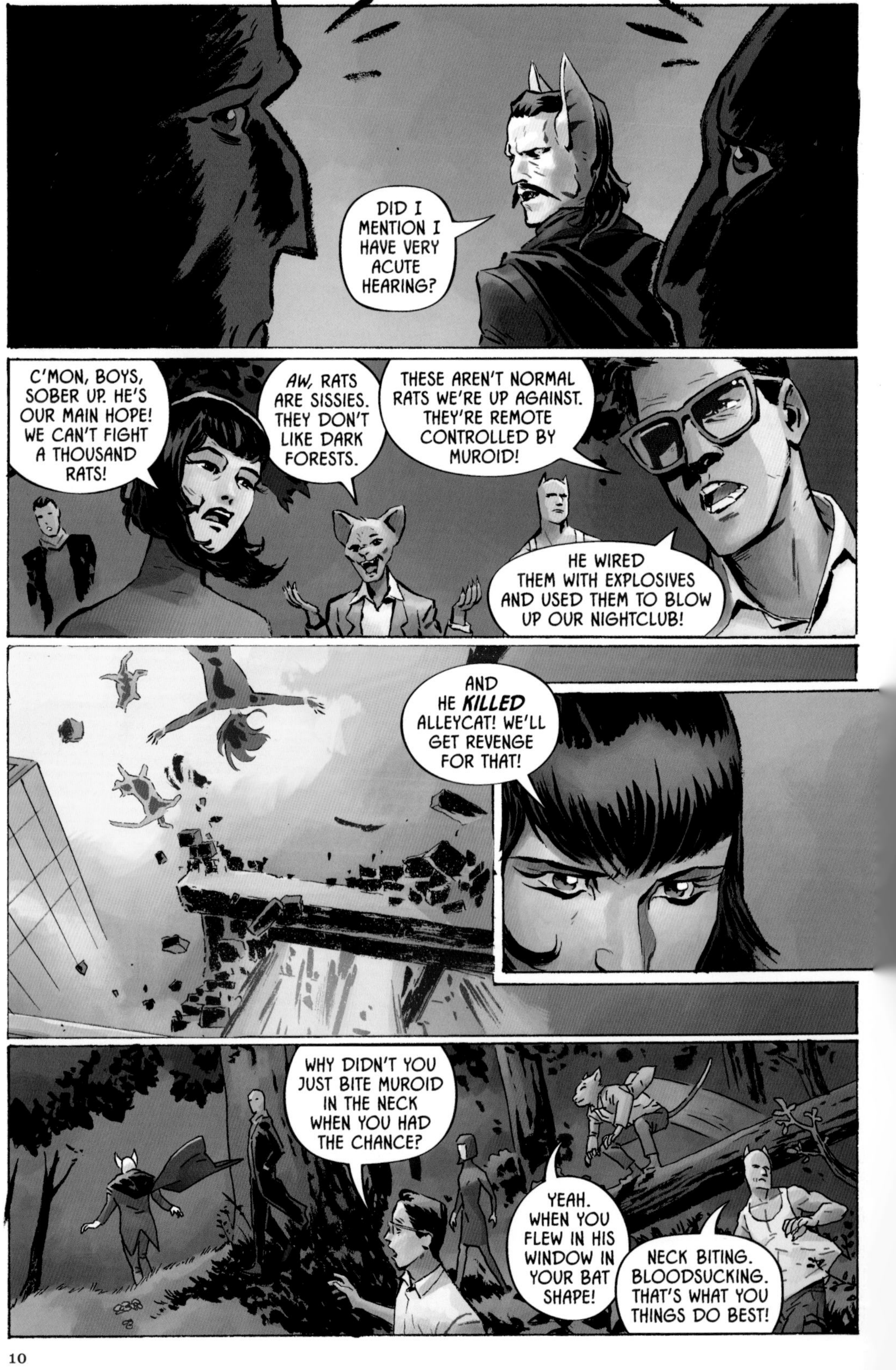
DID I MENTION I HAVE VERY ACUTE HEARING?
C'MON, BOYS, SOBER UP. HE'S OUR MAIN HOPE! WE CAN'T FIGHT A THOUSAND RATS!
AW, RATS ARE SISSIES. THEY DON'T LIKE DARK FORESTS.
THESE AREN'T NORMAL RATS WE'RE UP AGAINST. THEY'RE REMOTE CONTROLLED BY MUROID!
HE WIRED THEM WITH EXPLOSIVES AND USED THEM TO BLOW UP OUR NIGHTCLUB!
AND HE KILLED ALLEYCAT! WE'LL GET REVENGE FOR THAT!
WHY DIDN'T YOU JUST BITE MUROID IN THE NECK WHEN YOU HAD THE CHANCE?
YEAH. WHEN YOU FLEW IN HIS WINDOW IN YOUR BAT SHAPE!
NECK BITING. BLOODSUCKING. THAT'S WHAT YOU THINGS DO BEST!

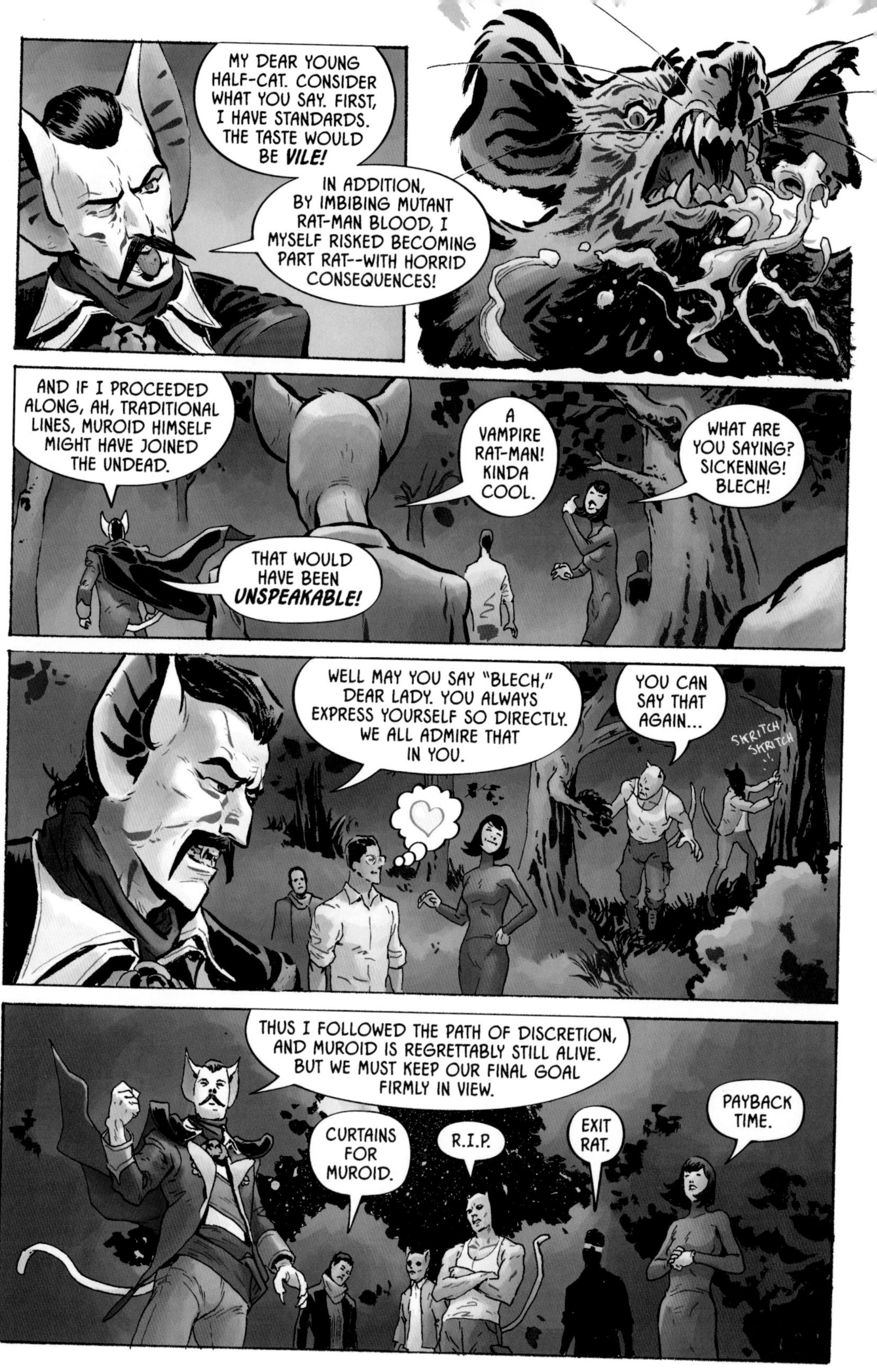
MY DEAR YOUNG HALF-CAT. CONSIDER WHAT YOU SAY. FIRST, I HAVE STANDARDS. THE TASTE WOULD BE *VILE!*
IN ADDITION, BY IMBIBING MUTANT RAT-MAN BLOOD, I MYSELF RISKED BECOMING PART RAT--WITH HORRID CONSEQUENCES!
AND IF I PROCEEDED ALONG, AH, TRADITIONAL LINES, MUROID HIMSELF MIGHT HAVE JOINED THE UNDEAD.
A VAMPIRE RAT-MAN! KINDA COOL.
WHAT ARE YOU SAYING? SICKENING! BLECH!
THAT WOULD HAVE BEEN *UNSPEAKABLE!*
WELL MAY YOU SAY "BLECH," DEAR LADY. YOU ALWAYS EXPRESS YOURSELF SO DIRECTLY. WE ALL ADMIRE THAT IN YOU.
YOU CAN SAY THAT AGAIN...
SKRITCH SKRITCH
THUS I FOLLOWED THE PATH OF DISCRETION, AND MUROID IS REGRETTABLY STILL ALIVE. BUT WE MUST KEEP OUR FINAL GOAL FIRMLY IN VIEW.
CURTAINS FOR MUROID.
R.I.P.
EXIT RAT.
PAYBACK TIME.

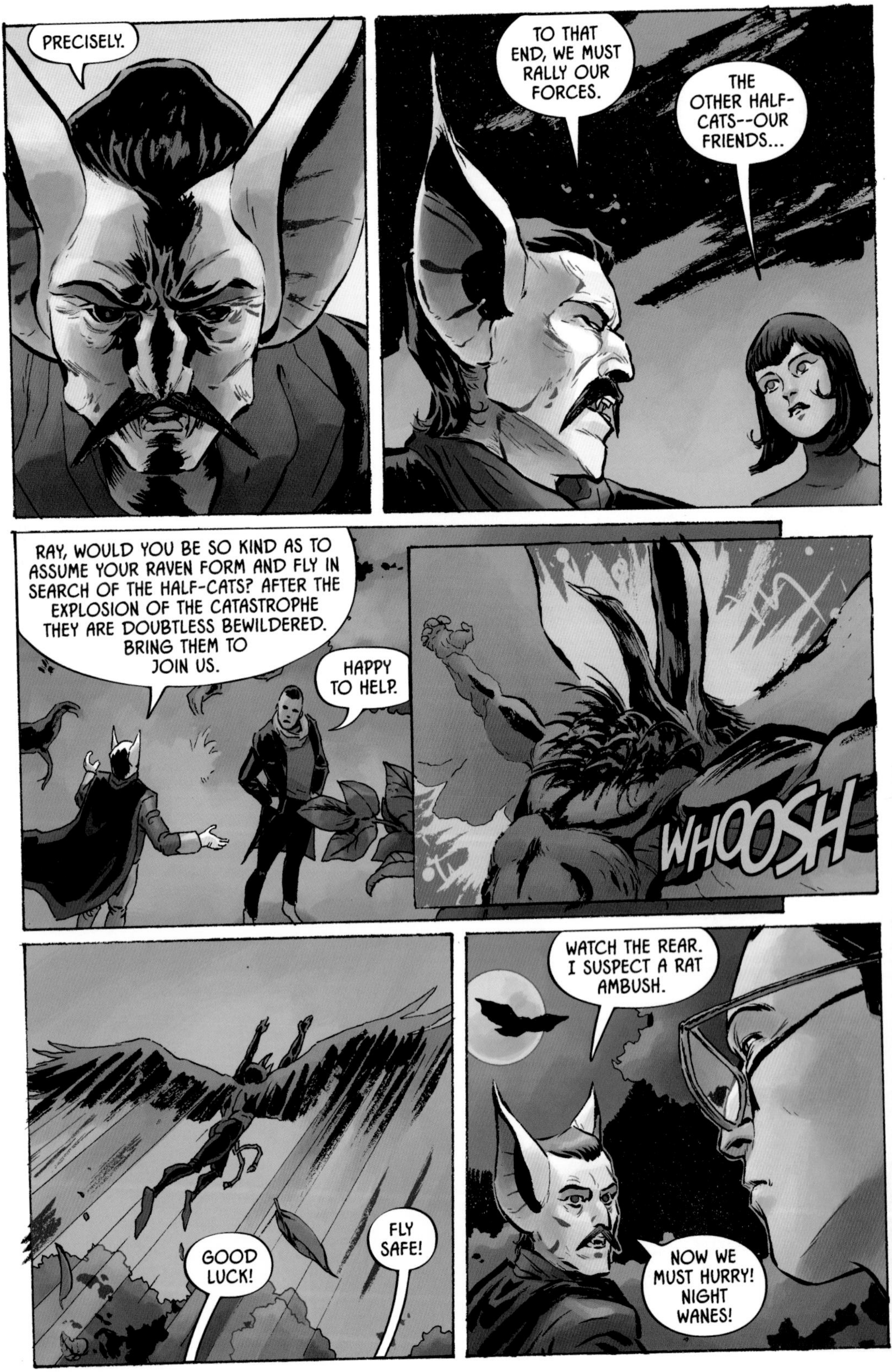
PRECISELY.
TO THAT END, WE MUST RALLY OUR FORCES.
THE OTHER HALF-CATS--OUR FRIENDS...
RAY, WOULD YOU BE SO KIND AS TO ASSUME YOUR RAVEN FORM AND FLY IN SEARCH OF THE HALF-CATS? AFTER THE EXPLOSION OF THE CATASTROPHE THEY ARE DOUBTLESS BEWILDERED. BRING THEM TO JOIN US.
HAPPY TO HELP.
WHOOSH
GOOD LUCK!
FLY SAFE!
WATCH THE REAR. I SUSPECT A RAT AMBUSH.
NOW WE MUST HURRY! NIGHT WANES!

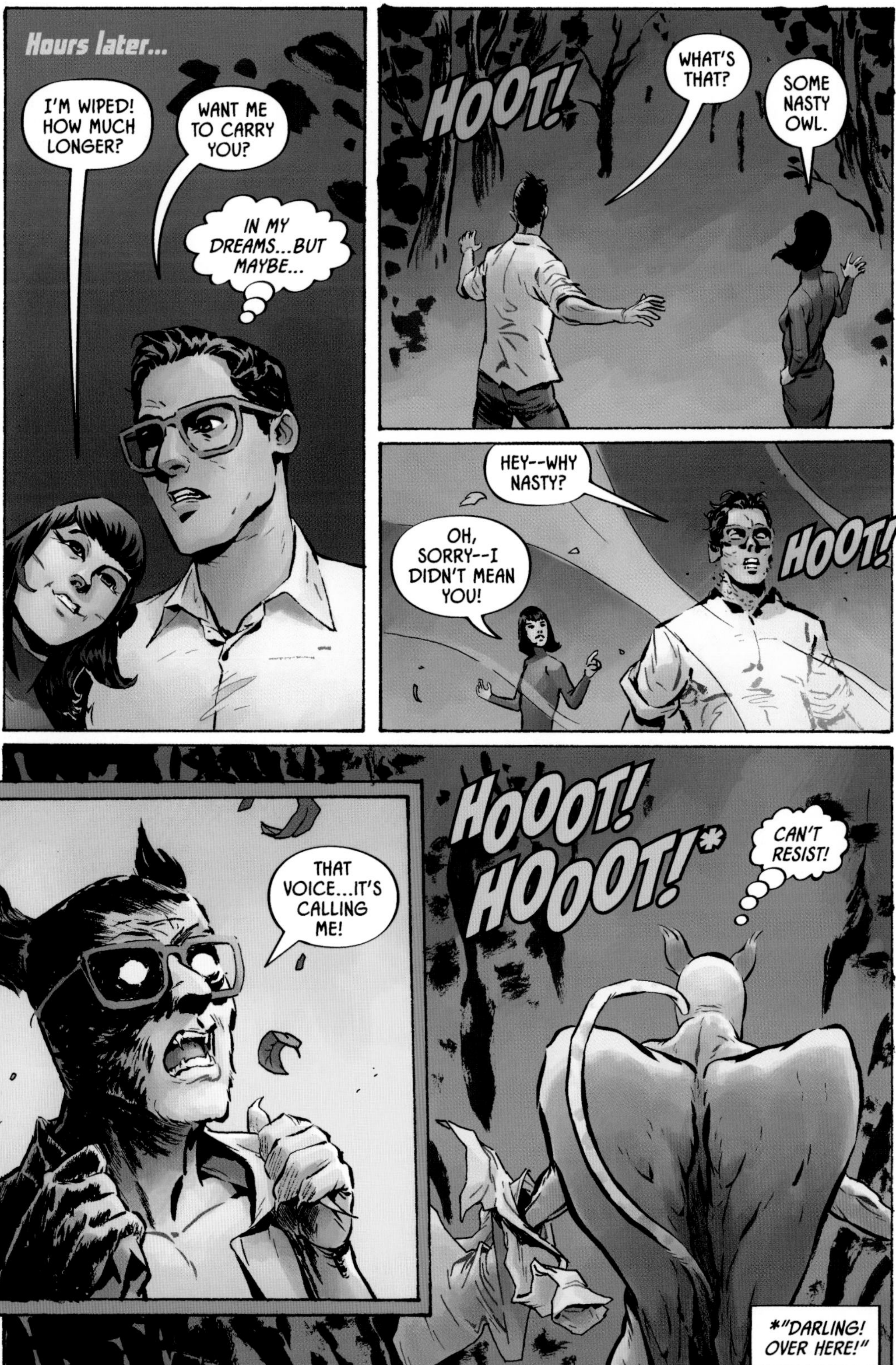
Hours later...
I'M WIPED! HOW MUCH LONGER?
WANT ME TO CARRY YOU?
IN MY DREAMS...BUT MAYBE...
HOOT!
WHAT'S THAT?
SOME NASTY OWL.
HEY--WHY NASTY?
OH, SORRY--I DIDN'T MEAN YOU!
HOOT!
HOOOT! HOOOT!*
THAT VOICE...IT'S CALLING ME!
CAN'T RESIST!
*"DARLING! OVER HERE!"

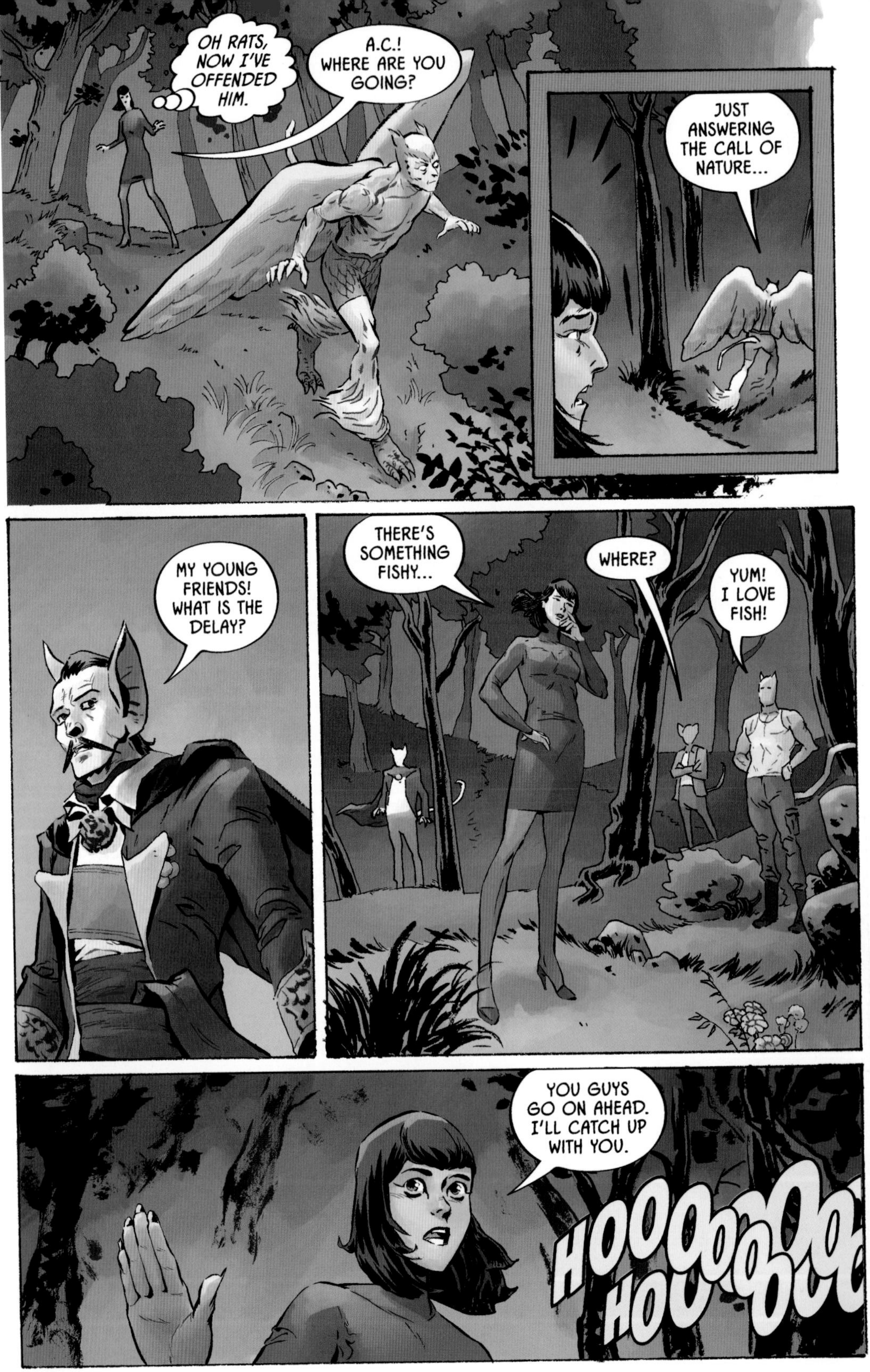
OH RATS, NOW I'VE OFFENDED HIM.
A.C.! WHERE ARE YOU GOING?
JUST ANSWERING THE CALL OF NATURE...
MY YOUNG FRIENDS! WHAT IS THE DELAY?
THERE'S SOMETHING FISHY...
WHERE?
YUM! I LOVE FISH!
YOU GUYS GO ON AHEAD. I'LL CATCH UP WITH YOU.
HOOOOOOOO HOOOOOOO

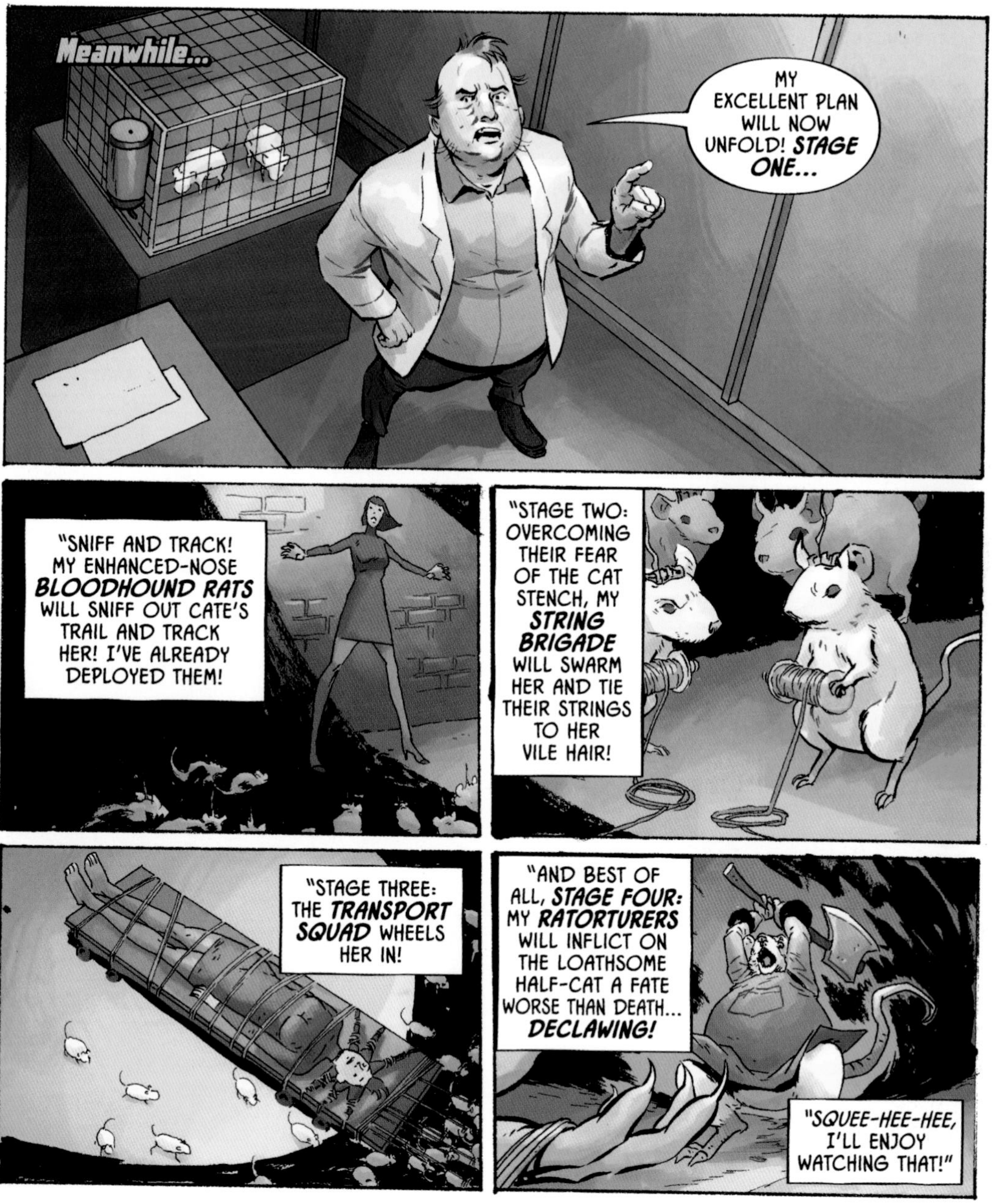
Meanwhile...
MY EXCELLENT PLAN WILL NOW UNFOLD! STAGE ONE...
"SNIFF AND TRACK! MY ENHANCED-NOSE BLOODHOUND RATS WILL SNIFF OUT CATE'S TRAIL AND TRACK HER! I'VE ALREADY DEPLOYED THEM!
"STAGE TWO: OVERCOMING THEIR FEAR OF THE CAT STENCH, MY STRING BRIGADE WILL SWARM HER AND TIE THEIR STRINGS TO HER VILE HAIR!
"STAGE THREE: THE TRANSPORT SQUAD WHEELS HER IN!
"AND BEST OF ALL, STAGE FOUR: MY RATORTURERS WILL INFLICT ON THE LOATHSOME HALF-CAT A FATE WORSE THAN DEATH... DECLAWING!
"SQUEE-HEE-HEE, I'LL ENJOY WATCHING THAT!"

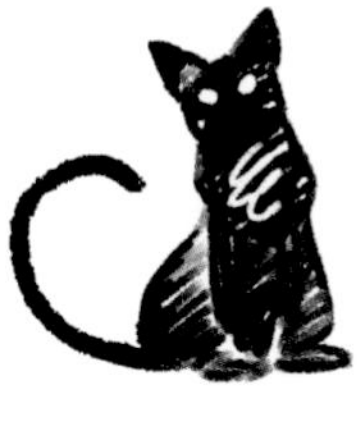

CATS NEED CLAWS

Declawing is a surgical procedure in which the last bones of a cat's toes, including the nail beds, are amputated. Scratching is a normal behavior for cats and serves several purposes. There are nonsurgical solutions to save your upholstery!
Read more at www.catsandbirds.ca

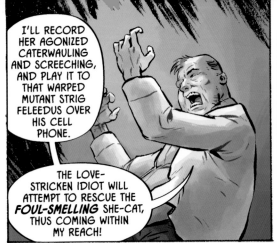

I'LL RECORD HER AGONIZED CATERWAULING AND SCREECHING, AND PLAY IT TO THAT WARPED MUTANT STRIG FELEEDUS OVER HIS CELL PHONE.

THE LOVE-STRICKEN IDIOT WILL ATTEMPT TO RESCUE THE *FOUL-SMELLING* SHE-CAT, THUS COMING WITHIN MY REACH!

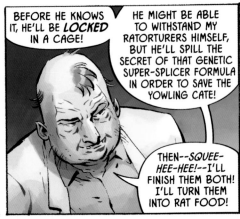

BEFORE HE KNOWS IT, HE'LL BE *LOCKED* IN A CAGE!

HE MIGHT BE ABLE TO WITHSTAND MY RATORTURERS HIMSELF, BUT HE'LL SPILL THE SECRET OF THAT GENETIC SUPER-SPLICER FORMULA IN ORDER TO SAVE THE YOWLING CATE!

THEN--*SQUEE-HEE-HEE!*--I'LL FINISH THEM BOTH! I'LL TURN THEM INTO RAT FOOD!

"AND THE WHOLE WORLD WILL SOON BE RAT-ATTRACTIVE! OURS FOR THE TAKING!"

AS FOR YOU, MY TREACHEROUS PETS, DON'T THINK I FAILED TO NOTICE YOUR COMMUNICATION WITH THAT RED-EYED BAT! ONCE I GET THE SUPER-SPLICER FORMULA, YOU'LL BE TRANSFORMED INTO TWO *RAT-A-LICIOUS* HOT RAT BABES IN NO TIME FLAT!

THEN I'LL PAY YOU BACK...I'LL KEEP YOU IN SLAVE COLLARS! YOU'LL CATER TO MY EVERY WHIM! OR ELSE! COVER ME WITH CHEESE SPREAD...NIBBLE IT OFF...THE PLEASURE WILL BE *MINE*, THE FEAR WILL BE YOURS!

THIS GUY IS NOT YOUR AVERAGE DREAMBOAT.

YOU THINK?

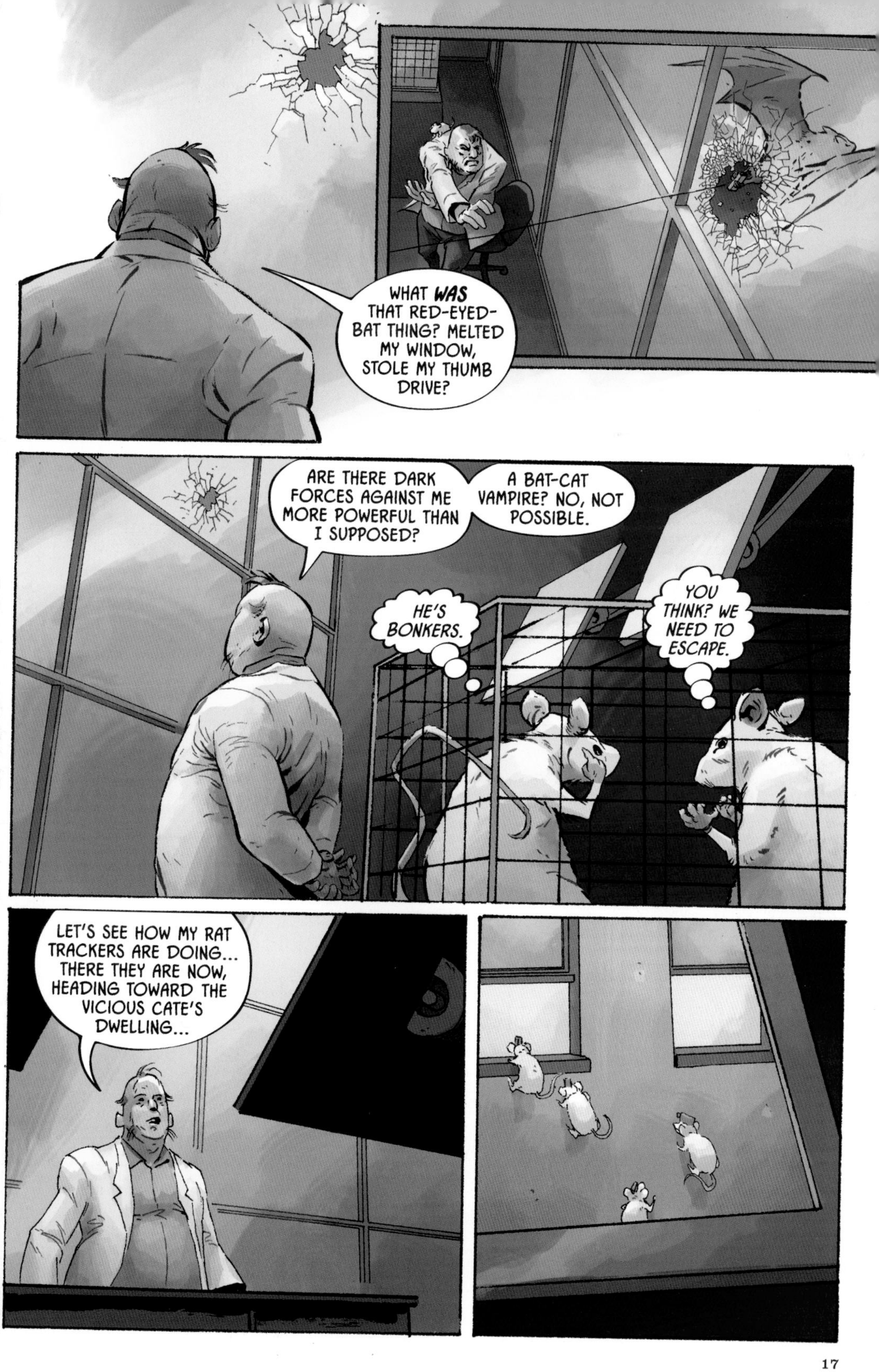
WHAT WAS THAT RED-EYED-BAT THING? MELTED MY WINDOW, STOLE MY THUMB DRIVE?
ARE THERE DARK FORCES AGAINST ME MORE POWERFUL THAN I SUPPOSED?
A BAT-CAT VAMPIRE? NO, NOT POSSIBLE.
HE'S BONKERS.
YOU THINK? WE NEED TO ESCAPE.
LET'S SEE HOW MY RAT TRACKERS ARE DOING... THERE THEY ARE NOW, HEADING TOWARD THE VICIOUS CATE'S DWELLING...

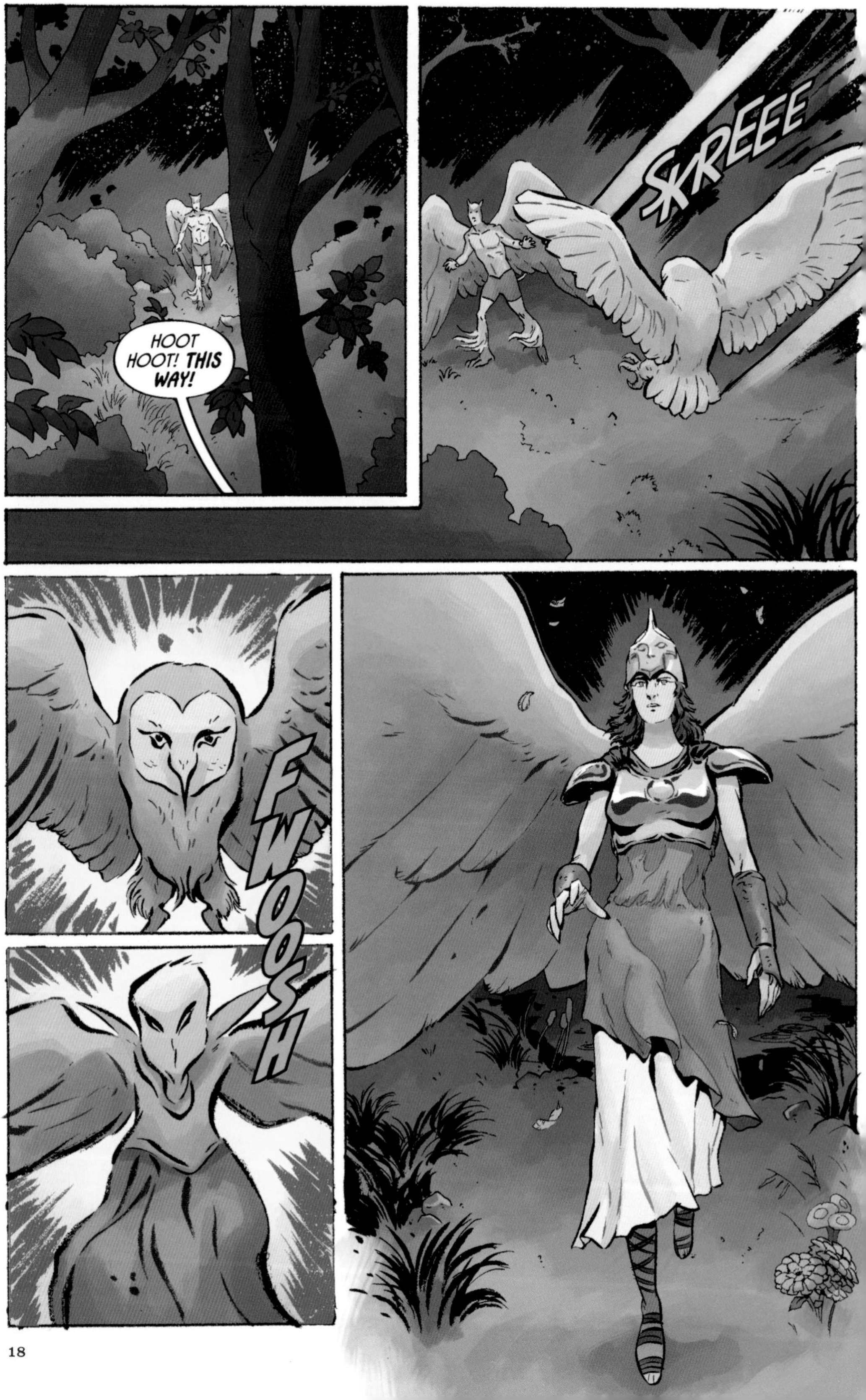
HOOT HOOT! THIS WAY!
SKREEE
FWOOSH

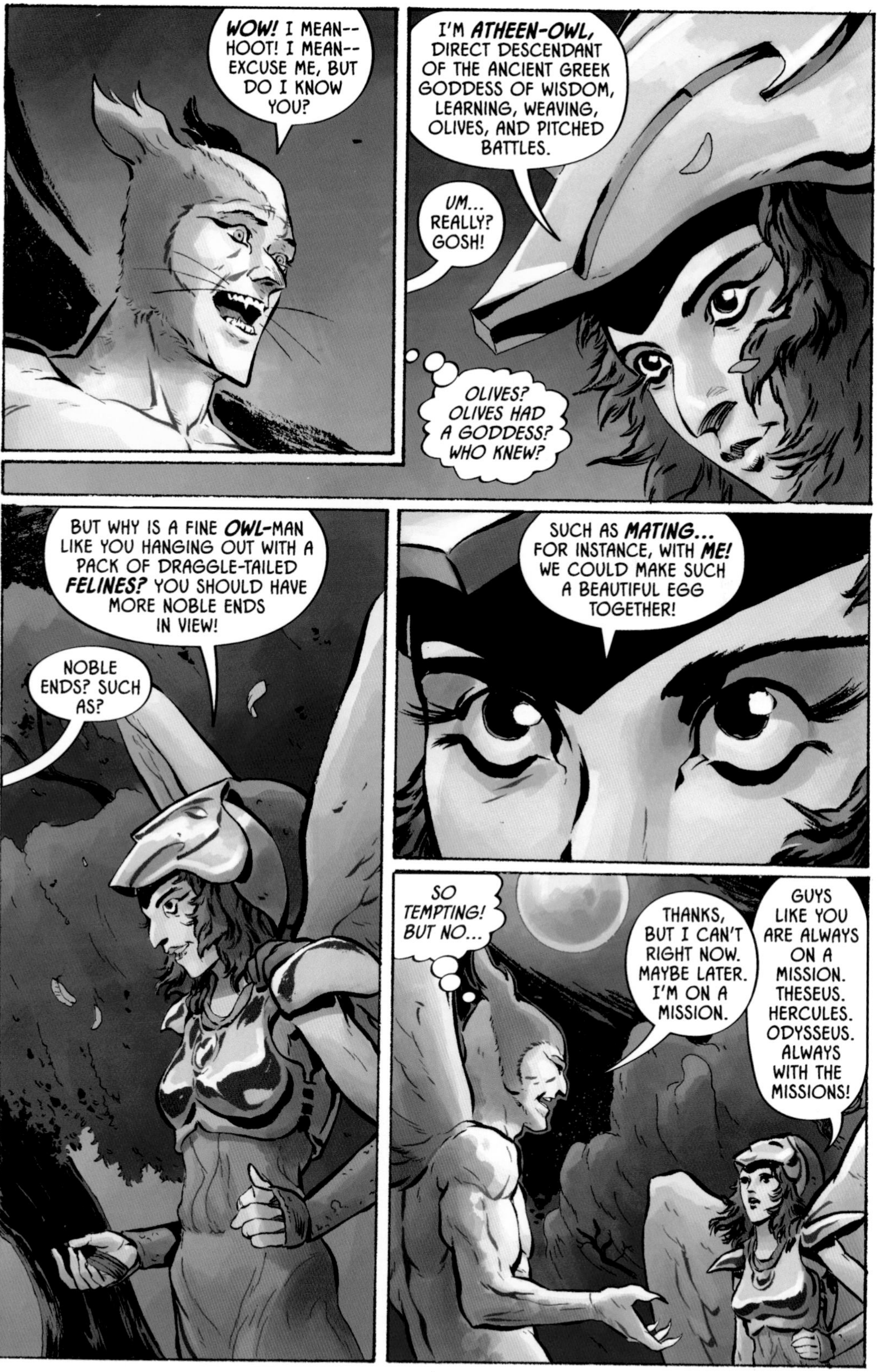
WOW! I MEAN-- HOOT! I MEAN-- EXCUSE ME, BUT DO I KNOW YOU?
I'M ATHEEN-OWL, DIRECT DESCENDANT OF THE ANCIENT GREEK GODDESS OF WISDOM, LEARNING, WEAVING, OLIVES, AND PITCHED BATTLES.
UM... REALLY? GOSH!
OLIVES? OLIVES HAD A GODDESS? WHO KNEW?
BUT WHY IS A FINE OWL-MAN LIKE YOU HANGING OUT WITH A PACK OF DRAGGLE-TAILED FELINES? YOU SHOULD HAVE MORE NOBLE ENDS IN VIEW!
NOBLE ENDS? SUCH AS?
SUCH AS MATING... FOR INSTANCE, WITH ME! WE COULD MAKE SUCH A BEAUTIFUL EGG TOGETHER!
SO TEMPTING! BUT NO...
THANKS, BUT I CAN'T RIGHT NOW. MAYBE LATER. I'M ON A MISSION.
GUYS LIKE YOU ARE ALWAYS ON A MISSION. THESEUS. HERCULES. ODYSSEUS. ALWAYS WITH THE MISSIONS!

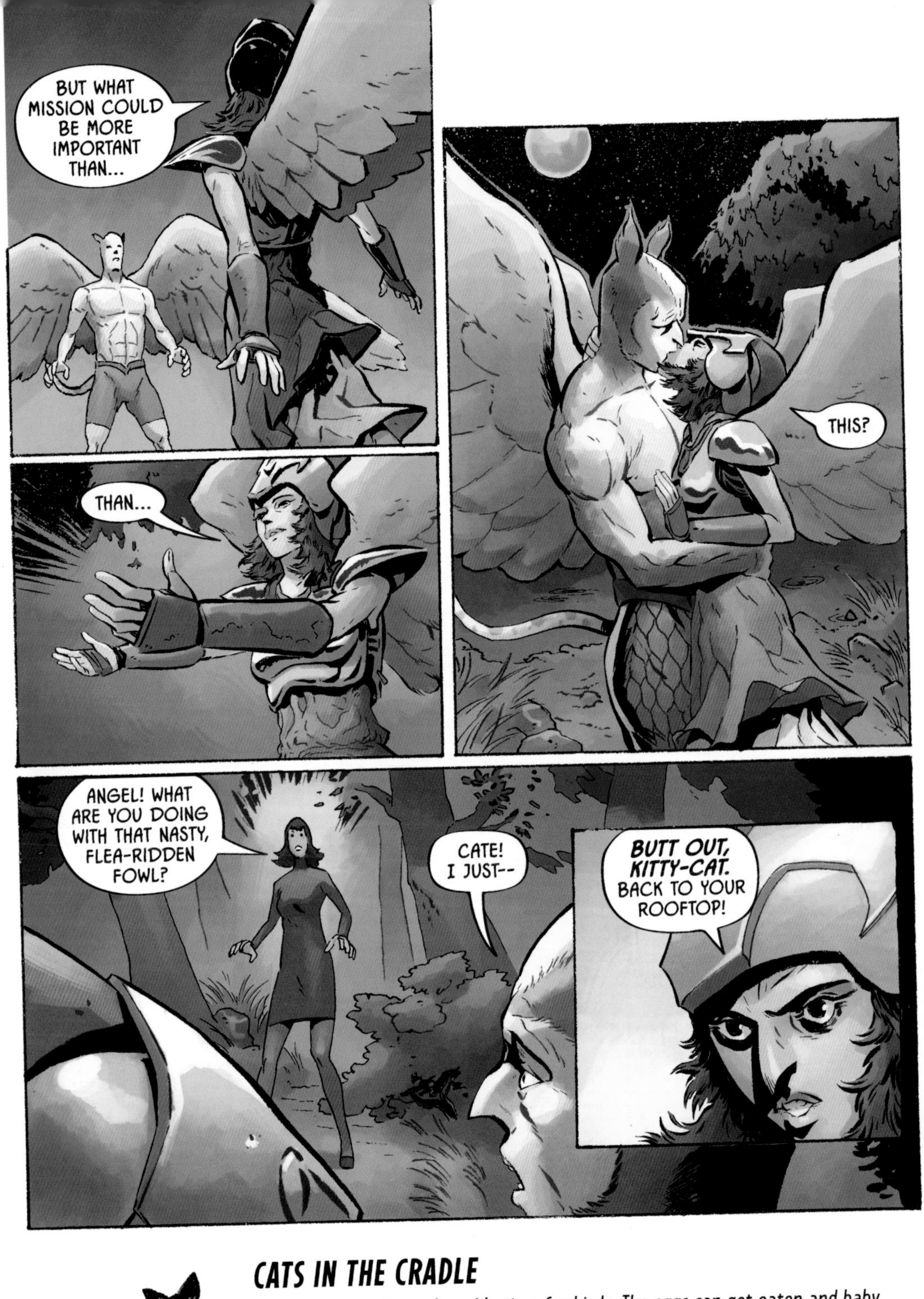
BUT WHAT MISSION COULD BE MORE IMPORTANT THAN...
THAN...
THIS?
ANGEL! WHAT ARE YOU DOING WITH THAT NASTY, FLEA-RIDDEN FOWL?
CATE! I JUST--
BUTT OUT, KITTY-CAT. BACK TO YOUR ROOFTOP!

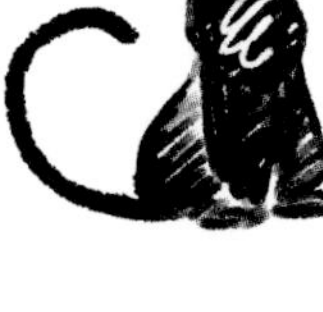

CATS IN THE CRADLE

Breeding season is a vulnerable time for birds. The eggs can get eaten and baby birds are very susceptible to predators. If young birds live long enough to leave the nest, they have no survival skills; they can't feed themselves yet, or fly well (if at all), or defend themselves.

Read more at www.catsandbirds.ca

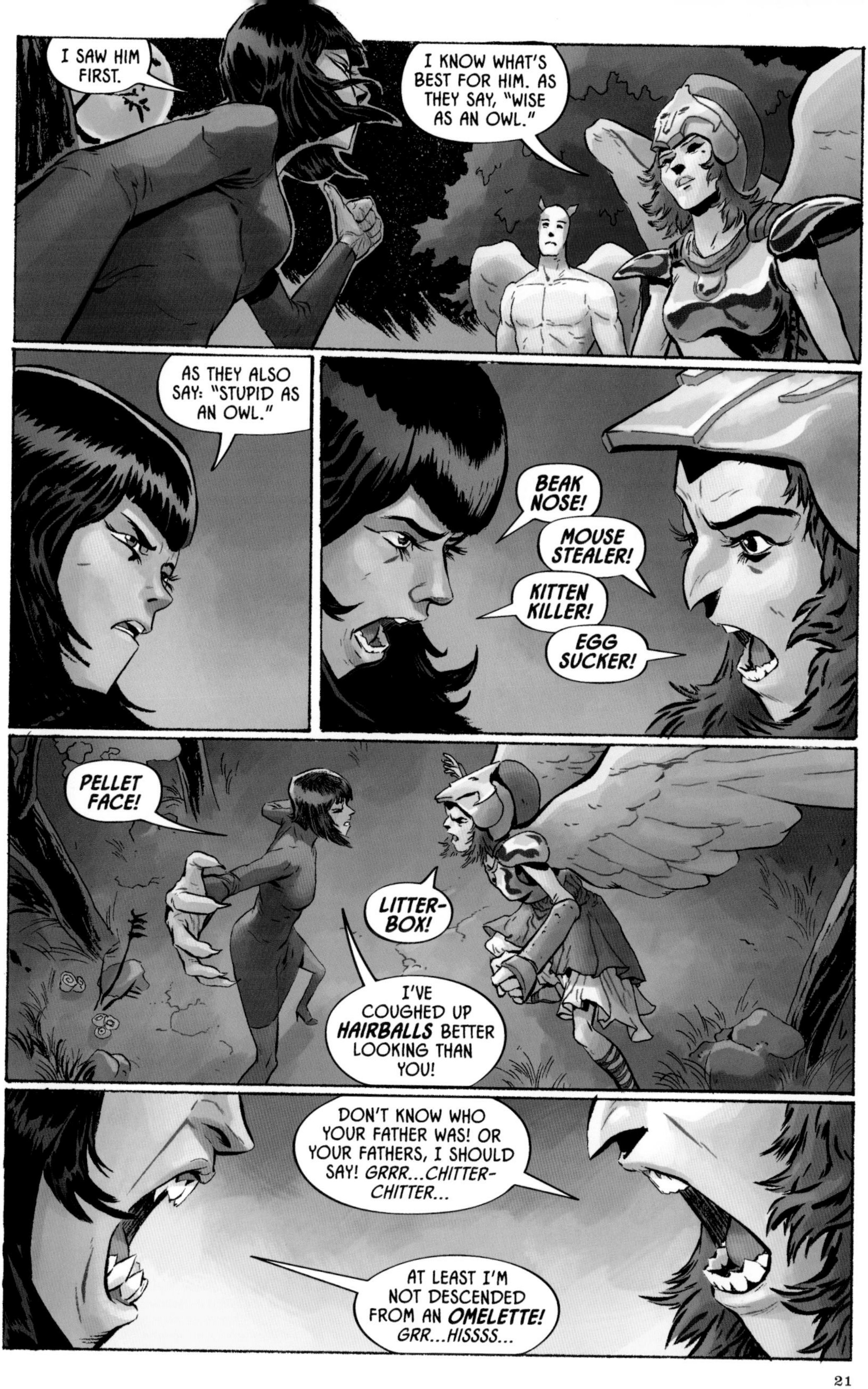
I SAW HIM FIRST.
I KNOW WHAT'S BEST FOR HIM. AS THEY SAY, "WISE AS AN OWL."
AS THEY ALSO SAY: "STUPID AS AN OWL."
BEAK NOSE!
MOUSE STEALER!
KITTEN KILLER!
EGG SUCKER!
PELLET FACE!
LITTER-BOX!
I'VE COUGHED UP HAIRBALLS BETTER LOOKING THAN YOU!
DON'T KNOW WHO YOUR FATHER WAS! OR YOUR FATHERS, I SHOULD SAY! GRRR...CHITTER-CHITTER...
AT LEAST I'M NOT DESCENDED FROM AN OMELETTE! GRR...HISSSS...

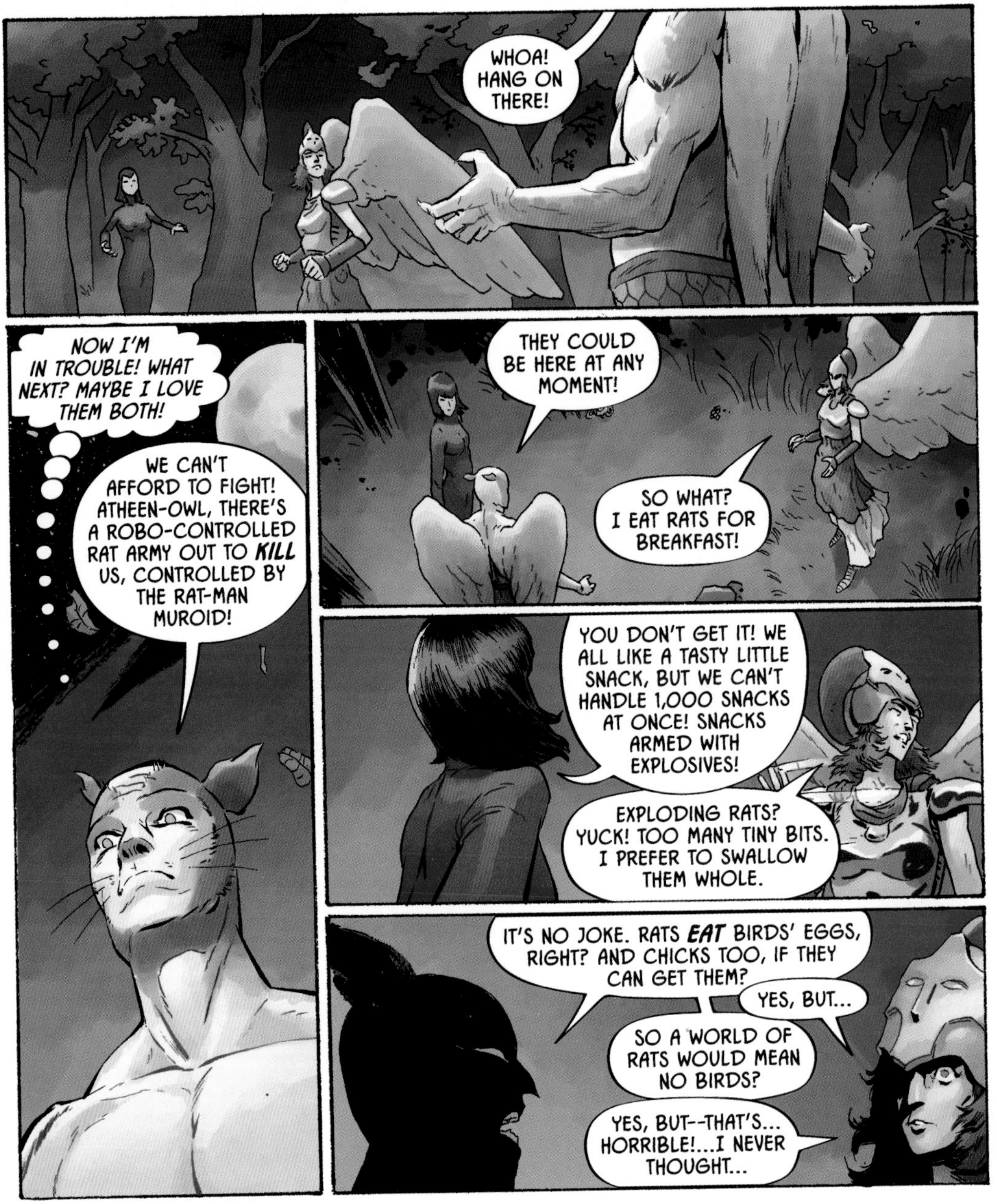

WHOA! HANG ON THERE!
NOW I'M IN TROUBLE! WHAT NEXT? MAYBE I LOVE THEM BOTH!
WE CAN'T AFFORD TO FIGHT! ATHEEN-OWL, THERE'S A ROBO-CONTROLLED RAT ARMY OUT TO KILL US, CONTROLLED BY THE RAT-MAN MUROID!
THEY COULD BE HERE AT ANY MOMENT!
SO WHAT? I EAT RATS FOR BREAKFAST!
YOU DON'T GET IT! WE ALL LIKE A TASTY LITTLE SNACK, BUT WE CAN'T HANDLE 1,000 SNACKS AT ONCE! SNACKS ARMED WITH EXPLOSIVES!
EXPLODING RATS? YUCK! TOO MANY TINY BITS. I PREFER TO SWALLOW THEM WHOLE.
IT'S NO JOKE. RATS EAT BIRDS' EGGS, RIGHT? AND CHICKS TOO, IF THEY CAN GET THEM?
YES, BUT...
SO A WORLD OF RATS WOULD MEAN NO BIRDS?
YES, BUT--THAT'S... HORRIBLE!...I NEVER THOUGHT...

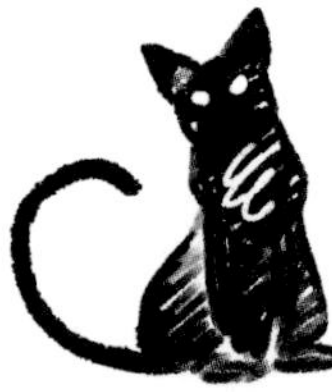

RATS AND CATS

140 bird species have gone extinct since AD 1500. Rats contributed to 41 extinctions and cats 34, making them the two most deadly factors. Extinctions partially or entirely caused by rats include species of lorikeet (Pacific Islands), white-winged sandpiper (Tahiti), bush wren and piopio (New Zealand), and robust white-eye (Lord Howe Island). Read more at www.birdlife.org and www.sciencedirect.com

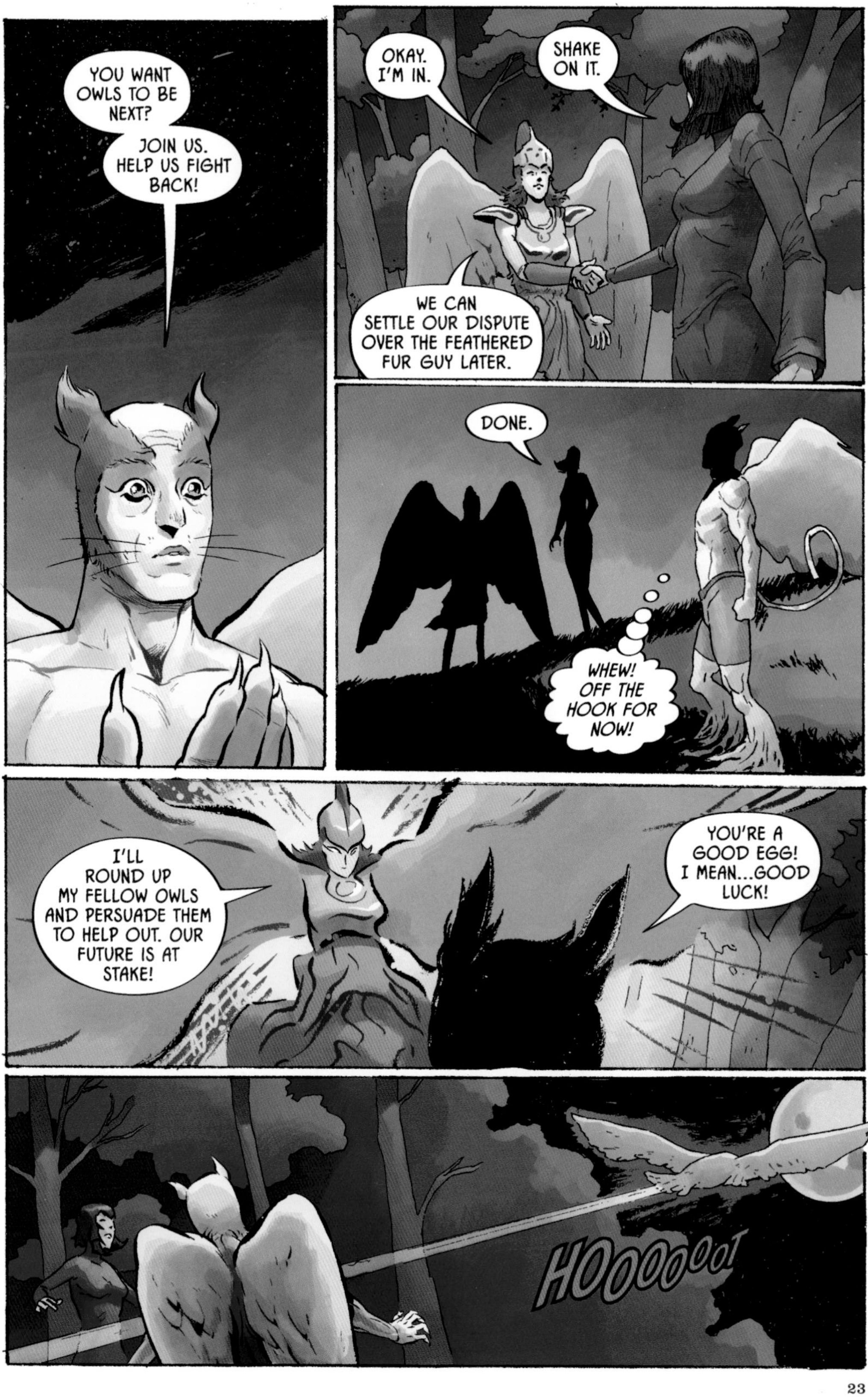
YOU WANT OWLS TO BE NEXT?
JOIN US. HELP US FIGHT BACK!
OKAY. I'M IN.
SHAKE ON IT.
WE CAN SETTLE OUR DISPUTE OVER THE FEATHERED FUR GUY LATER.
DONE.
WHEW! OFF THE HOOK FOR NOW!
I'LL ROUND UP MY FELLOW OWLS AND PERSUADE THEM TO HELP OUT. OUR FUTURE IS AT STAKE!
YOU'RE A GOOD EGG! I MEAN...GOOD LUCK!
HOOOOoot

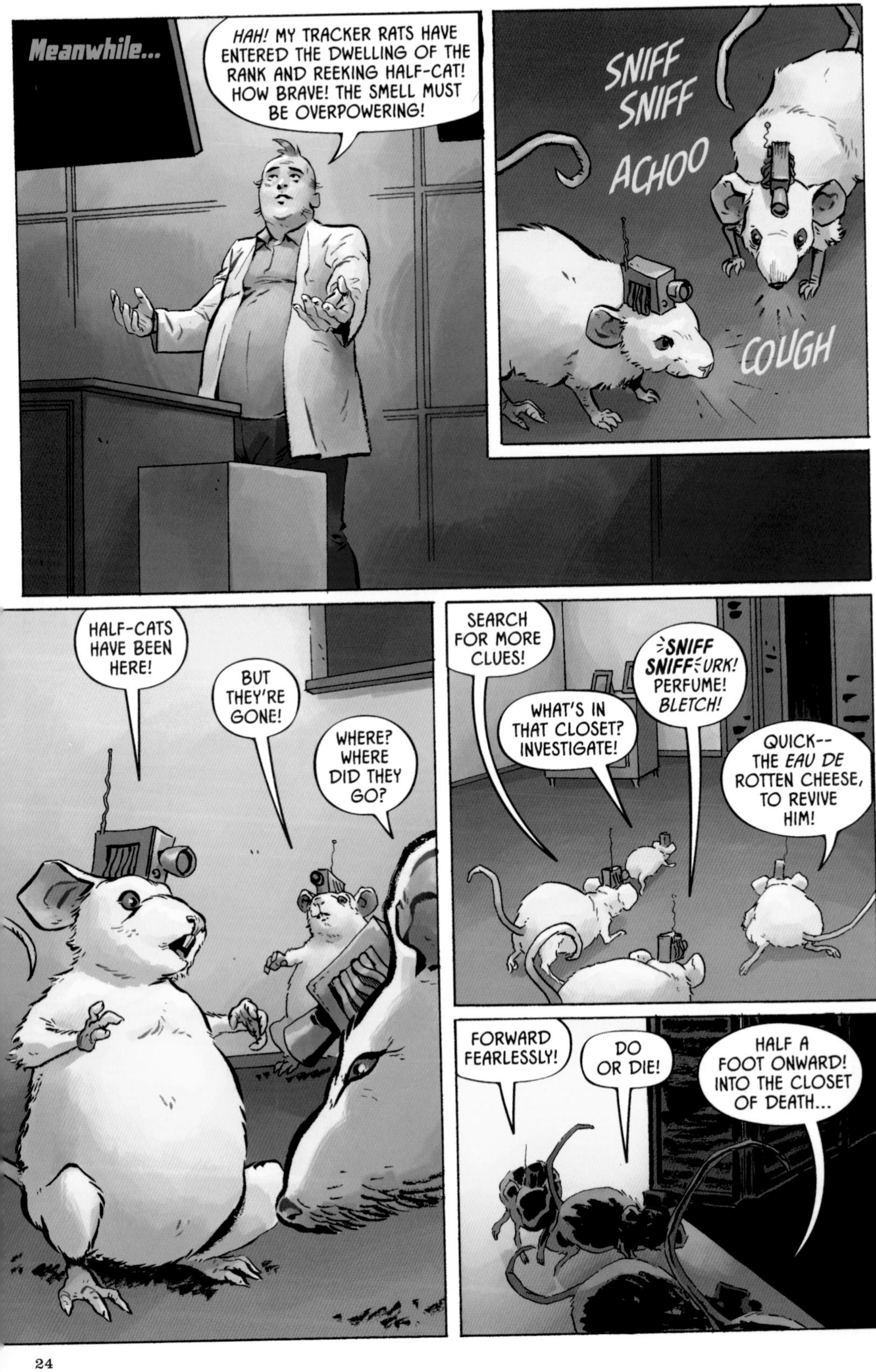
Meanwhile...
HAH! MY TRACKER RATS HAVE ENTERED THE DWELLING OF THE RANK AND REEKING HALF-CAT! HOW BRAVE! THE SMELL MUST BE OVERPOWERING!
SNIFF SNIFF
ACHOO
COUGH
HALF-CATS HAVE BEEN HERE!
BUT THEY'RE GONE!
WHERE? WHERE DID THEY GO?
SEARCH FOR MORE CLUES!
SNIFF SNIFF URK! PERFUME! BLETCH!
WHAT'S IN THAT CLOSET? INVESTIGATE!
QUICK-- THE EAU DE ROTTEN CHEESE, TO REVIVE HIM!
FORWARD FEARLESSLY!
DO OR DIE!
HALF A FOOT ONWARD! INTO THE CLOSET OF DEATH...

SQUEAK

SQUEAK

SQUEAK

WHAT THE HECK HAS GOT INTO THEM?

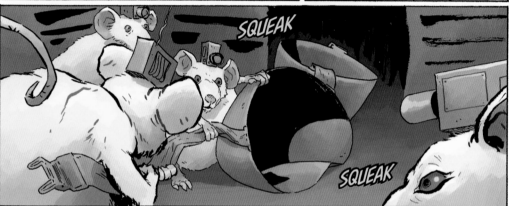

SQUEAK

SQUEAK

WHAT'S THE MATTER WITH YOU? WHAT ARE YOU DOING WITH THAT BRA? HAVEN'T YOU EVER SEEN A BRA BEFORE?

SQUEAK

SQUEAK

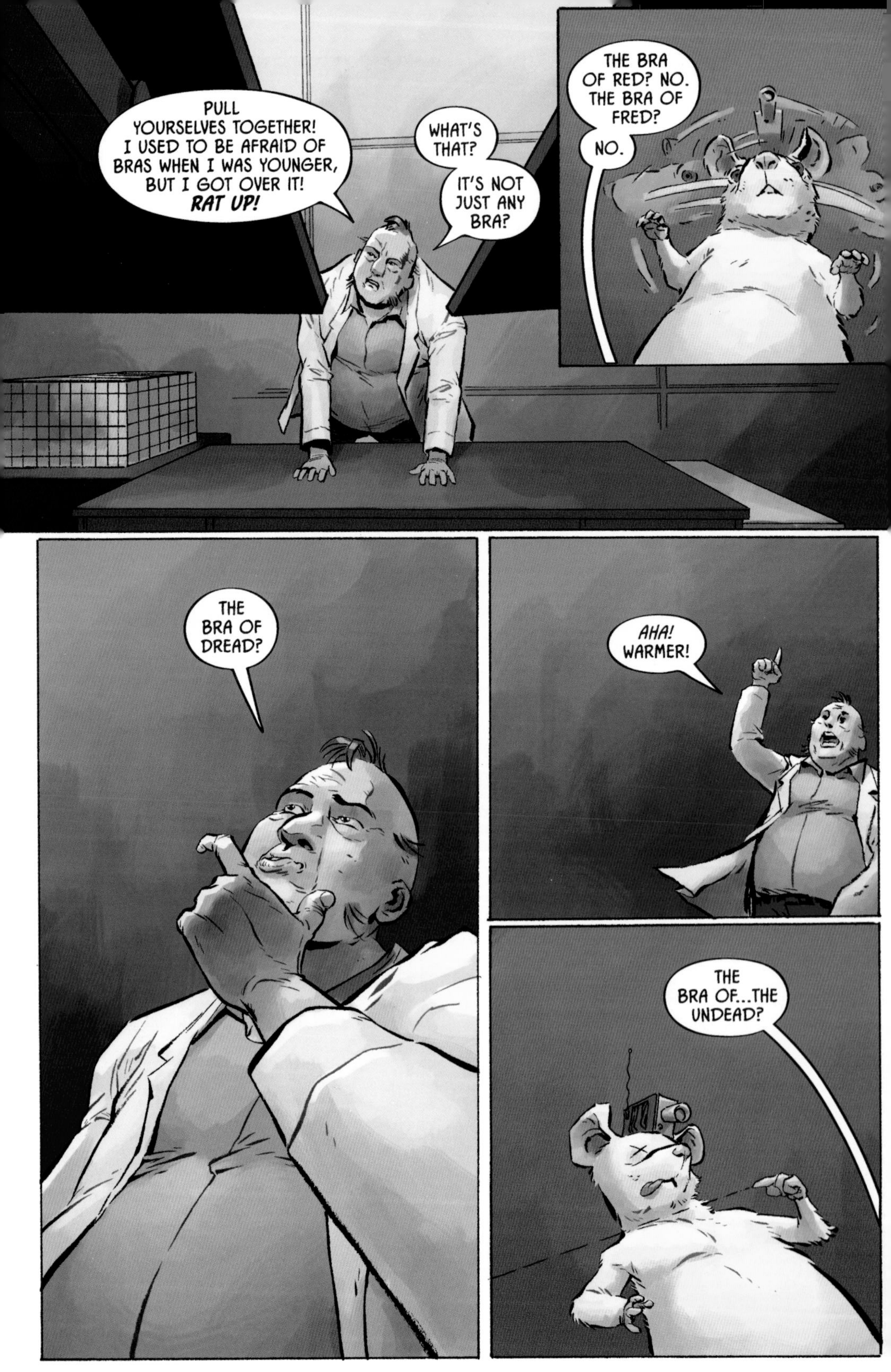
PULL YOURSELVES TOGETHER! I USED TO BE AFRAID OF BRAS WHEN I WAS YOUNGER, BUT I GOT OVER IT! RAT UP!
WHAT'S THAT?
IT'S NOT JUST ANY BRA?
THE BRA OF RED? NO. THE BRA OF FRED?
NO.
THE BRA OF DREAD?
AHA! WARMER!
THE BRA OF...THE UNDEAD?

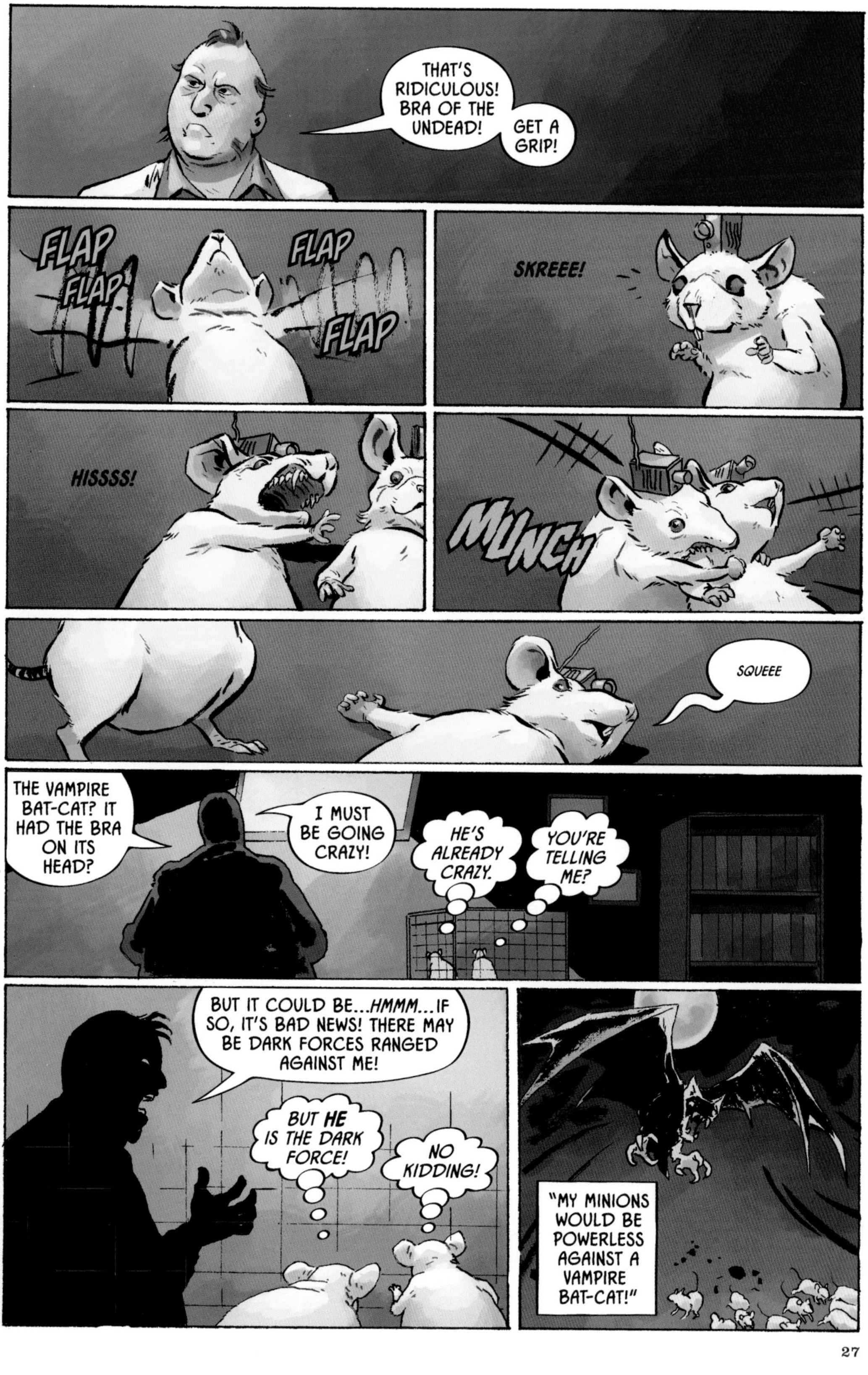
THAT'S RIDICULOUS! BRA OF THE UNDEAD!
GET A GRIP!
FLAP
FLAP
FLAP
FLAP
SKREEE!
HISSSS!
MUNCH
SQUEEE
THE VAMPIRE BAT-CAT? IT HAD THE BRA ON ITS HEAD?
I MUST BE GOING CRAZY!
HE'S ALREADY CRAZY.
YOU'RE TELLING ME?
BUT IT COULD BE...HMMM...IF SO, IT'S BAD NEWS! THERE MAY BE DARK FORCES RANGED AGAINST ME!
BUT HE IS THE DARK FORCE!
NO KIDDING!
"MY MINIONS WOULD BE POWERLESS AGAINST A VAMPIRE BAT-CAT!"

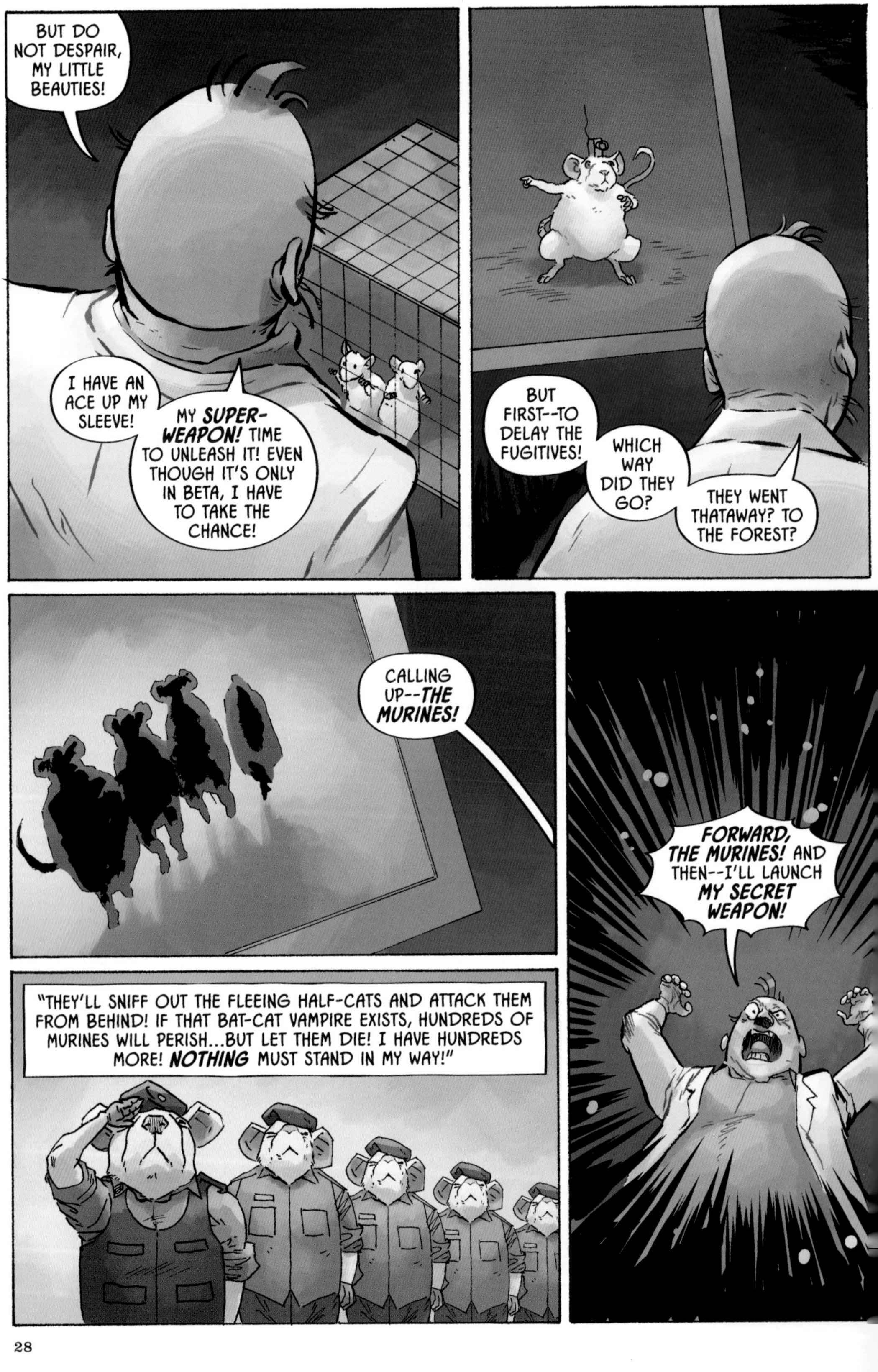
BUT DO NOT DESPAIR, MY LITTLE BEAUTIES!
I HAVE AN ACE UP MY SLEEVE!
MY SUPER-WEAPON! TIME TO UNLEASH IT! EVEN THOUGH IT'S ONLY IN BETA, I HAVE TO TAKE THE CHANCE!
BUT FIRST--TO DELAY THE FUGITIVES!
WHICH WAY DID THEY GO?
THEY WENT THATAWAY? TO THE FOREST?
CALLING UP--THE MURINES!
"THEY'LL SNIFF OUT THE FLEEING HALF-CATS AND ATTACK THEM FROM BEHIND! IF THAT BAT-CAT VAMPIRE EXISTS, HUNDREDS OF MURINES WILL PERISH...BUT LET THEM DIE! I HAVE HUNDREDS MORE! NOTHING MUST STAND IN MY WAY!"
FORWARD, THE MURINES! AND THEN--I'LL LAUNCH MY SECRET WEAPON!

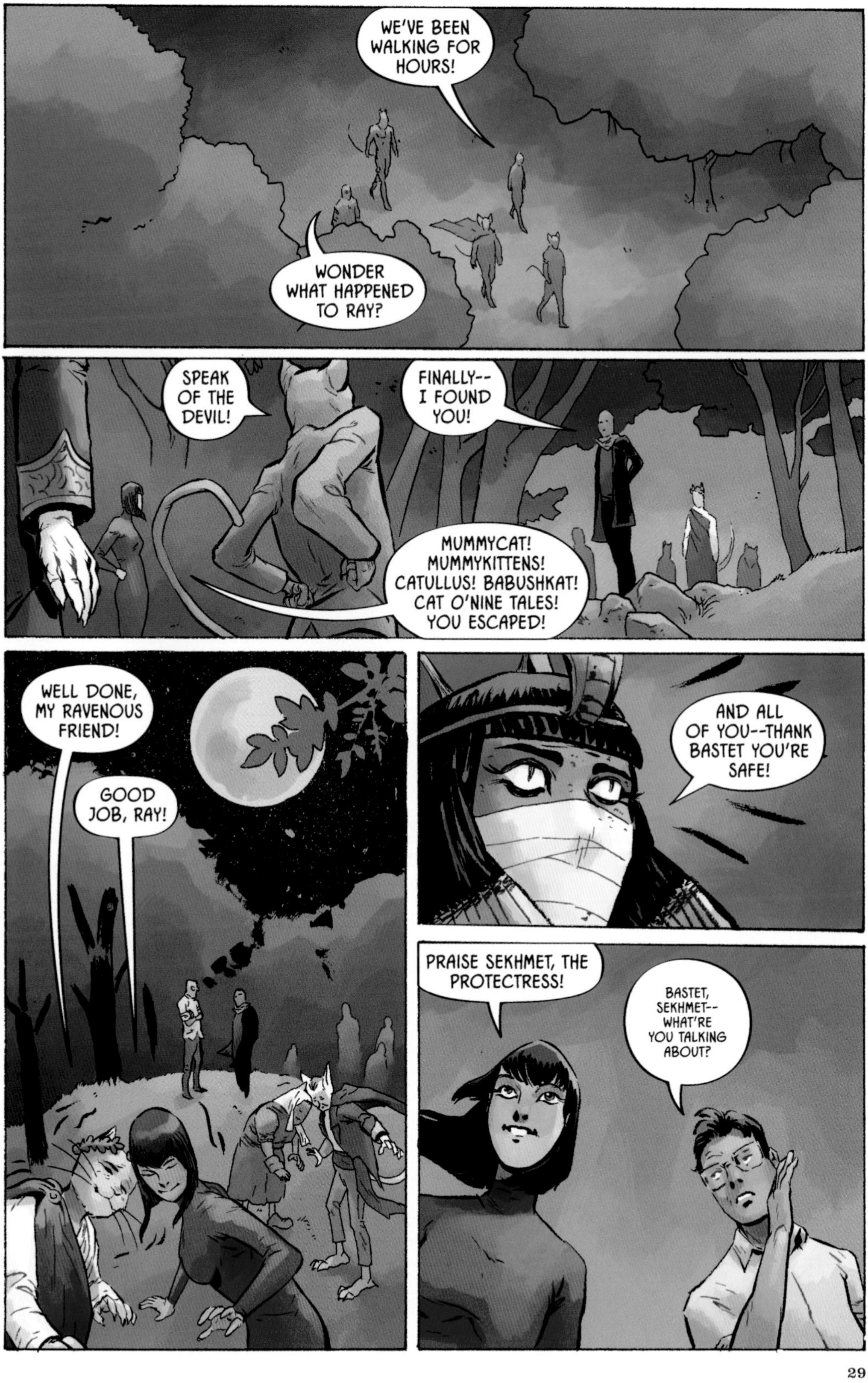
WE'VE BEEN WALKING FOR HOURS!
WONDER WHAT HAPPENED TO RAY?
SPEAK OF THE DEVIL!
FINALLY-- I FOUND YOU!
MUMMYCAT! MUMMYKITTENS! CATULLUS! BABUSHKAT! CAT O'NINE TALES! YOU ESCAPED!
WELL DONE, MY RAVENOUS FRIEND!
GOOD JOB, RAY!
AND ALL OF YOU--THANK BASTET YOU'RE SAFE!
PRAISE SEKHMET, THE PROTECTRESS!
BASTET, SEKHMET-- WHAT'RE YOU TALKING ABOUT?

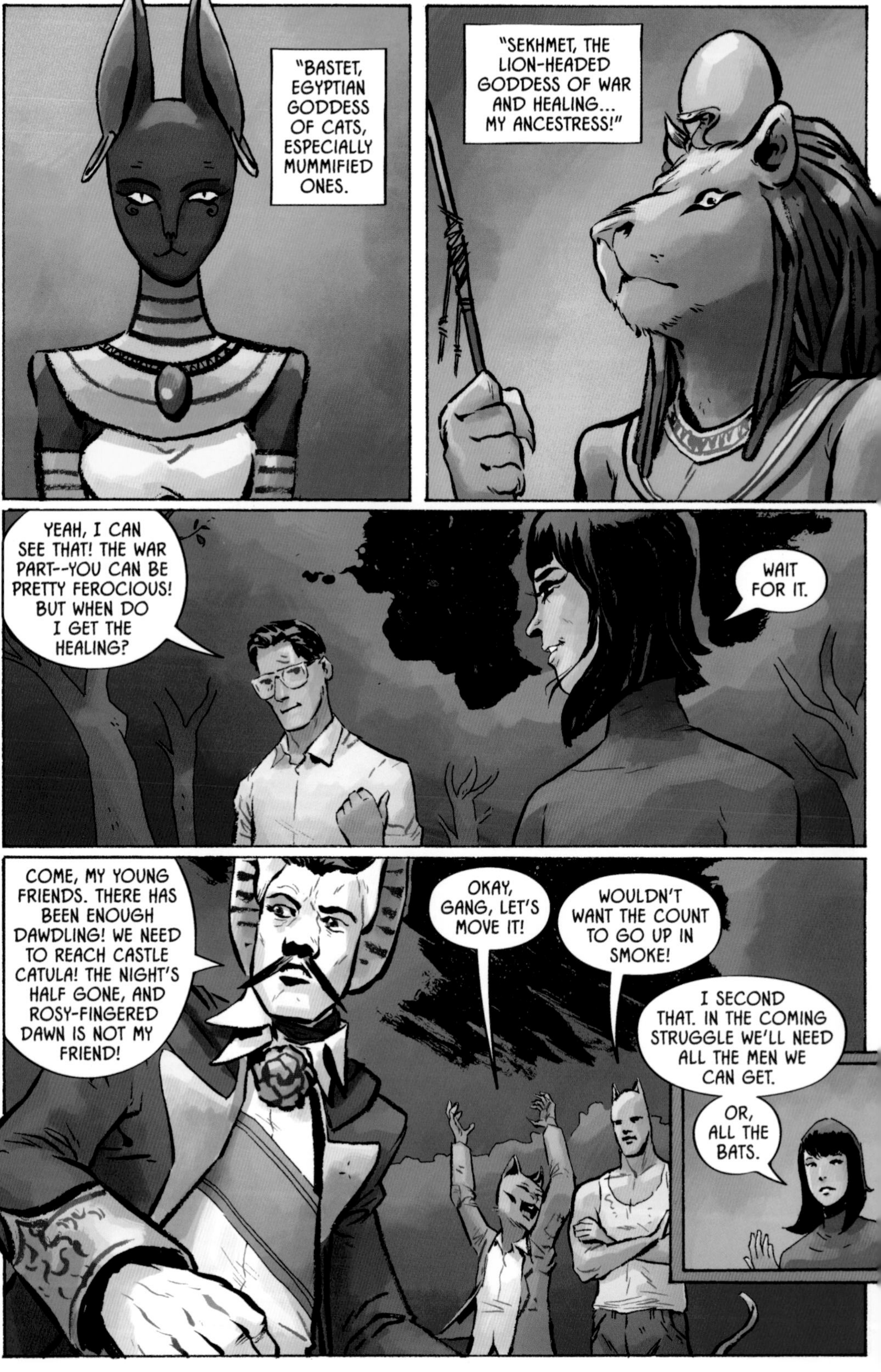
"BASTET, EGYPTIAN GODDESS OF CATS, ESPECIALLY MUMMIFIED ONES.
"SEKHMET, THE LION-HEADED GODDESS OF WAR AND HEALING... MY ANCESTRESS!"
YEAH, I CAN SEE THAT! THE WAR PART--YOU CAN BE PRETTY FEROCIOUS! BUT WHEN DO I GET THE HEALING?
WAIT FOR IT.
COME, MY YOUNG FRIENDS. THERE HAS BEEN ENOUGH DAWDLING! WE NEED TO REACH CASTLE CATULA! THE NIGHT'S HALF GONE, AND ROSY-FINGERED DAWN IS NOT MY FRIEND!
OKAY, GANG, LET'S MOVE IT!
WOULDN'T WANT THE COUNT TO GO UP IN SMOKE!
I SECOND THAT. IN THE COMING STRUGGLE WE'LL NEED ALL THE MEN WE CAN GET.
OR, ALL THE BATS.

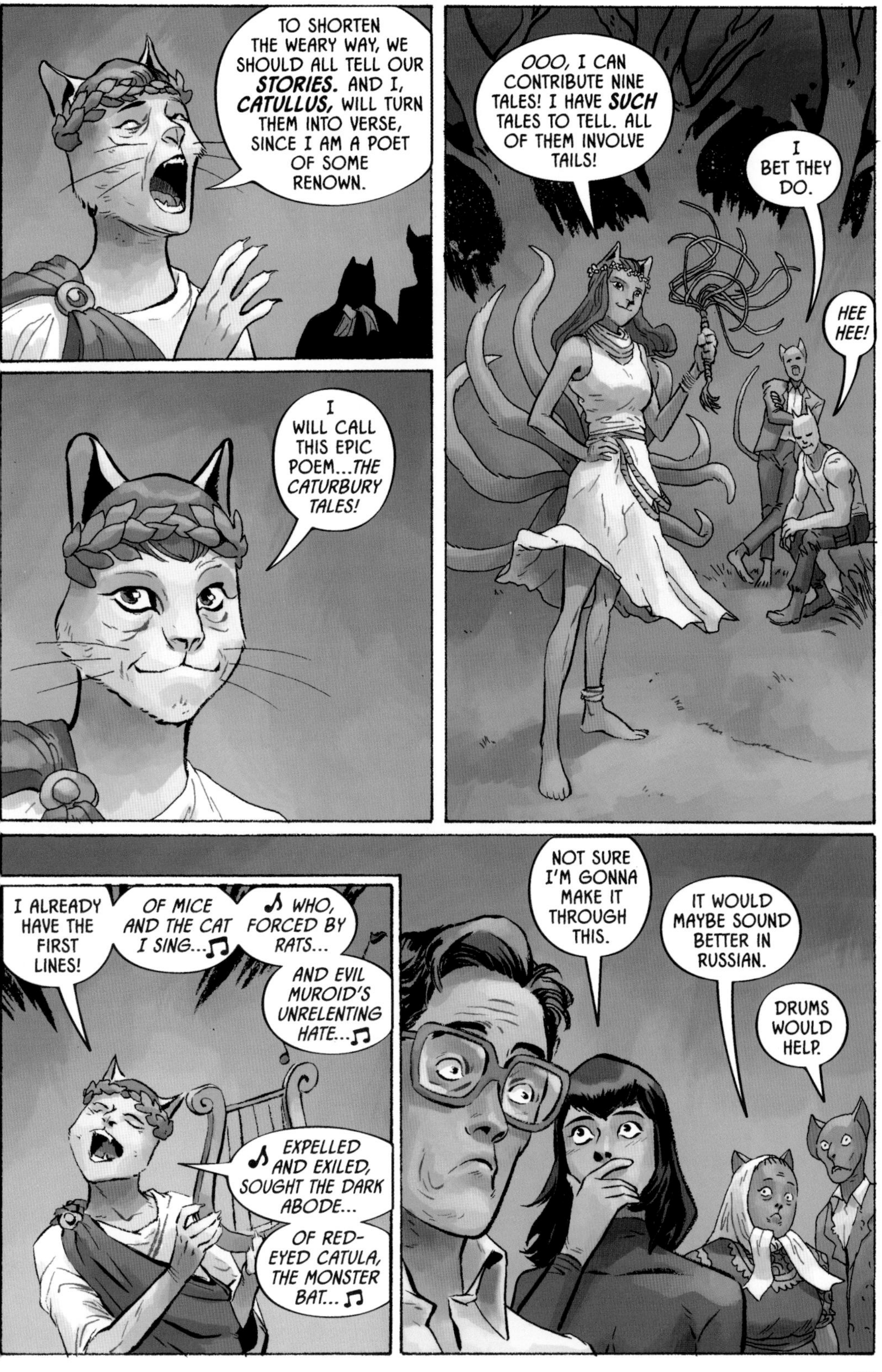
TO SHORTEN THE WEARY WAY, WE SHOULD ALL TELL OUR **STORIES.** AND I, **CATULLUS,** WILL TURN THEM INTO VERSE, SINCE I AM A POET OF SOME RENOWN.
OOO, I CAN CONTRIBUTE NINE TALES! I HAVE **SUCH** TALES TO TELL. ALL OF THEM INVOLVE TAILS!
I BET THEY DO.
HEE HEE!
I WILL CALL THIS EPIC POEM...*THE CATURBURY TALES!*
NOT SURE I'M GONNA MAKE IT THROUGH THIS.
IT WOULD MAYBE SOUND BETTER IN RUSSIAN.
DRUMS WOULD HELP.
I ALREADY HAVE THE FIRST LINES!
OF MICE AND THE CAT I SING...♫
♪ WHO, FORCED BY RATS...
AND EVIL MUROID'S UNRELENTING HATE...♫
♪ EXPELLED AND EXILED, SOUGHT THE DARK ABODE...
OF RED-EYED CATULA, THE MONSTER BAT...♫

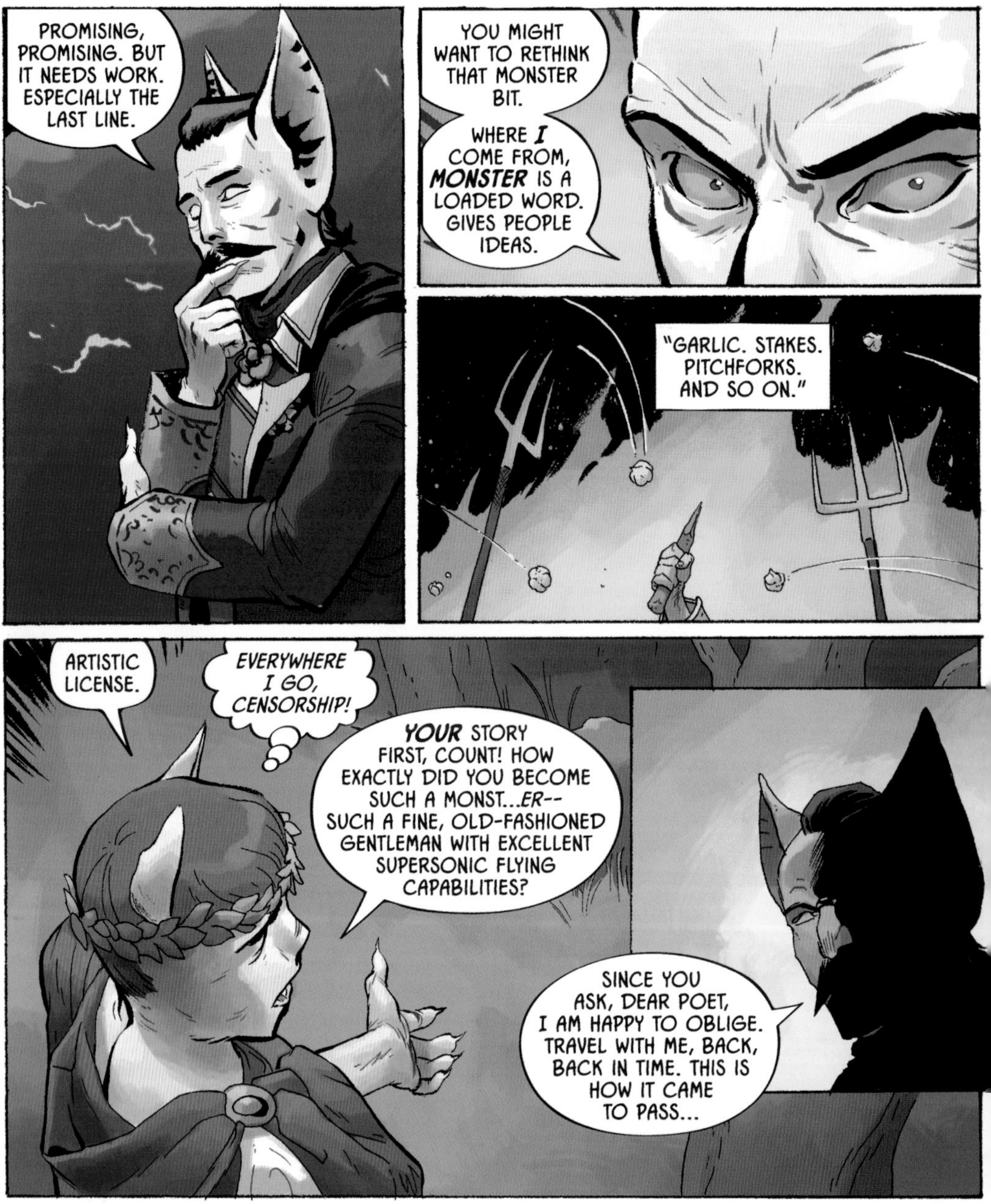
PROMISING, PROMISING. BUT IT NEEDS WORK. ESPECIALLY THE LAST LINE.
YOU MIGHT WANT TO RETHINK THAT MONSTER BIT.
WHERE *I* COME FROM, **MONSTER** IS A LOADED WORD. GIVES PEOPLE IDEAS.
"GARLIC. STAKES. PITCHFORKS. AND SO ON."
ARTISTIC LICENSE.
EVERYWHERE I GO, CENSORSHIP!
YOUR STORY FIRST, COUNT! HOW EXACTLY DID YOU BECOME SUCH A MONST...*ER*-- SUCH A FINE, OLD-FASHIONED GENTLEMAN WITH EXCELLENT SUPERSONIC FLYING CAPABILITIES?
SINCE YOU ASK, DEAR POET, I AM HAPPY TO OBLIGE. TRAVEL WITH ME, BACK, BACK IN TIME. THIS IS HOW IT CAME TO PASS...

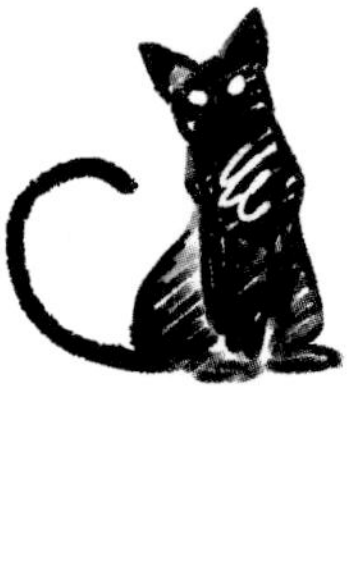

MONSTERS?

Cats are hunters, but they're not monsters—they're just doing what comes naturally. Cat owners are responsible for their pets' behavior, indoors and out, just as with dogs.
Read more at www.catsandbirds.ca

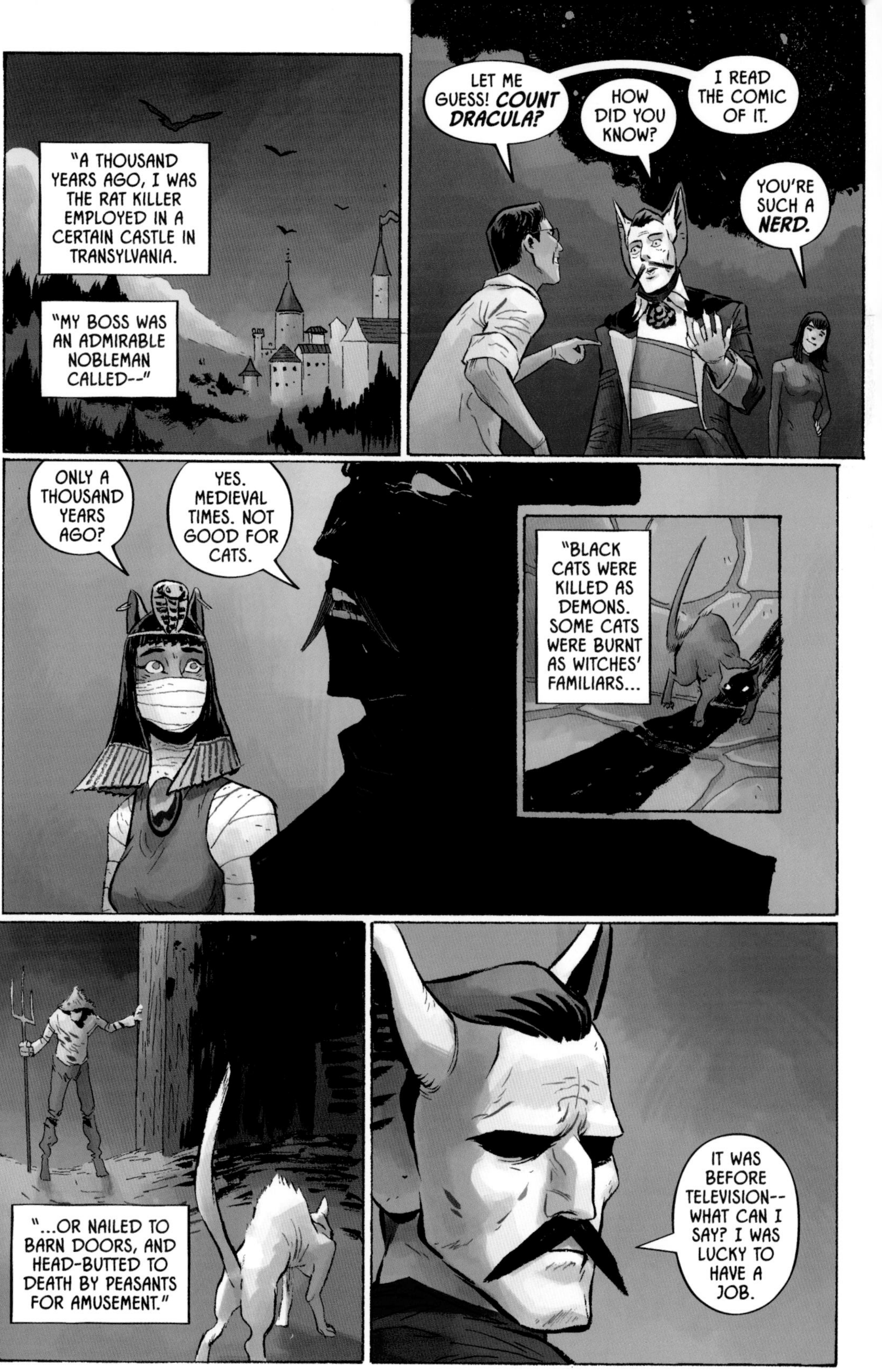

"A THOUSAND YEARS AGO, I WAS THE RAT KILLER EMPLOYED IN A CERTAIN CASTLE IN TRANSYLVANIA.
"MY BOSS WAS AN ADMIRABLE NOBLEMAN CALLED--"
LET ME GUESS! COUNT DRACULA?
HOW DID YOU KNOW?
I READ THE COMIC OF IT.
YOU'RE SUCH A NERD.
ONLY A THOUSAND YEARS AGO?
YES. MEDIEVAL TIMES. NOT GOOD FOR CATS.
"BLACK CATS WERE KILLED AS DEMONS. SOME CATS WERE BURNT AS WITCHES' FAMILIARS...
"...OR NAILED TO BARN DOORS, AND HEAD-BUTTED TO DEATH BY PEASANTS FOR AMUSEMENT."
IT WAS BEFORE TELEVISION-- WHAT CAN I SAY? I WAS LUCKY TO HAVE A JOB.

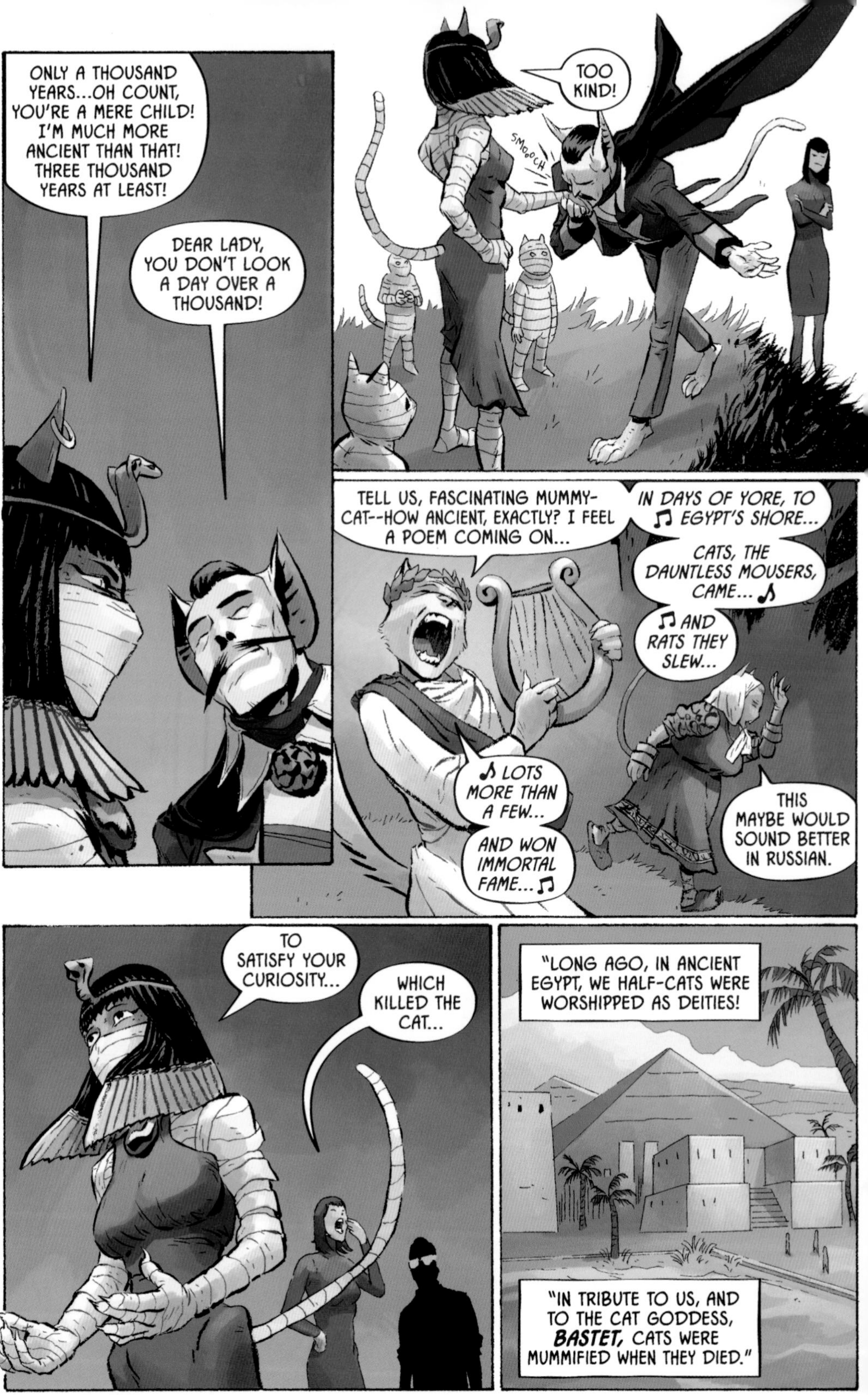
ONLY A THOUSAND YEARS...OH COUNT, YOU'RE A MERE CHILD! I'M MUCH MORE ANCIENT THAN THAT! THREE THOUSAND YEARS AT LEAST!
DEAR LADY, YOU DON'T LOOK A DAY OVER A THOUSAND!
TOO KIND!
SMOOOCH
TELL US, FASCINATING MUMMY-CAT--HOW ANCIENT, EXACTLY? I FEEL A POEM COMING ON...
IN DAYS OF YORE, TO ♫ EGYPT'S SHORE...
CATS, THE DAUNTLESS MOUSERS, CAME... ♪
♫ AND RATS THEY SLEW...
♪ LOTS MORE THAN A FEW...
AND WON IMMORTAL FAME... ♫
THIS MAYBE WOULD SOUND BETTER IN RUSSIAN.
TO SATISFY YOUR CURIOSITY...
WHICH KILLED THE CAT...
"LONG AGO, IN ANCIENT EGYPT, WE HALF-CATS WERE WORSHIPPED AS DEITIES!
"IN TRIBUTE TO US, AND TO THE CAT GODDESS, **BASTET,** CATS WERE MUMMIFIED WHEN THEY DIED."

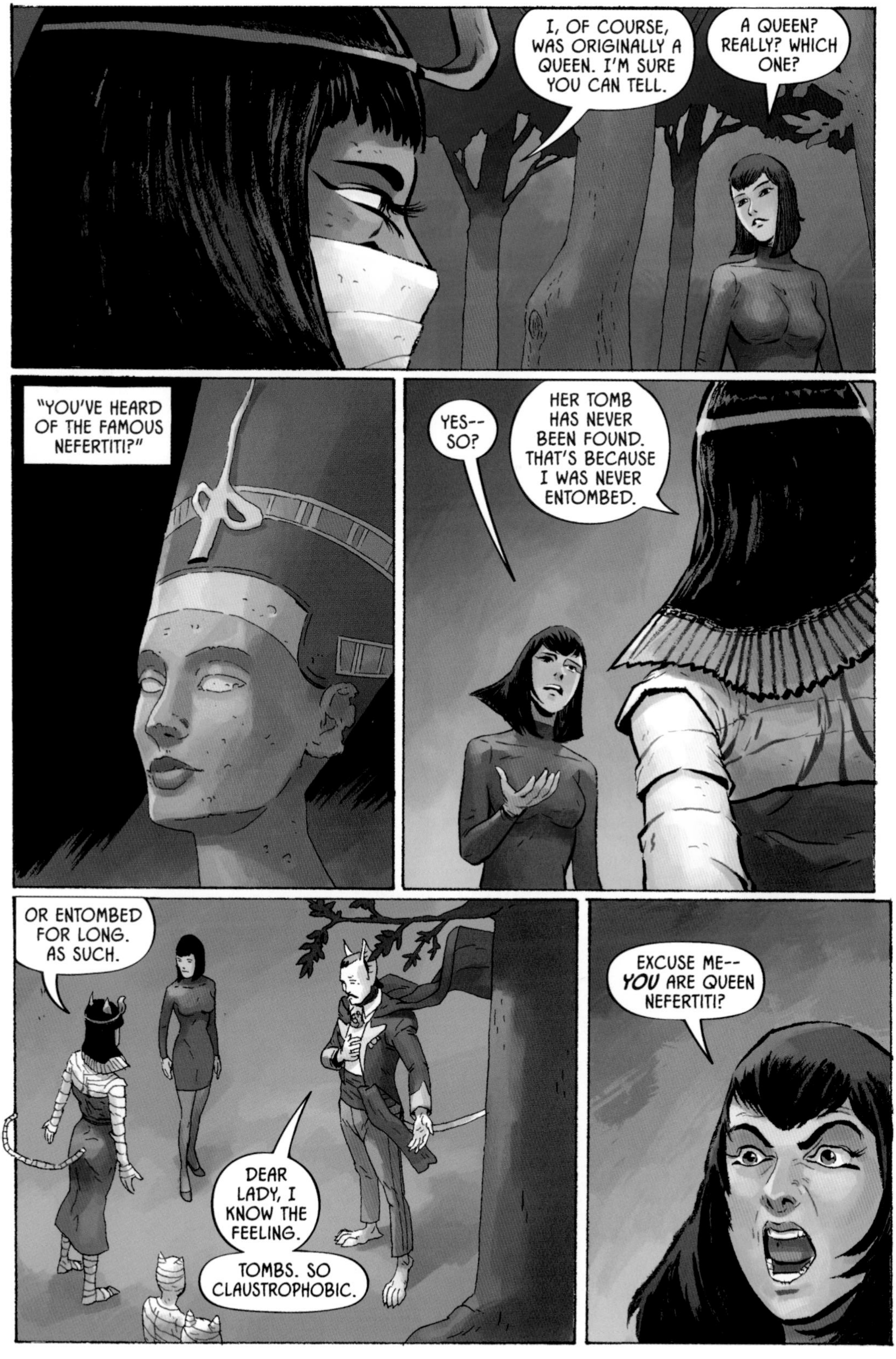
I, OF COURSE, WAS ORIGINALLY A QUEEN. I'M SURE YOU CAN TELL.
A QUEEN? REALLY? WHICH ONE?
"YOU'VE HEARD OF THE FAMOUS NEFERTITI?"
YES-- SO?
HER TOMB HAS NEVER BEEN FOUND. THAT'S BECAUSE I WAS NEVER ENTOMBED.
OR ENTOMBED FOR LONG. AS SUCH.
DEAR LADY, I KNOW THE FEELING.
TOMBS. SO CLAUSTROPHOBIC.
EXCUSE ME-- *YOU* ARE QUEEN NEFERTITI?

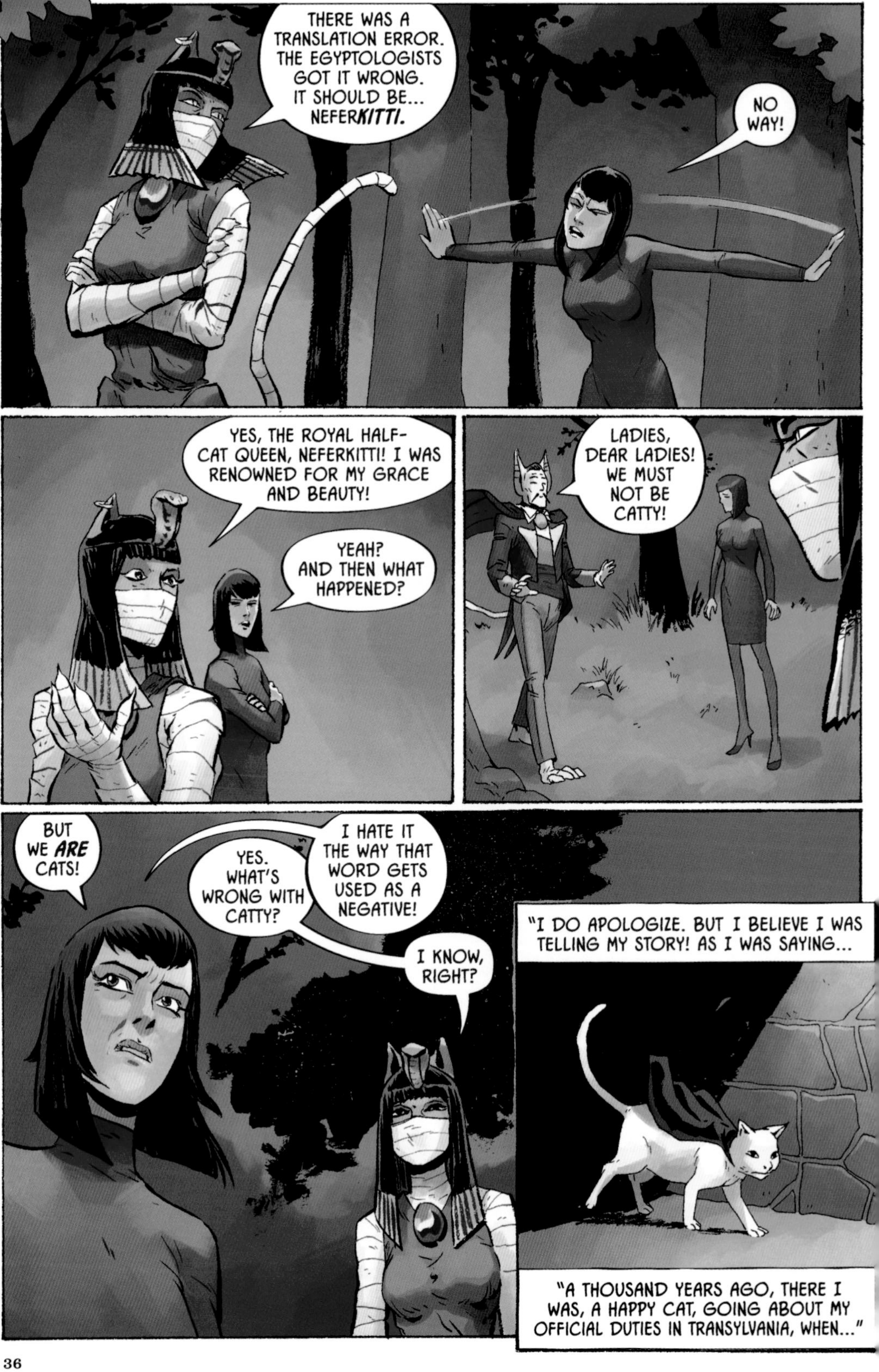
THERE WAS A TRANSLATION ERROR. THE EGYPTOLOGISTS GOT IT WRONG. IT SHOULD BE... NEFER*KITTI.*
NO WAY!
YES, THE ROYAL HALF-CAT QUEEN, NEFERKITTI! I WAS RENOWNED FOR MY GRACE AND BEAUTY!
YEAH? AND THEN WHAT HAPPENED?
LADIES, DEAR LADIES! WE MUST NOT BE CATTY!
BUT WE *ARE* CATS!
YES. WHAT'S WRONG WITH CATTY?
I HATE IT THE WAY THAT WORD GETS USED AS A NEGATIVE!
I KNOW, RIGHT?
"I DO APOLOGIZE. BUT I BELIEVE I WAS TELLING MY STORY! AS I WAS SAYING...
"A THOUSAND YEARS AGO, THERE I WAS, A HAPPY CAT, GOING ABOUT MY OFFICIAL DUTIES IN TRANSYLVANIA, WHEN..."

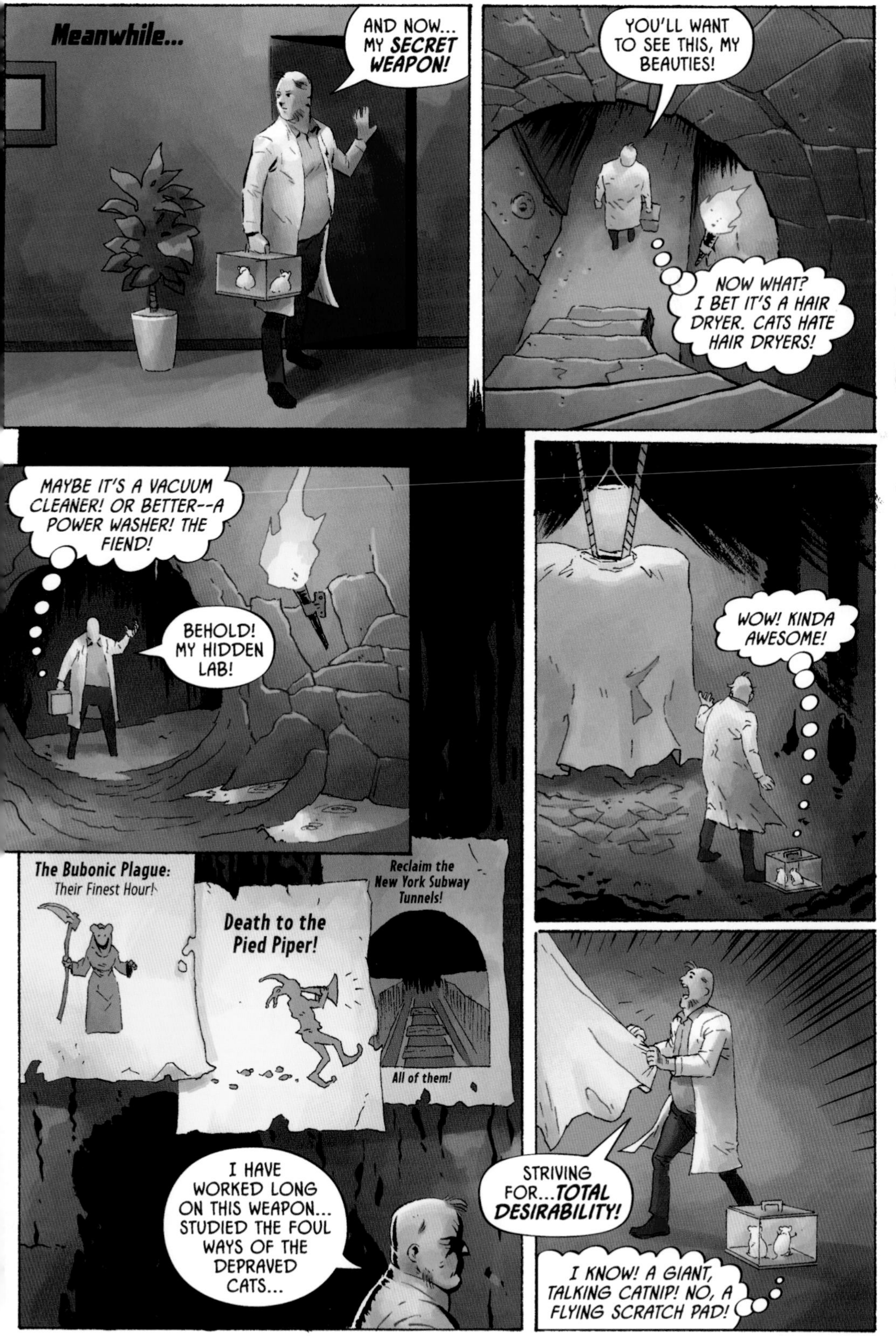
Meanwhile...
AND NOW... MY SECRET WEAPON!
YOU'LL WANT TO SEE THIS, MY BEAUTIES!
NOW WHAT? I BET IT'S A HAIR DRYER. CATS HATE HAIR DRYERS!
MAYBE IT'S A VACUUM CLEANER! OR BETTER--A POWER WASHER! THE FIEND!
BEHOLD! MY HIDDEN LAB!
WOW! KINDA AWESOME!
The Bubonic Plague: Their Finest Hour!
Death to the Pied Piper!
Reclaim the New York Subway Tunnels!
All of them!
I HAVE WORKED LONG ON THIS WEAPON... STUDIED THE FOUL WAYS OF THE DEPRAVED CATS...
STRIVING FOR...TOTAL DESIRABILITY!
I KNOW! A GIANT, TALKING CATNIP! NO, A FLYING SCRATCH PAD!

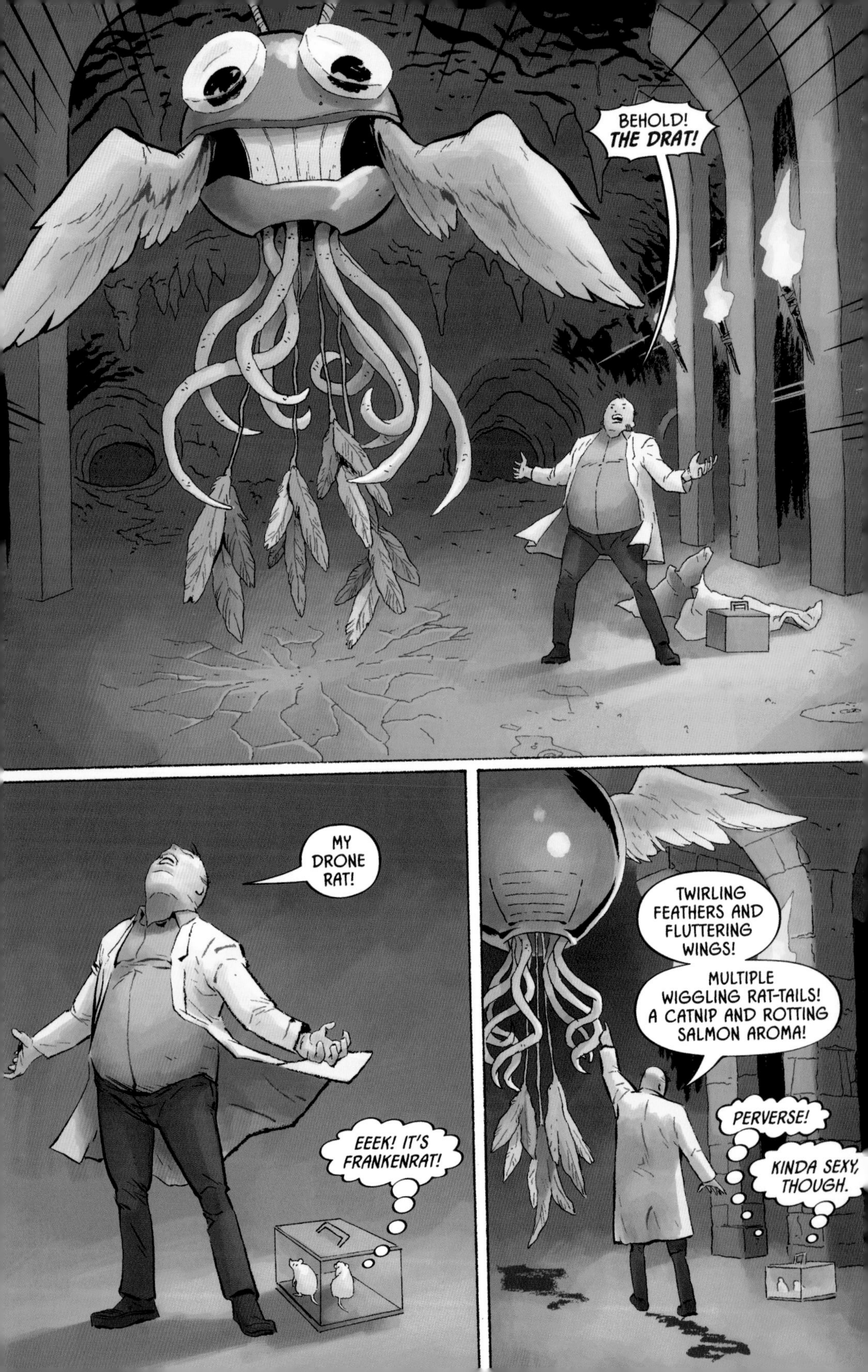
BEHOLD! THE DRAT!
MY DRONE RAT!
EEEK! IT'S FRANKENRAT!
TWIRLING FEATHERS AND FLUTTERING WINGS!
MULTIPLE WIGGLING RAT-TAILS! A CATNIP AND ROTTING SALMON AROMA!
PERVERSE!
KINDA SEXY, THOUGH.

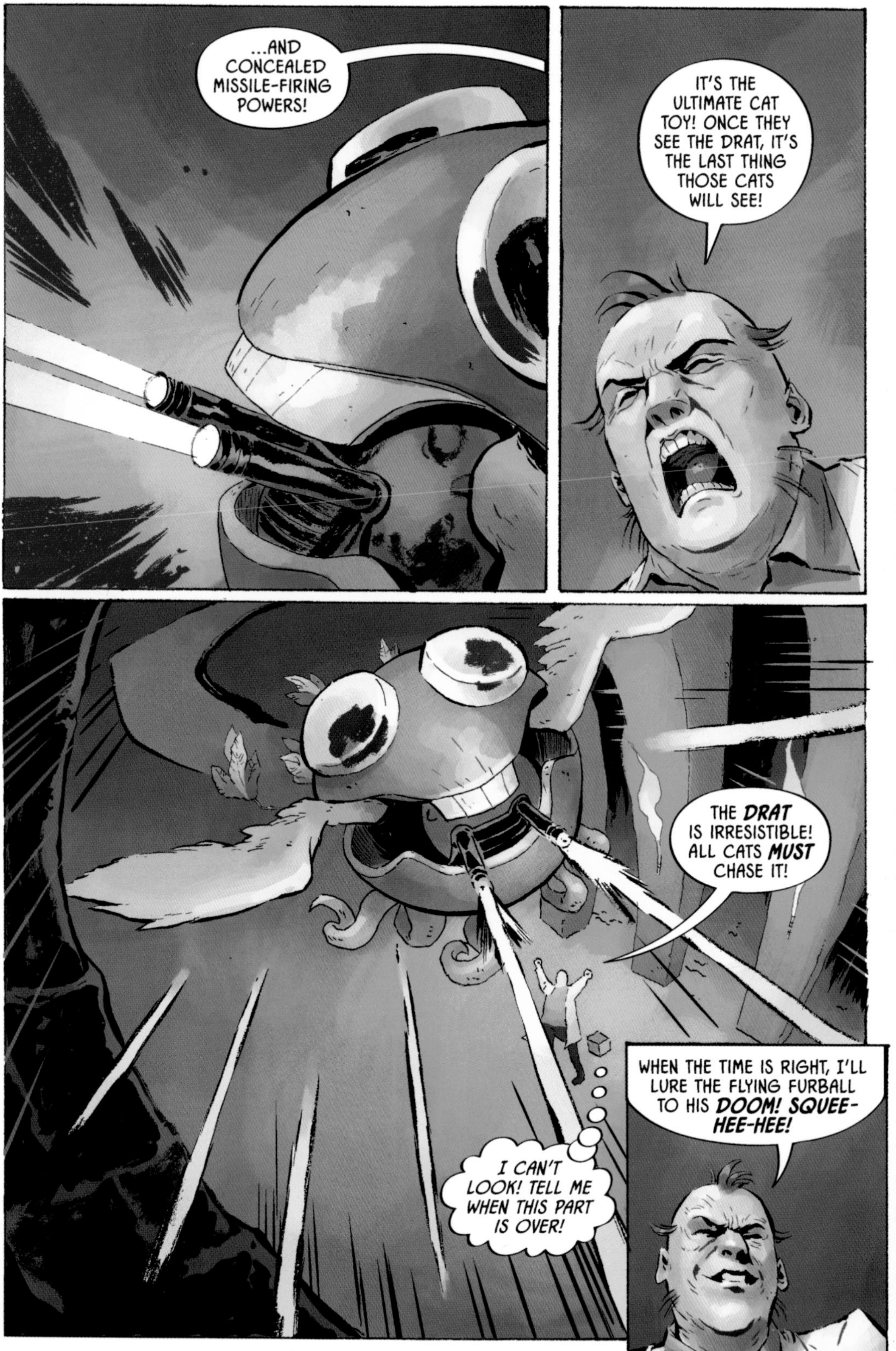
...AND CONCEALED MISSILE-FIRING POWERS!
IT'S THE ULTIMATE CAT TOY! ONCE THEY SEE THE DRAT, IT'S THE LAST THING THOSE CATS WILL SEE!
THE **DRAT** IS IRRESISTIBLE! ALL CATS **MUST** CHASE IT!
WHEN THE TIME IS RIGHT, I'LL LURE THE FLYING FURBALL TO HIS **DOOM! SQUEE-HEE-HEE!**
I CAN'T LOOK! TELL ME WHEN THIS PART IS OVER!

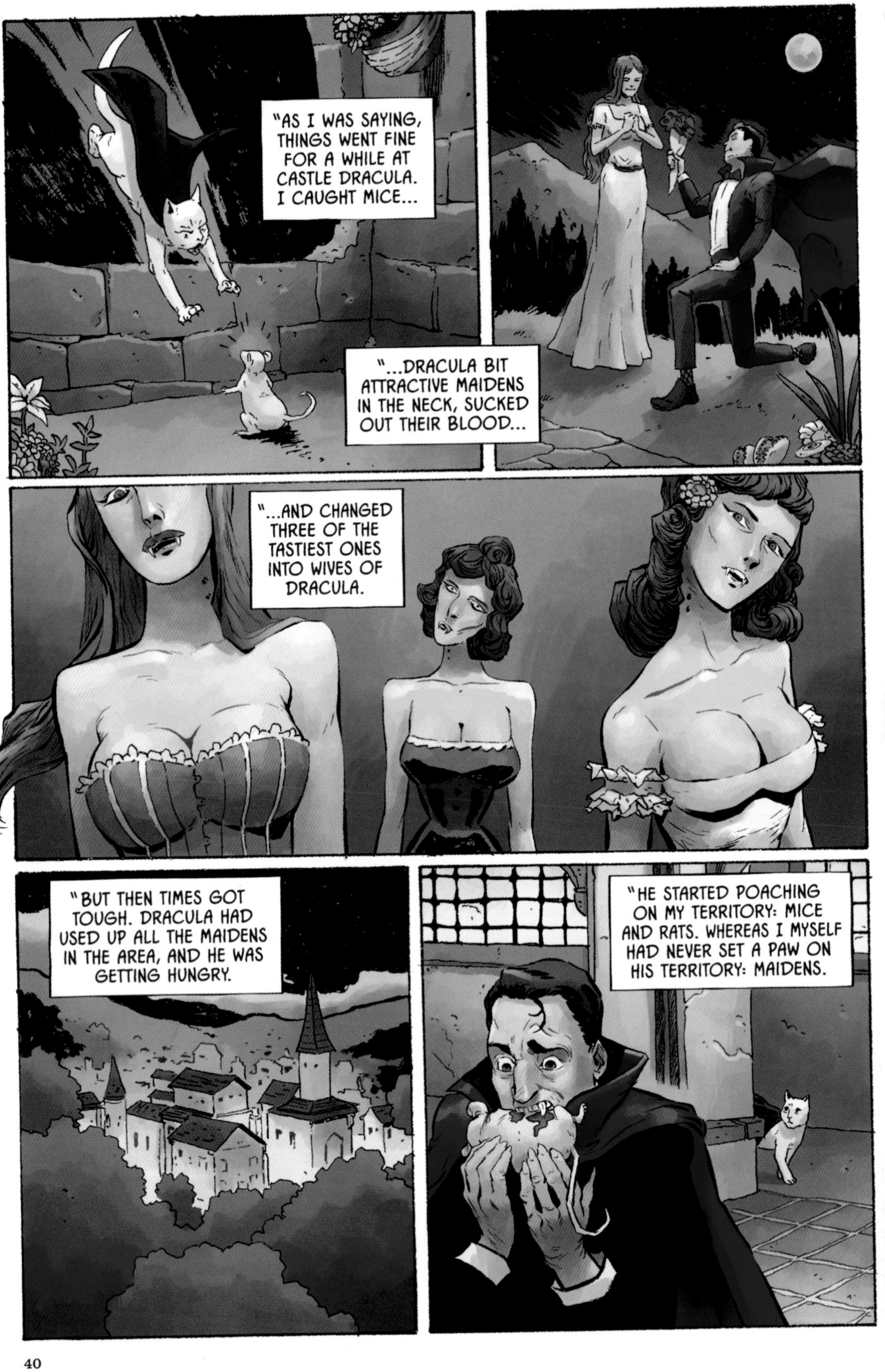
"AS I WAS SAYING, THINGS WENT FINE FOR A WHILE AT CASTLE DRACULA. I CAUGHT MICE...
"...DRACULA BIT ATTRACTIVE MAIDENS IN THE NECK, SUCKED OUT THEIR BLOOD...
"...AND CHANGED THREE OF THE TASTIEST ONES INTO WIVES OF DRACULA.
"BUT THEN TIMES GOT TOUGH. DRACULA HAD USED UP ALL THE MAIDENS IN THE AREA, AND HE WAS GETTING HUNGRY.
"HE STARTED POACHING ON MY TERRITORY: MICE AND RATS. WHEREAS I MYSELF HAD NEVER SET A PAW ON HIS TERRITORY: MAIDENS.

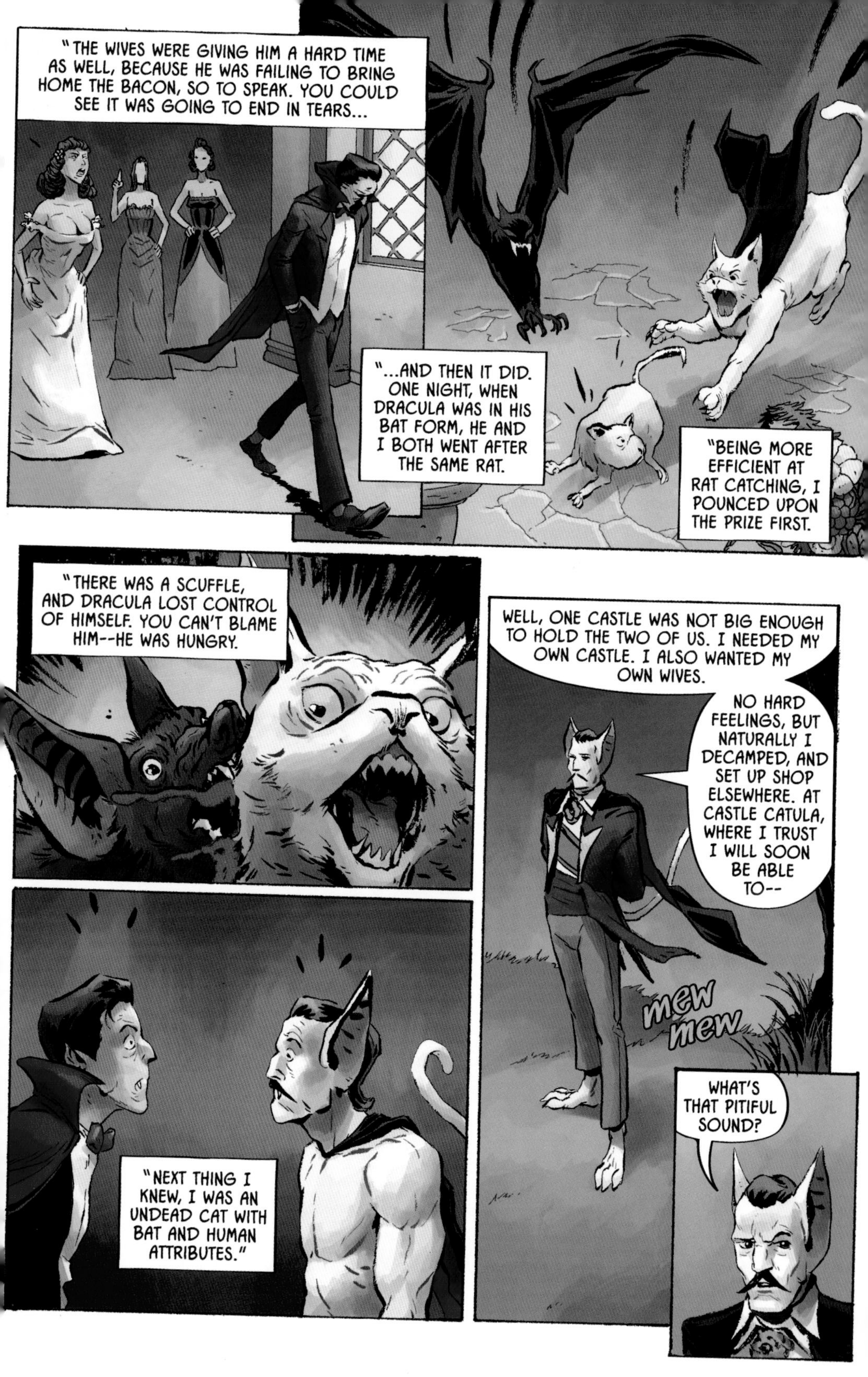
"THE WIVES WERE GIVING HIM A HARD TIME AS WELL, BECAUSE HE WAS FAILING TO BRING HOME THE BACON, SO TO SPEAK. YOU COULD SEE IT WAS GOING TO END IN TEARS...
"...AND THEN IT DID. ONE NIGHT, WHEN DRACULA WAS IN HIS BAT FORM, HE AND I BOTH WENT AFTER THE SAME RAT.
"BEING MORE EFFICIENT AT RAT CATCHING, I POUNCED UPON THE PRIZE FIRST.
"THERE WAS A SCUFFLE, AND DRACULA LOST CONTROL OF HIMSELF. YOU CAN'T BLAME HIM--HE WAS HUNGRY.
"NEXT THING I KNEW, I WAS AN UNDEAD CAT WITH BAT AND HUMAN ATTRIBUTES."
WELL, ONE CASTLE WAS NOT BIG ENOUGH TO HOLD THE TWO OF US. I NEEDED MY OWN CASTLE. I ALSO WANTED MY OWN WIVES.
NO HARD FEELINGS, BUT NATURALLY I DECAMPED, AND SET UP SHOP ELSEWHERE. AT CASTLE CATULA, WHERE I TRUST I WILL SOON BE ABLE TO--
mew mew
WHAT'S THAT PITIFUL SOUND?

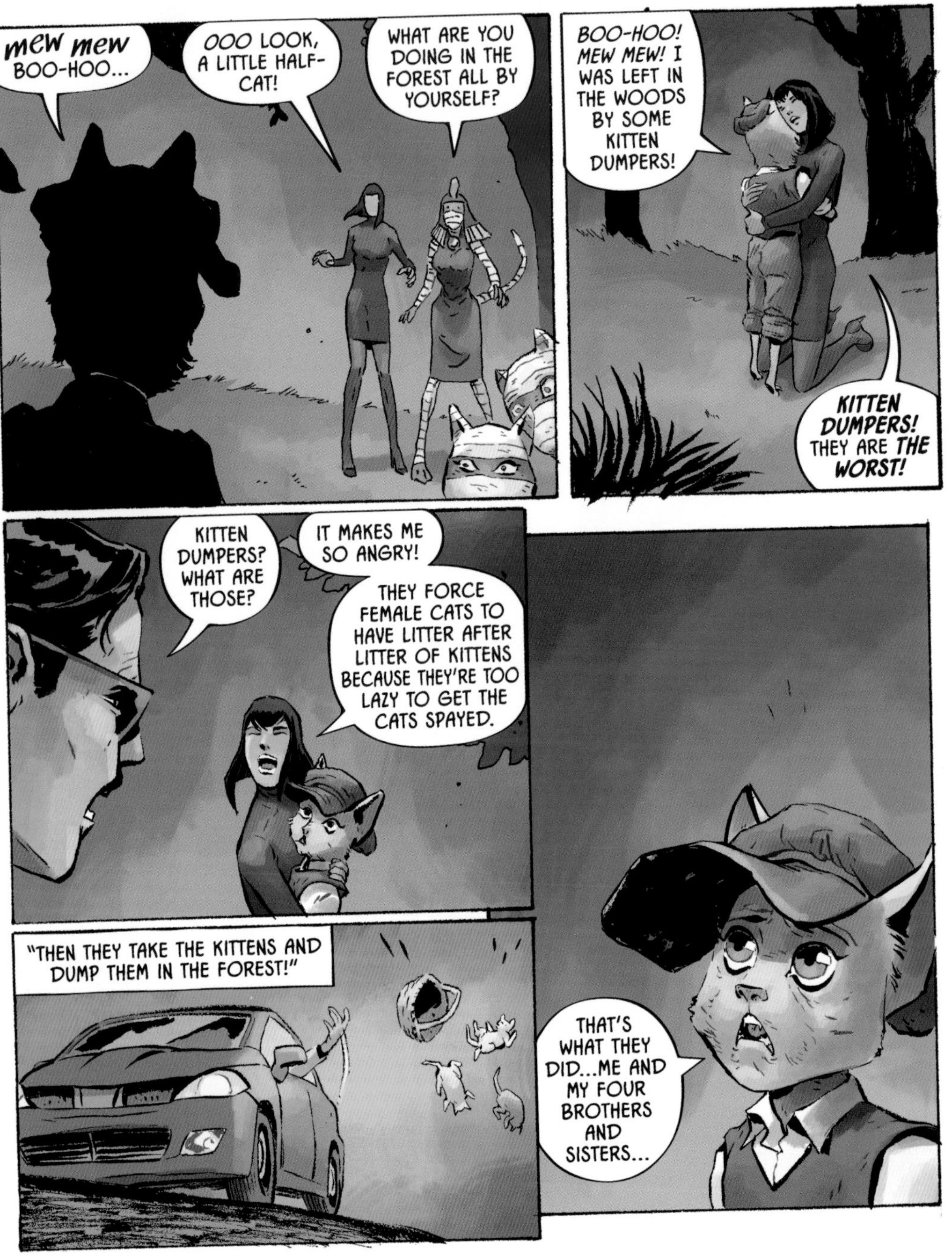
mew mew
BOO-HOO...
OOO LOOK, A LITTLE HALF-CAT!
WHAT ARE YOU DOING IN THE FOREST ALL BY YOURSELF?
BOO-HOO! MEW MEW! I WAS LEFT IN THE WOODS BY SOME KITTEN DUMPERS!
KITTEN DUMPERS! THEY ARE THE WORST!
KITTEN DUMPERS? WHAT ARE THOSE?
IT MAKES ME SO ANGRY!
THEY FORCE FEMALE CATS TO HAVE LITTER AFTER LITTER OF KITTENS BECAUSE THEY'RE TOO LAZY TO GET THE CATS SPAYED.
"THEN THEY TAKE THE KITTENS AND DUMP THEM IN THE FOREST!"
THAT'S WHAT THEY DID...ME AND MY FOUR BROTHERS AND SISTERS...

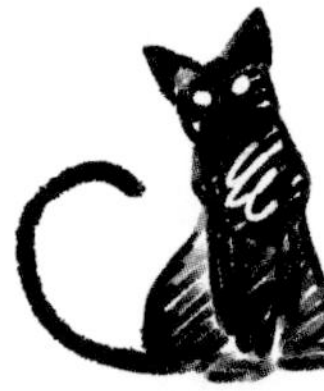

CAT ABANDON

Cats may behave with abandon, but cat abandonment is animal cruelty and contributes to the feral cat population. Abandoning an animal is illegal in Canada and most states in the US. Take any unwanted cats to a shelter, and get your new cat there, too! Read more at www.catsandbirds.ca

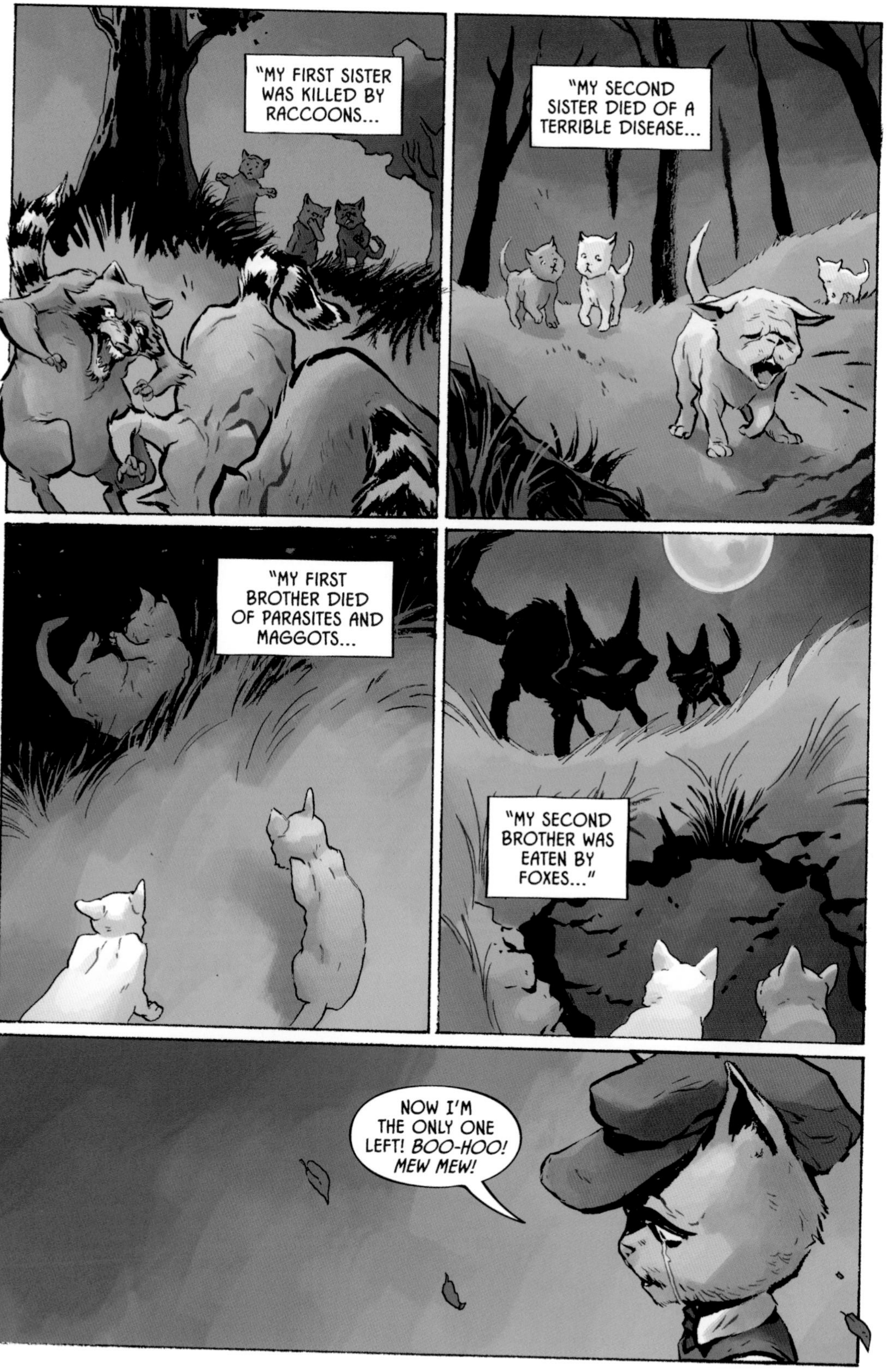
"MY FIRST SISTER WAS KILLED BY RACCOONS...
"MY SECOND SISTER DIED OF A TERRIBLE DISEASE...
"MY FIRST BROTHER DIED OF PARASITES AND MAGGOTS...
"MY SECOND BROTHER WAS EATEN BY FOXES..."
NOW I'M THE ONLY ONE LEFT! *BOO-HOO! MEW MEW!*

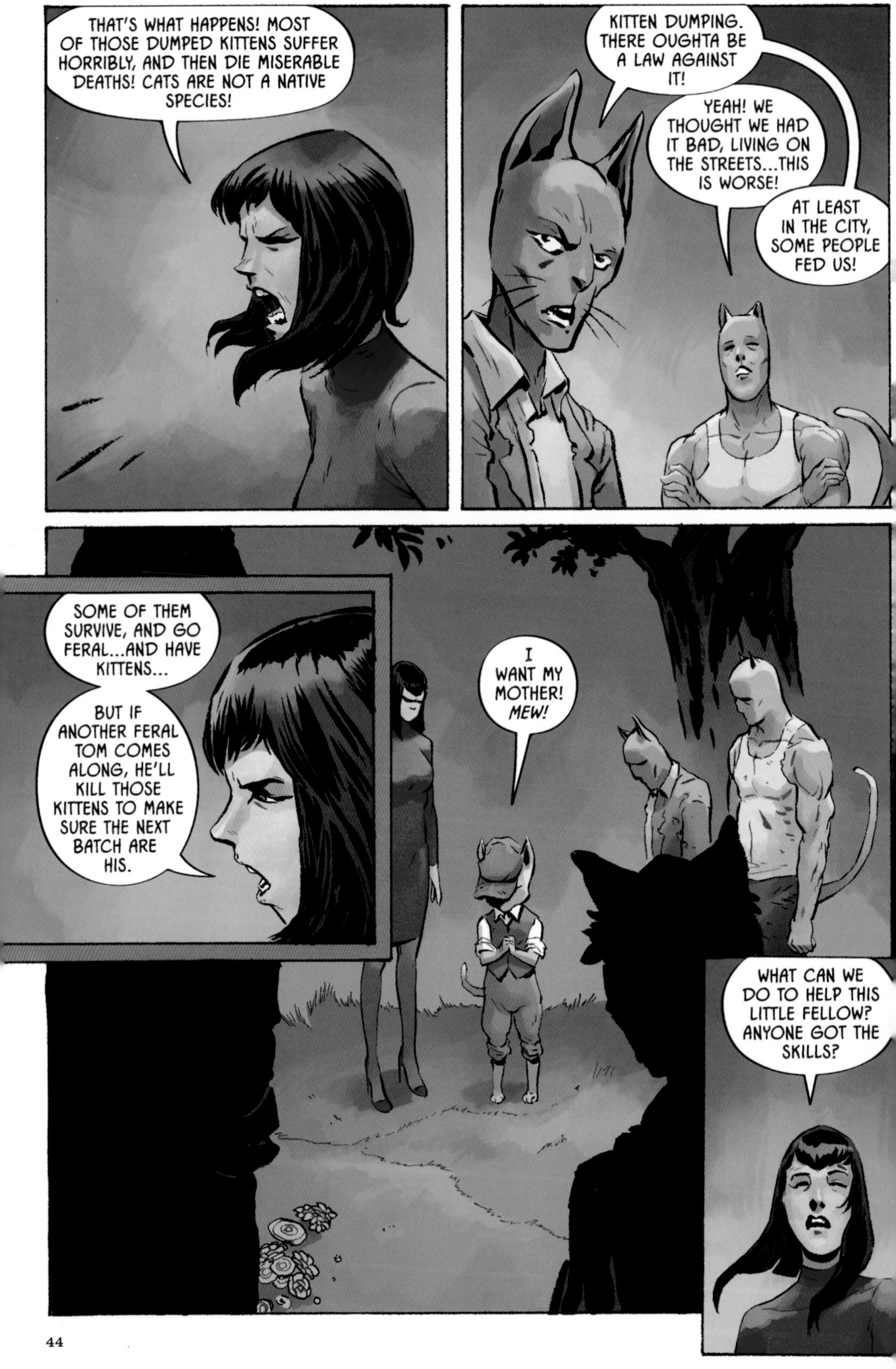
THAT'S WHAT HAPPENS! MOST OF THOSE DUMPED KITTENS SUFFER HORRIBLY, AND THEN DIE MISERABLE DEATHS! CATS ARE NOT A NATIVE SPECIES!
KITTEN DUMPING. THERE OUGHTA BE A LAW AGAINST IT!
YEAH! WE THOUGHT WE HAD IT BAD, LIVING ON THE STREETS...THIS IS WORSE!
AT LEAST IN THE CITY, SOME PEOPLE FED US!
SOME OF THEM SURVIVE, AND GO FERAL...AND HAVE KITTENS...
BUT IF ANOTHER FERAL TOM COMES ALONG, HE'LL KILL THOSE KITTENS TO MAKE SURE THE NEXT BATCH ARE HIS.
I WANT MY MOTHER! *MEW!*
WHAT CAN WE DO TO HELP THIS LITTLE FELLOW? ANYONE GOT THE SKILLS?

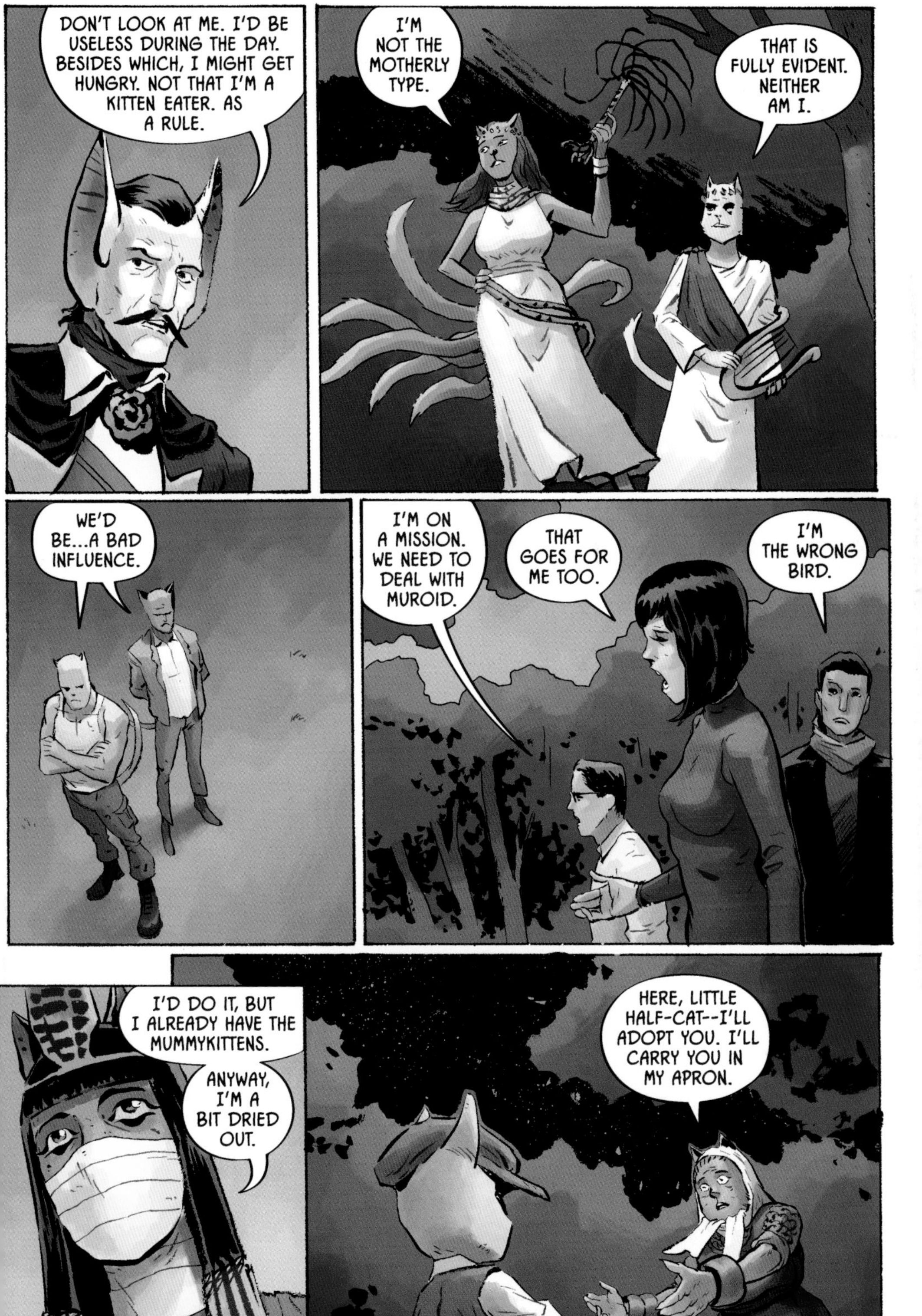
DON'T LOOK AT ME. I'D BE USELESS DURING THE DAY. BESIDES WHICH, I MIGHT GET HUNGRY. NOT THAT I'M A KITTEN EATER. AS A RULE.
I'M NOT THE MOTHERLY TYPE.
THAT IS FULLY EVIDENT. NEITHER AM I.
WE'D BE...A BAD INFLUENCE.
I'M ON A MISSION. WE NEED TO DEAL WITH MUROID.
THAT GOES FOR ME TOO.
I'M THE WRONG BIRD.
I'D DO IT, BUT I ALREADY HAVE THE MUMMYKITTENS.
ANYWAY, I'M A BIT DRIED OUT.
HERE, LITTLE HALF-CAT--I'LL ADOPT YOU. I'LL CARRY YOU IN MY APRON.

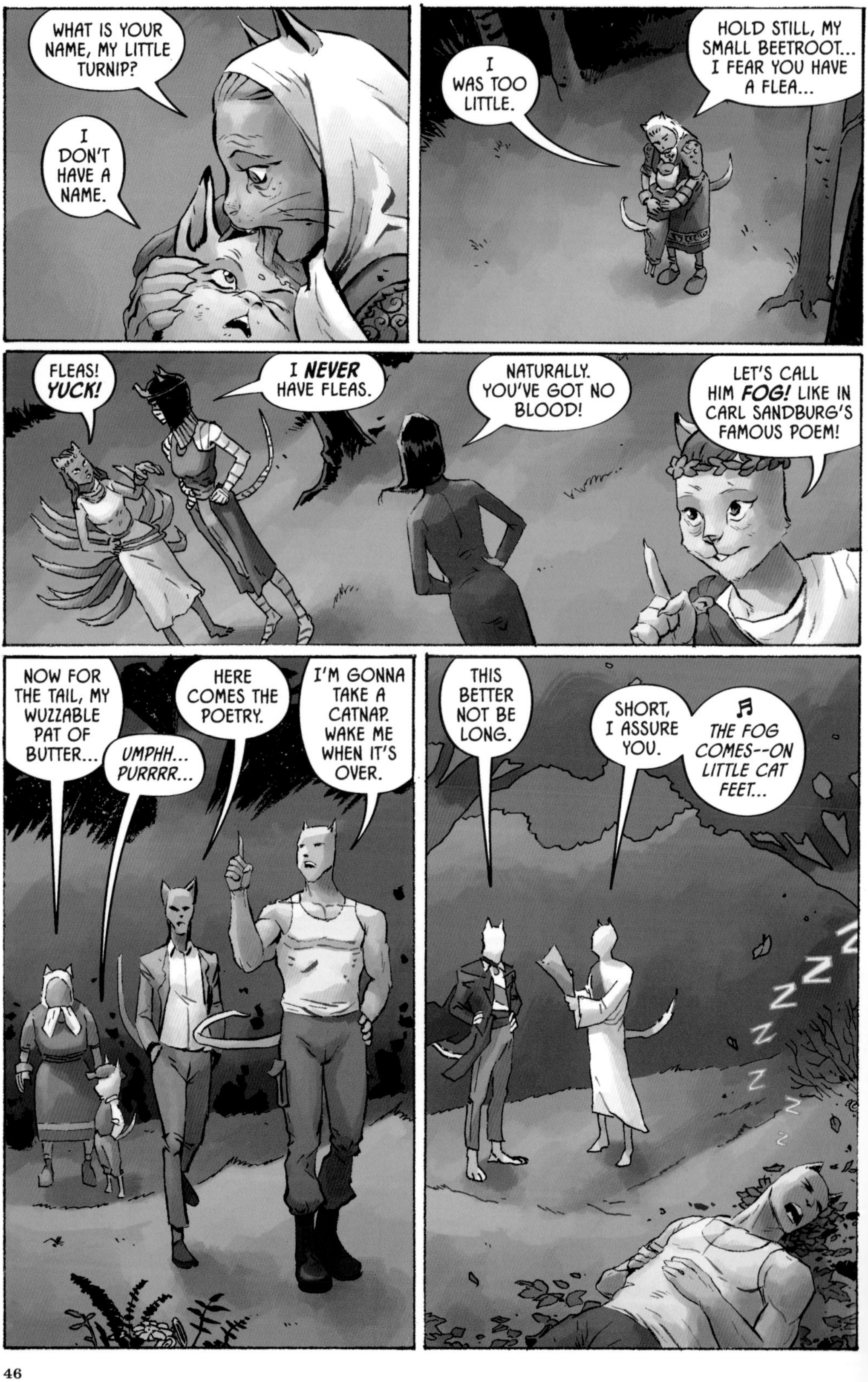
WHAT IS YOUR NAME, MY LITTLE TURNIP?
I DON'T HAVE A NAME.
I WAS TOO LITTLE.
HOLD STILL, MY SMALL BEETROOT... I FEAR YOU HAVE A FLEA...
FLEAS! *YUCK!*
I ***NEVER*** HAVE FLEAS.
NATURALLY. YOU'VE GOT NO BLOOD!
LET'S CALL HIM ***FOG!*** LIKE IN CARL SANDBURG'S FAMOUS POEM!
NOW FOR THE TAIL, MY WUZZABLE PAT OF BUTTER...
UMPHH... PURRRR...
HERE COMES THE POETRY.
I'M GONNA TAKE A CATNAP. WAKE ME WHEN IT'S OVER.
THIS BETTER NOT BE LONG.
SHORT, I ASSURE YOU.
♫ *THE FOG COMES--ON LITTLE CAT FEET...*
Z Z Z Z Z Z Z Z Z

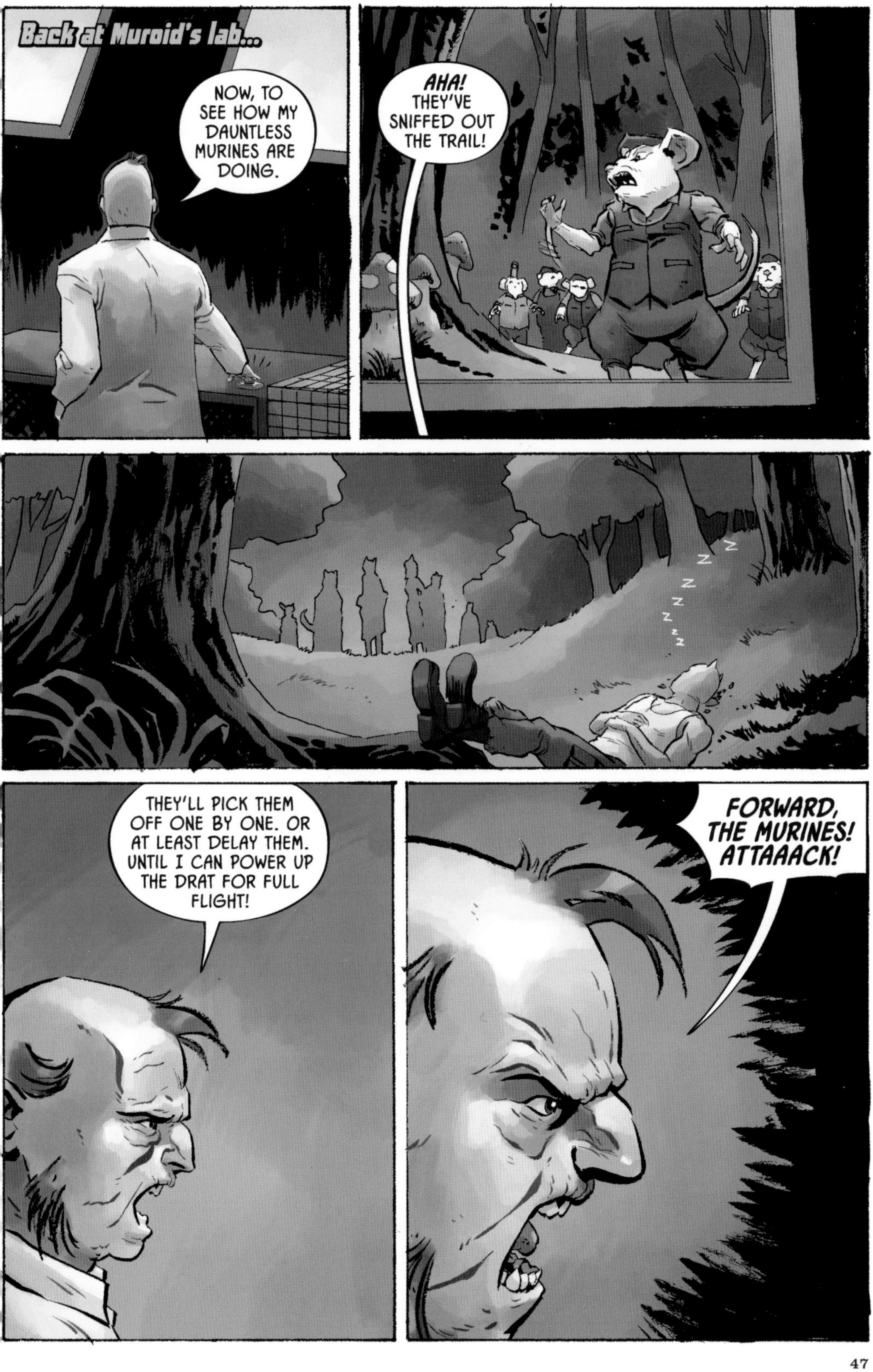
Back at Muroid's lab...
NOW, TO SEE HOW MY DAUNTLESS MURINES ARE DOING.
AHA! THEY'VE SNIFFED OUT THE TRAIL!
Z Z Z Z Z Z Z Z
THEY'LL PICK THEM OFF ONE BY ONE. OR AT LEAST DELAY THEM. UNTIL I CAN POWER UP THE DRAT FOR FULL FLIGHT!
FORWARD, THE MURINES! ATTAAACK!

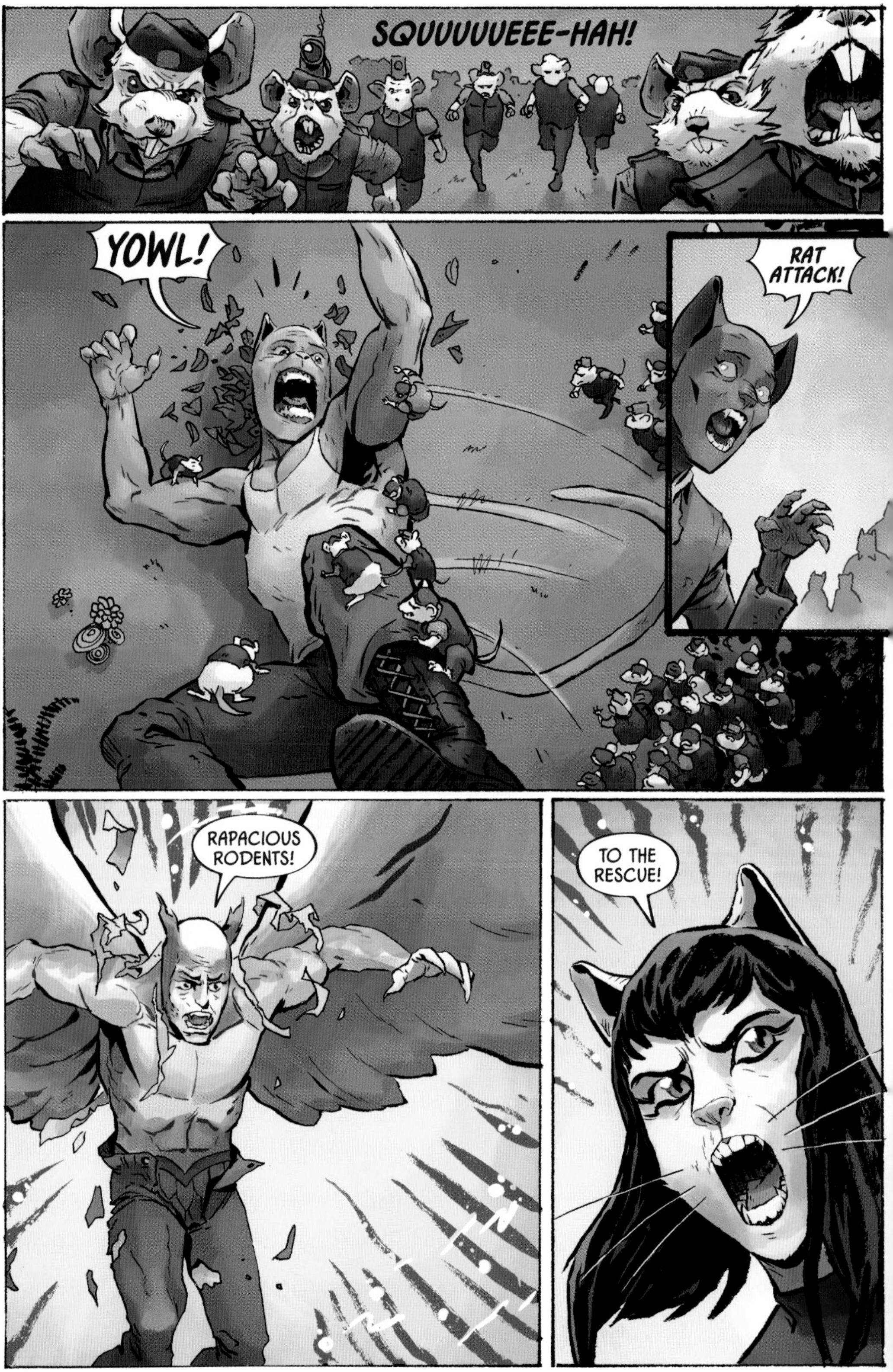
SQUUUUUEEE-HAH!
YOWL!
RAT ATTACK!
RAPACIOUS RODENTS!
TO THE RESCUE!

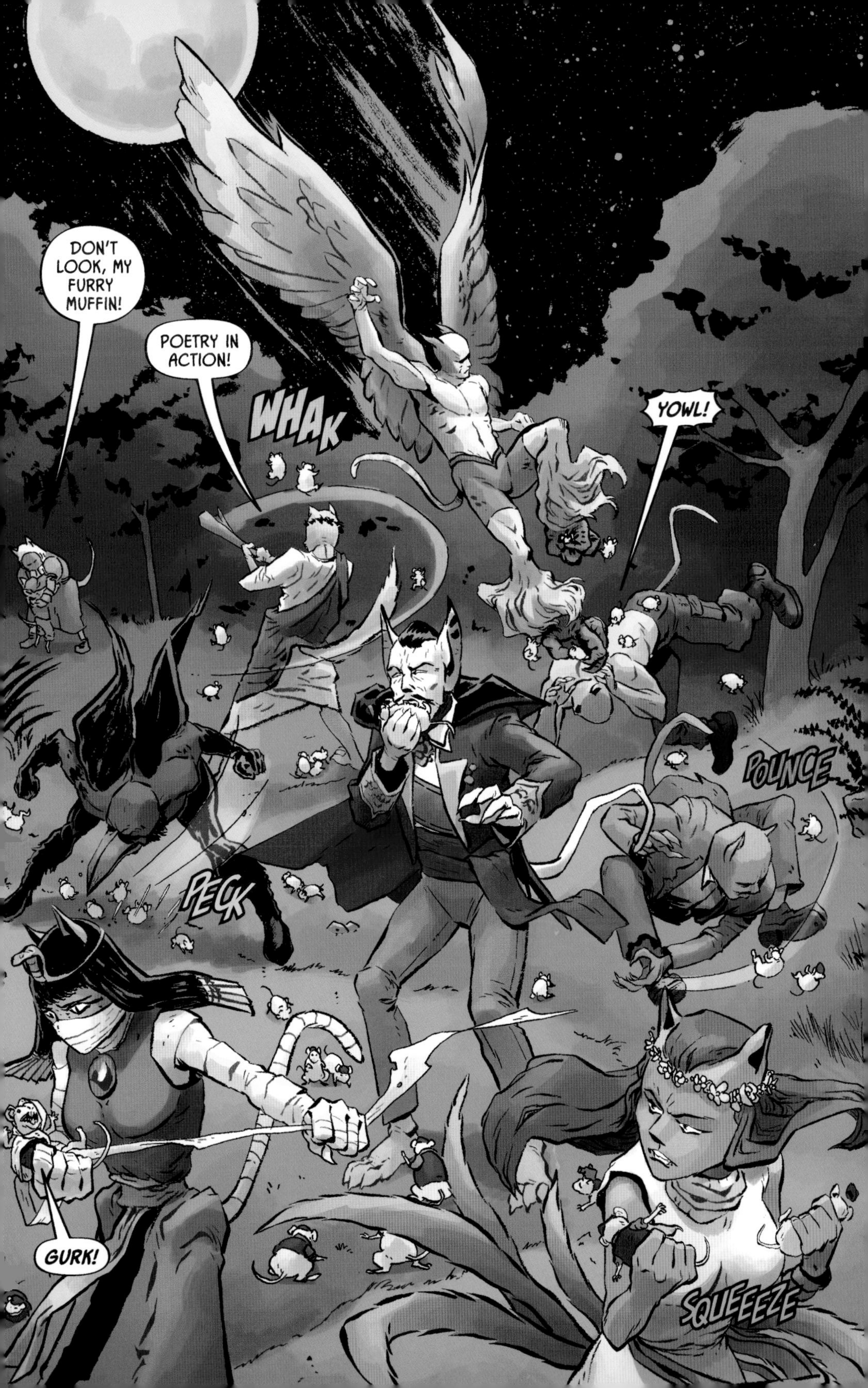
DON'T LOOK, MY FURRY MUFFIN!
POETRY IN ACTION!
WHAK
YOWL!
POUNCE
PECK
GURK!
SQUEEEZE

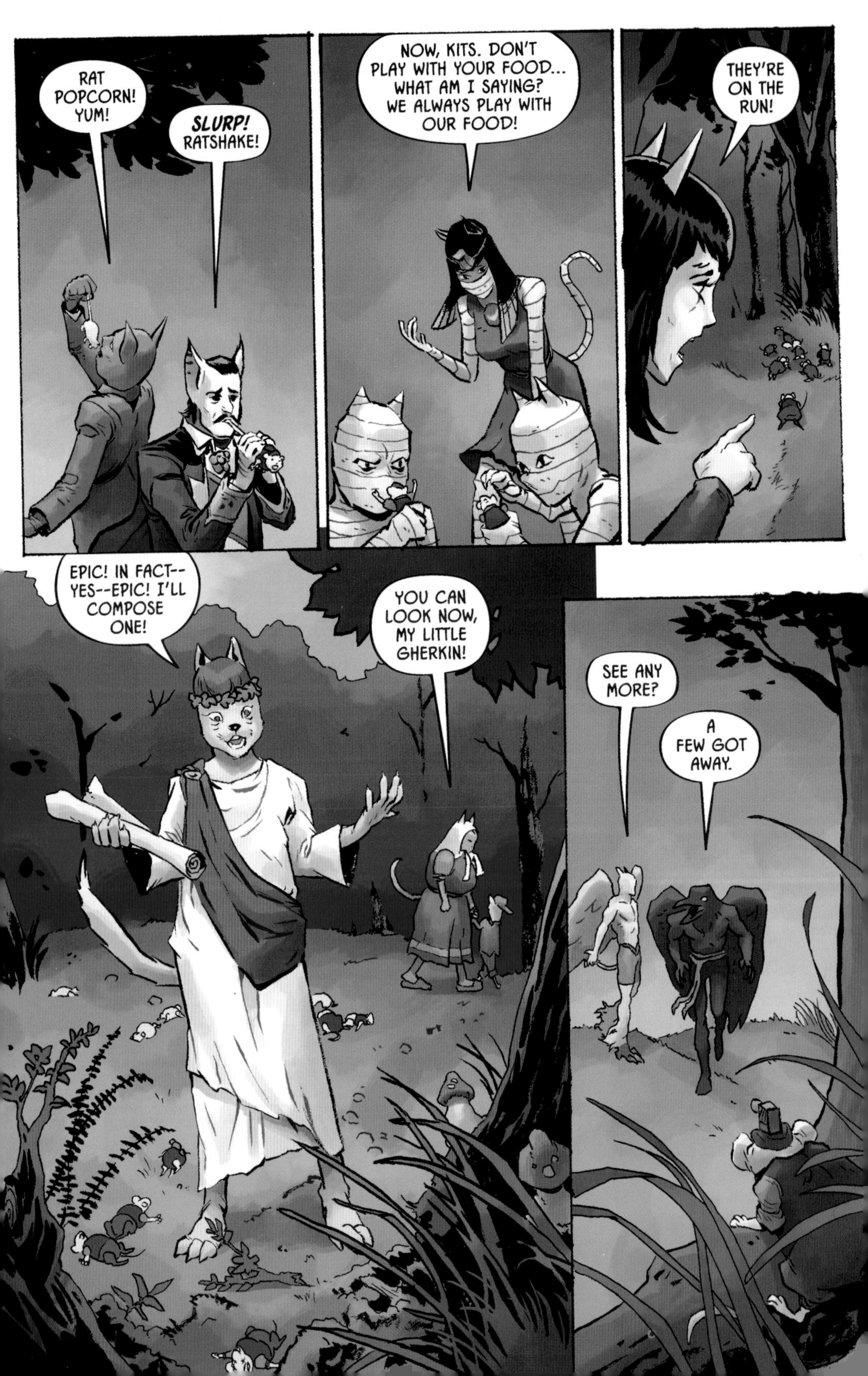
RAT POPCORN! YUM!
SLURP! RATSHAKE!
NOW, KITS. DON'T PLAY WITH YOUR FOOD... WHAT AM I SAYING? WE ALWAYS PLAY WITH OUR FOOD!
THEY'RE ON THE RUN!
EPIC! IN FACT--YES--EPIC! I'LL COMPOSE ONE!
YOU CAN LOOK NOW, MY LITTLE GHERKIN!
SEE ANY MORE?
A FEW GOT AWAY.

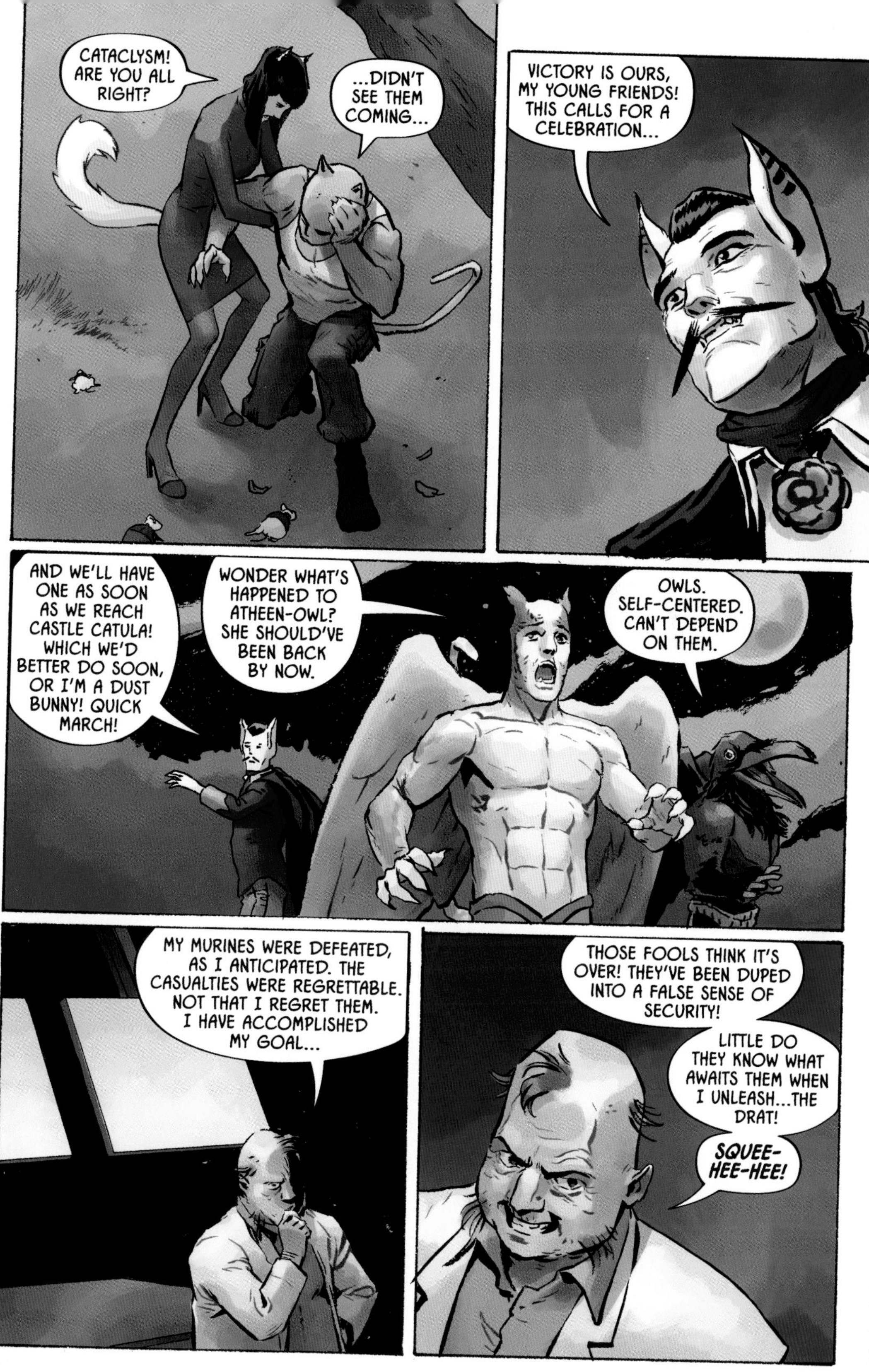
CATACLYSM! ARE YOU ALL RIGHT?
...DIDN'T SEE THEM COMING...
VICTORY IS OURS, MY YOUNG FRIENDS! THIS CALLS FOR A CELEBRATION...
AND WE'LL HAVE ONE AS SOON AS WE REACH CASTLE CATULA! WHICH WE'D BETTER DO SOON, OR I'M A DUST BUNNY! QUICK MARCH!
WONDER WHAT'S HAPPENED TO ATHEEN-OWL? SHE SHOULD'VE BEEN BACK BY NOW.
OWLS. SELF-CENTERED. CAN'T DEPEND ON THEM.
MY MURINES WERE DEFEATED, AS I ANTICIPATED. THE CASUALTIES WERE REGRETTABLE. NOT THAT I REGRET THEM. I HAVE ACCOMPLISHED MY GOAL...
THOSE FOOLS THINK IT'S OVER! THEY'VE BEEN DUPED INTO A FALSE SENSE OF SECURITY!
LITTLE DO THEY KNOW WHAT AWAITS THEM WHEN I UNLEASH...THE DRAT!
SQUEE-HEE-HEE!

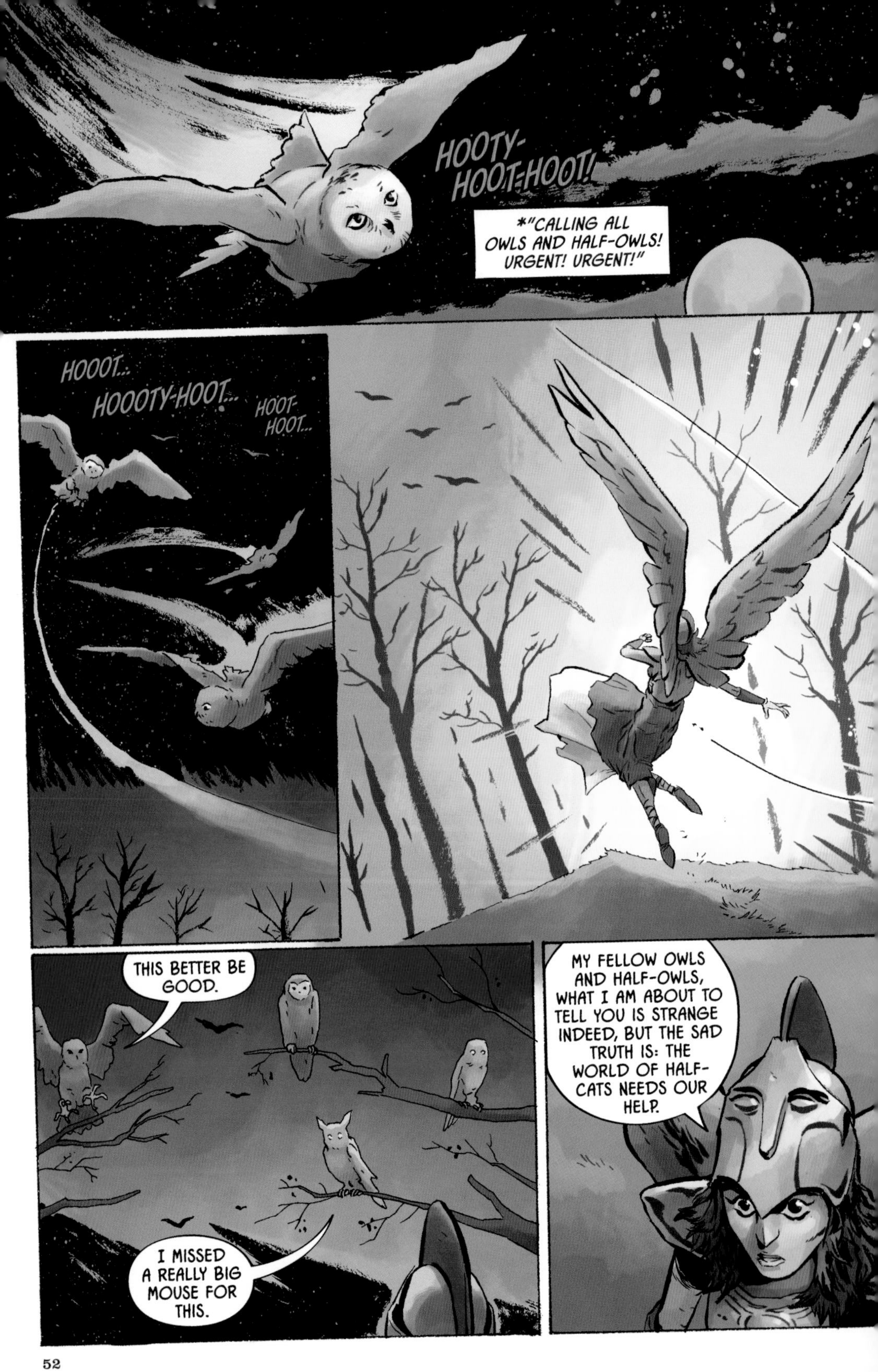
HOOTY-HOOT-HOOT!*
*"CALLING ALL OWLS AND HALF-OWLS! URGENT! URGENT!"
HOOOT...
HOOOTY-HOOT...
HOOT-HOOT...
THIS BETTER BE GOOD.
I MISSED A REALLY BIG MOUSE FOR THIS.
MY FELLOW OWLS AND HALF-OWLS, WHAT I AM ABOUT TO TELL YOU IS STRANGE INDEED, BUT THE SAD TRUTH IS: THE WORLD OF HALF-CATS NEEDS OUR HELP.

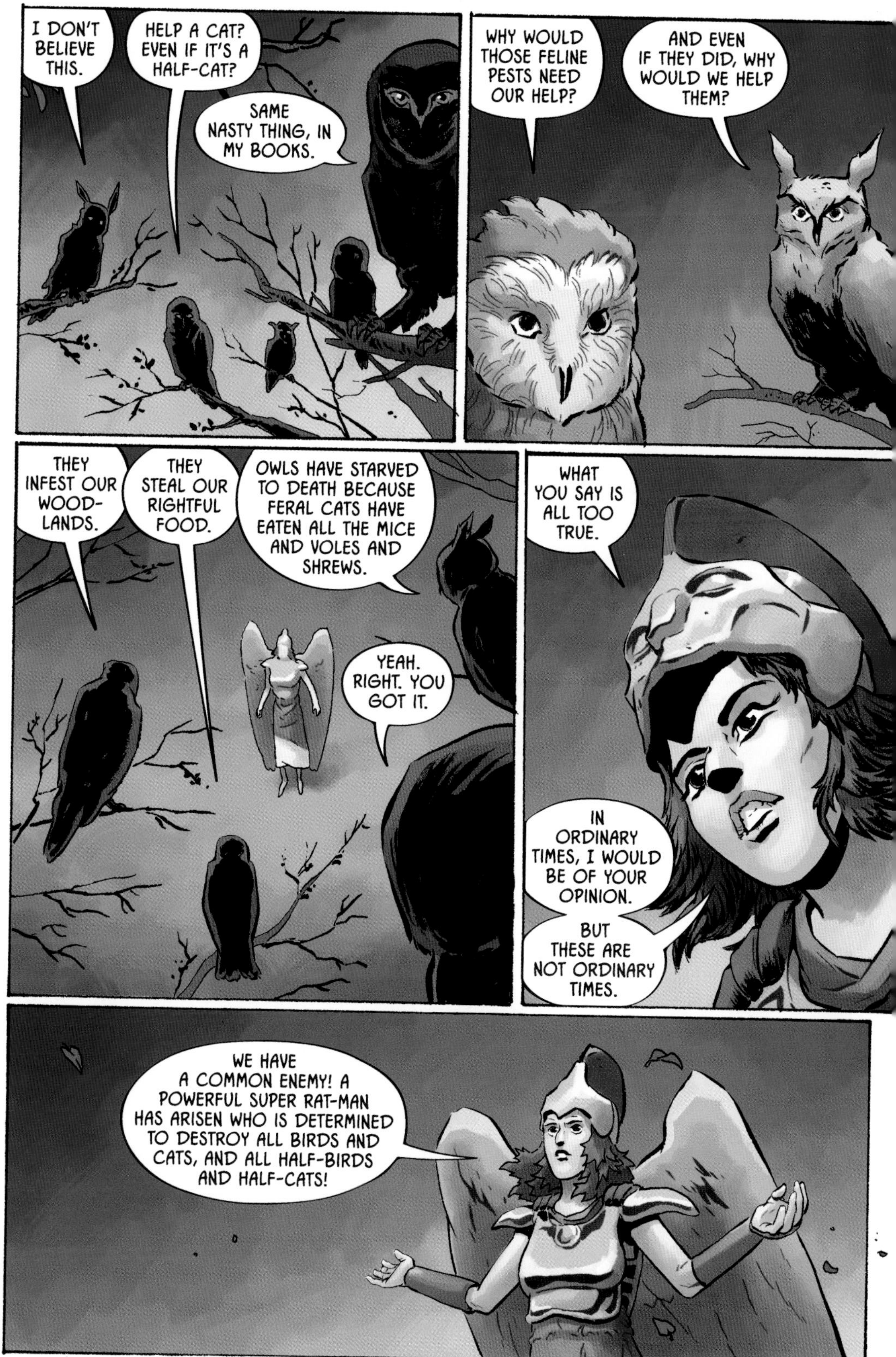
I DON'T BELIEVE THIS.
HELP A CAT? EVEN IF IT'S A HALF-CAT?
SAME NASTY THING, IN MY BOOKS.
WHY WOULD THOSE FELINE PESTS NEED OUR HELP?
AND EVEN IF THEY DID, WHY WOULD WE HELP THEM?
THEY INFEST OUR WOOD-LANDS.
THEY STEAL OUR RIGHTFUL FOOD.
OWLS HAVE STARVED TO DEATH BECAUSE FERAL CATS HAVE EATEN ALL THE MICE AND VOLES AND SHREWS.
YEAH. RIGHT. YOU GOT IT.
WHAT YOU SAY IS ALL TOO TRUE.
IN ORDINARY TIMES, I WOULD BE OF YOUR OPINION.
BUT THESE ARE NOT ORDINARY TIMES.
WE HAVE A COMMON ENEMY! A POWERFUL SUPER RAT-MAN HAS ARISEN WHO IS DETERMINED TO DESTROY ALL BIRDS AND CATS, AND ALL HALF-BIRDS AND HALF-CATS!

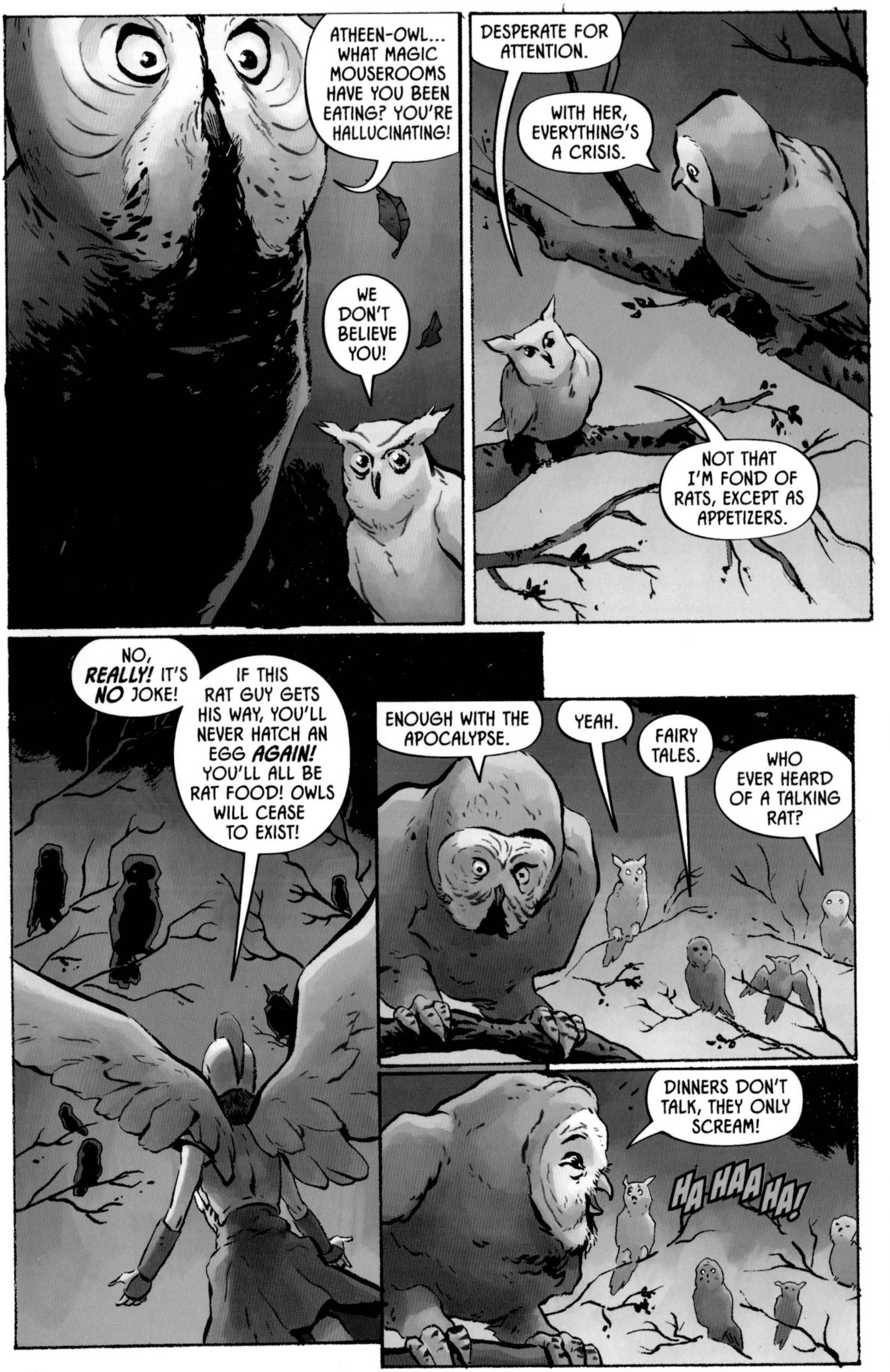
ATHEEN-OWL... WHAT MAGIC MOUSEROOMS HAVE YOU BEEN EATING? YOU'RE HALLUCINATING!
WE DON'T BELIEVE YOU!
DESPERATE FOR ATTENTION.
WITH HER, EVERYTHING'S A CRISIS.
NOT THAT I'M FOND OF RATS, EXCEPT AS APPETIZERS.
NO, **REALLY!** IT'S **NO** JOKE!
IF THIS RAT GUY GETS HIS WAY, YOU'LL NEVER HATCH AN EGG **AGAIN!** YOU'LL ALL BE RAT FOOD! OWLS WILL CEASE TO EXIST!
ENOUGH WITH THE APOCALYPSE.
YEAH.
FAIRY TALES.
WHO EVER HEARD OF A TALKING RAT?
DINNERS DON'T TALK, THEY ONLY SCREAM!
HA HAA HA!

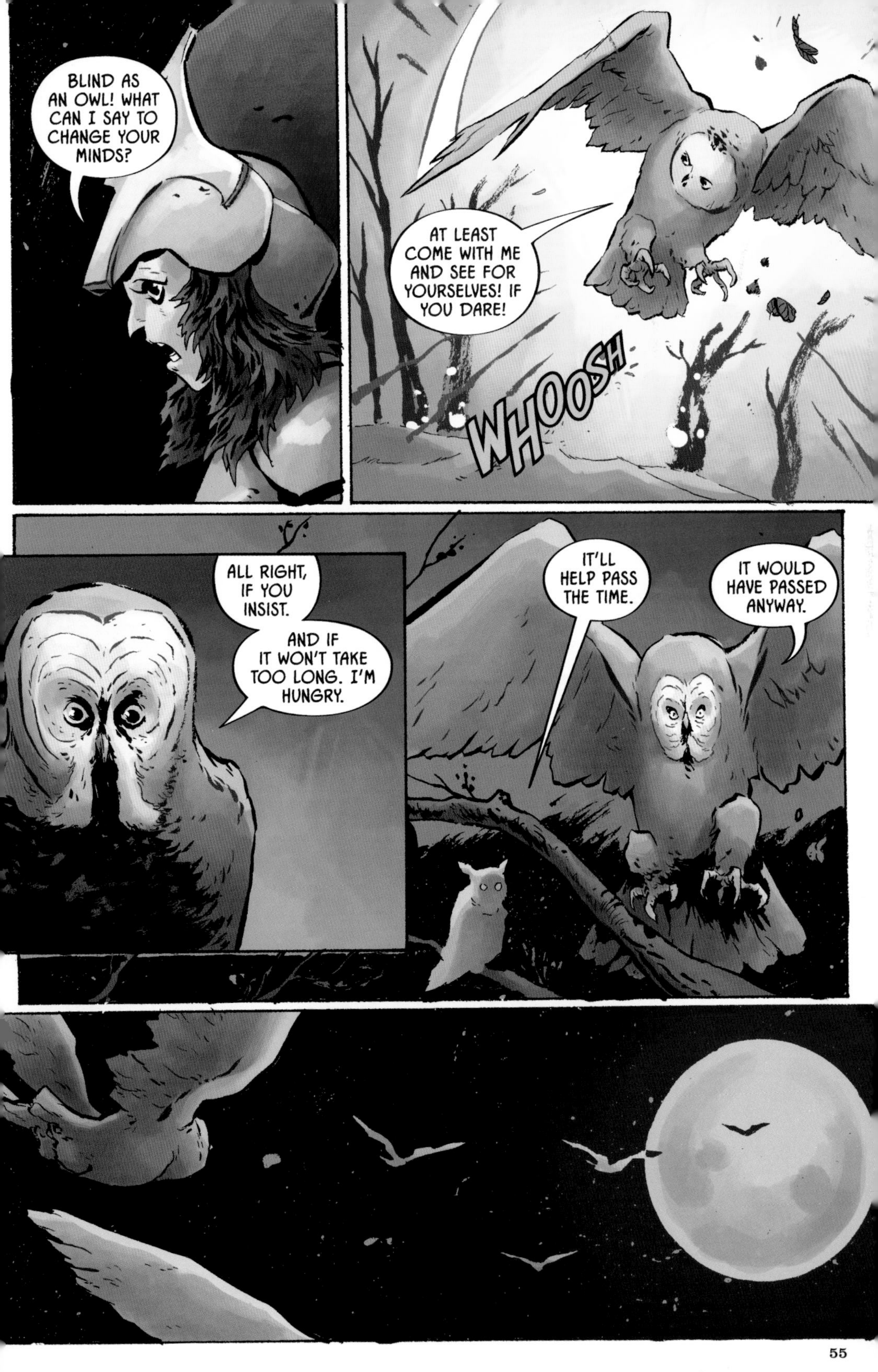
BLIND AS AN OWL! WHAT CAN I SAY TO CHANGE YOUR MINDS?
AT LEAST COME WITH ME AND SEE FOR YOURSELVES! IF YOU DARE!
WHOOSH
ALL RIGHT, IF YOU INSIST.
AND IF IT WON'T TAKE TOO LONG. I'M HUNGRY.
IT'LL HELP PASS THE TIME.
IT WOULD HAVE PASSED ANYWAY.

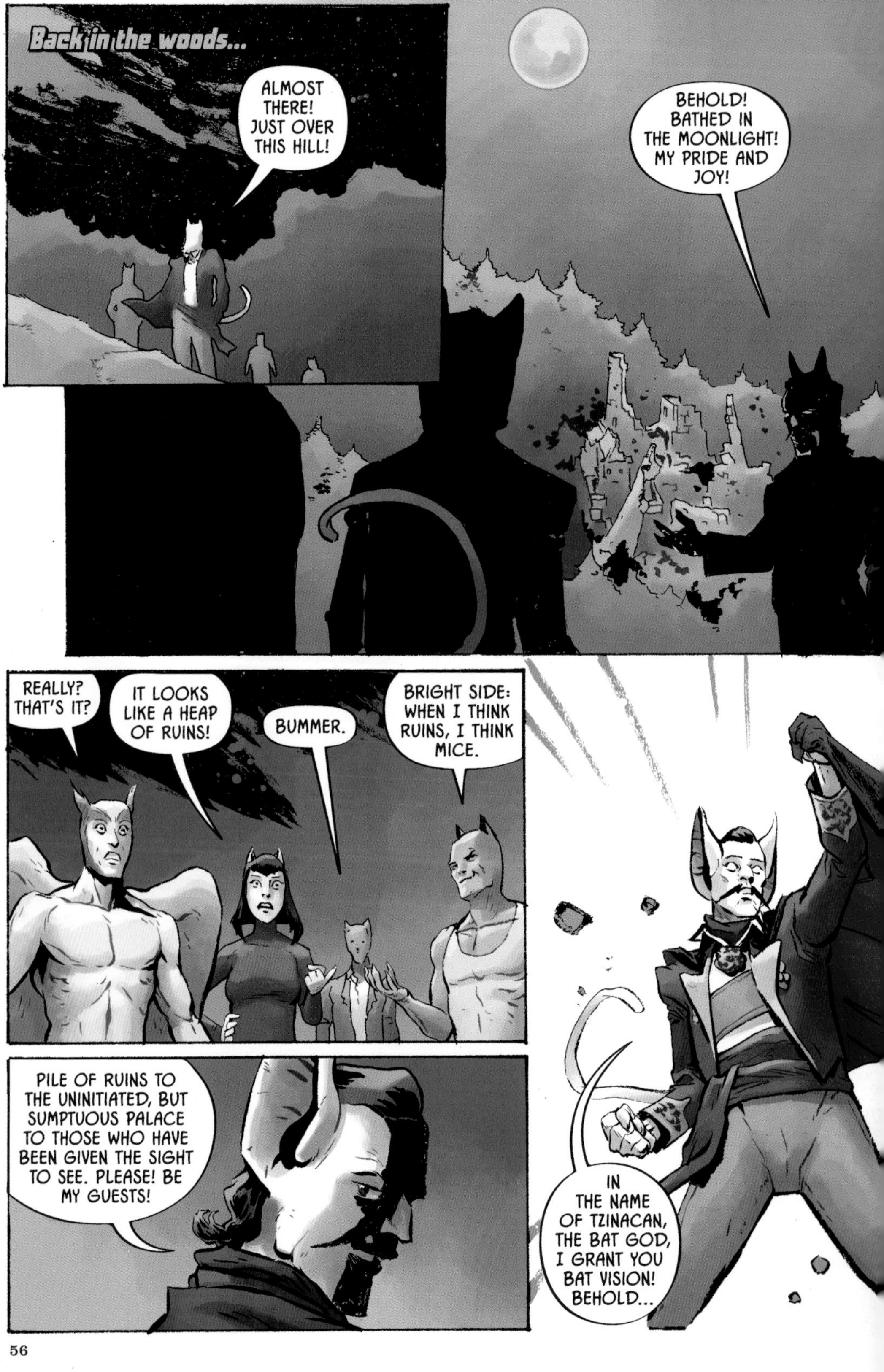
Back in the woods...
ALMOST THERE! JUST OVER THIS HILL!
BEHOLD! BATHED IN THE MOONLIGHT! MY PRIDE AND JOY!
REALLY? THAT'S IT?
IT LOOKS LIKE A HEAP OF RUINS!
BUMMER.
BRIGHT SIDE: WHEN I THINK RUINS, I THINK MICE.
PILE OF RUINS TO THE UNINITIATED, BUT SUMPTUOUS PALACE TO THOSE WHO HAVE BEEN GIVEN THE SIGHT TO SEE. PLEASE! BE MY GUESTS!
IN THE NAME OF TZINACAN, THE BAT GOD, I GRANT YOU BAT VISION! BEHOLD...

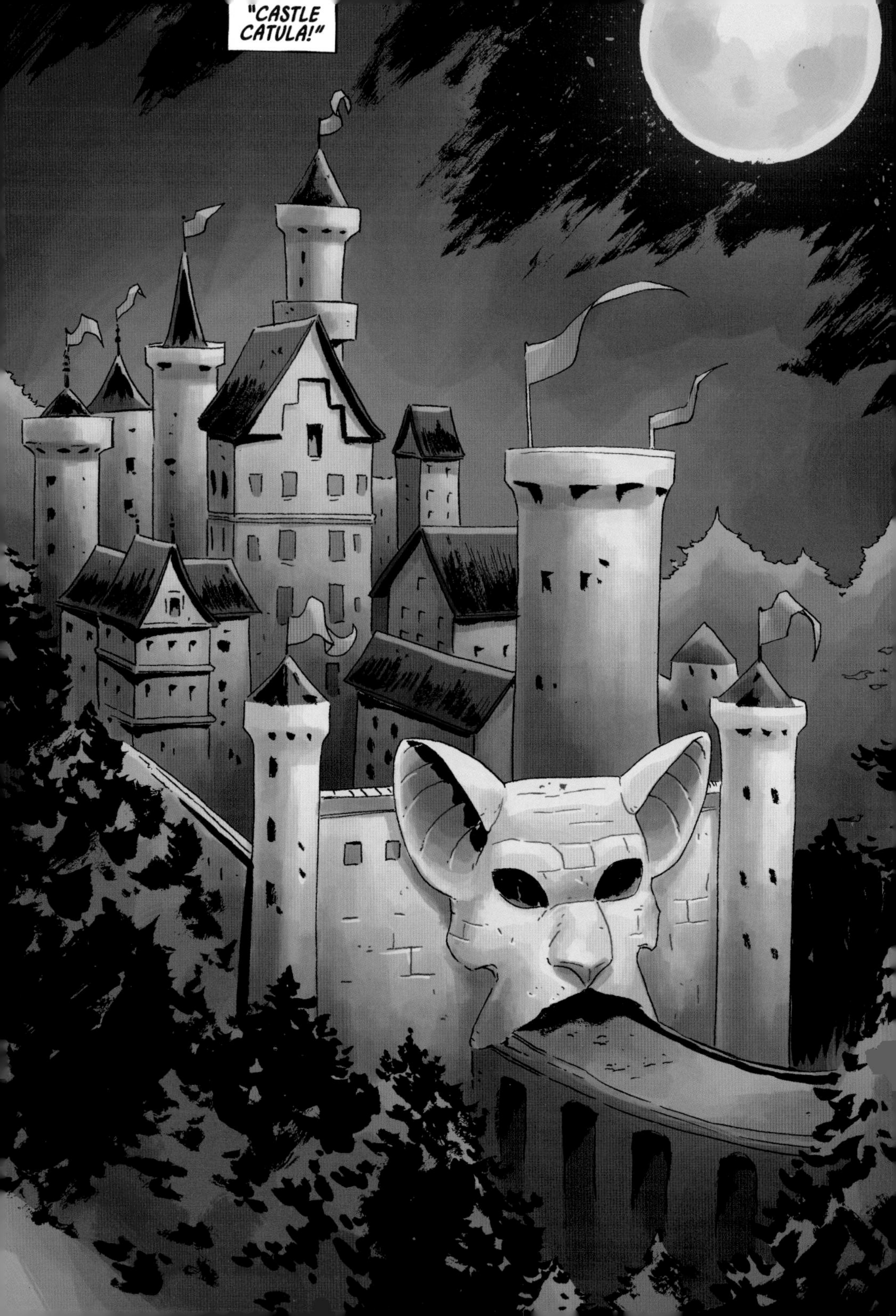
"CASTLE CATULA!"

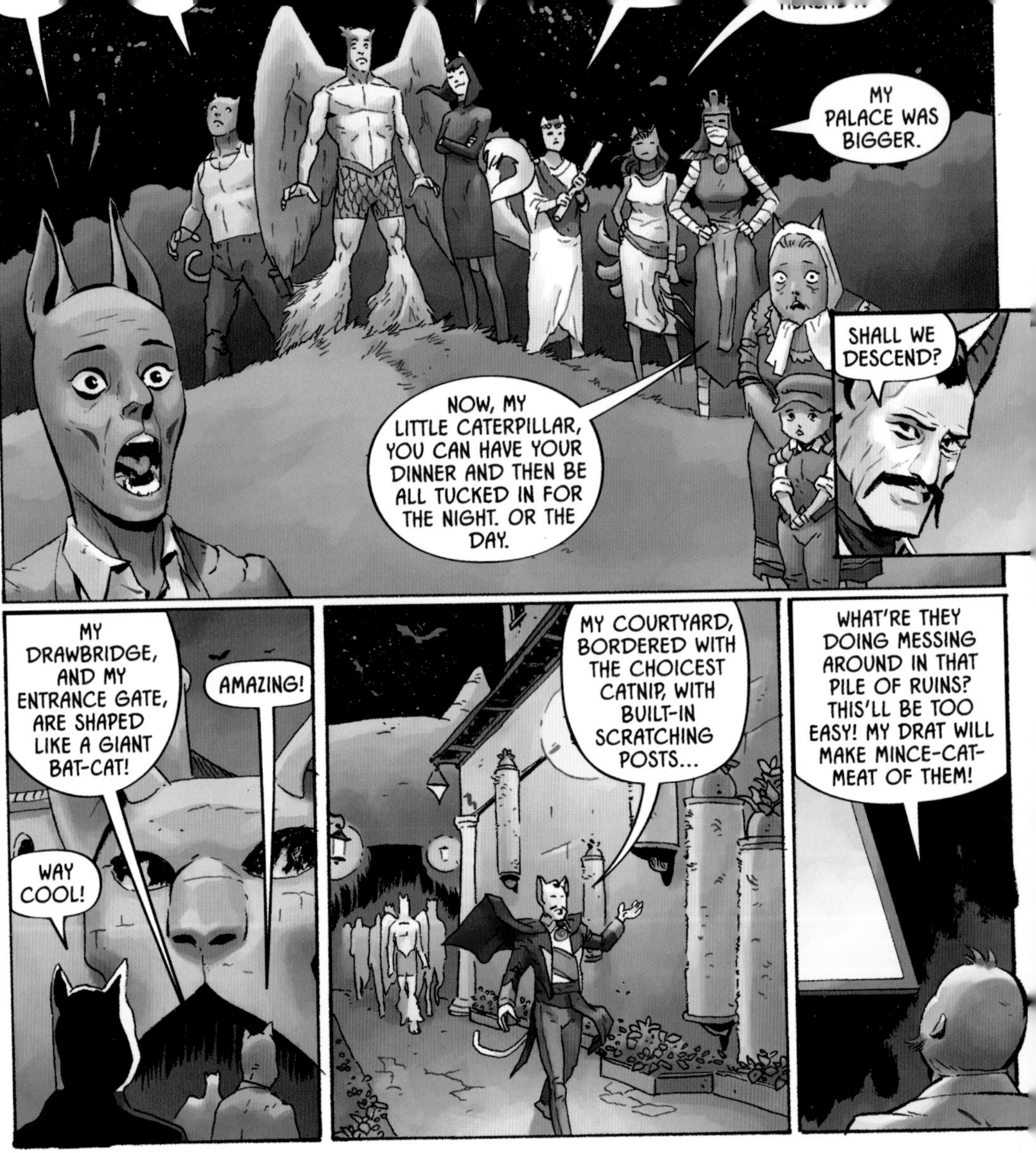
MY PALACE WAS BIGGER.
NOW, MY LITTLE CATERPILLAR, YOU CAN HAVE YOUR DINNER AND THEN BE ALL TUCKED IN FOR THE NIGHT. OR THE DAY.
SHALL WE DESCEND?
MY DRAWBRIDGE, AND MY ENTRANCE GATE, ARE SHAPED LIKE A GIANT BAT-CAT!
AMAZING!
WAY COOL!
MY COURTYARD, BORDERED WITH THE CHOICEST CATNIP, WITH BUILT-IN SCRATCHING POSTS...
WHAT'RE THEY DOING MESSING AROUND IN THAT PILE OF RUINS? THIS'LL BE TOO EASY! MY DRAT WILL MAKE MINCE-CAT-MEAT OF THEM!

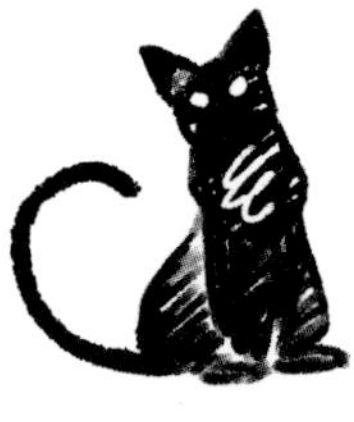

SAFE OUTDOOR CATS!

Cat enclosures, "catios," and cat walkways are all wonderful ways to let your cat enjoy the great outdoors without exposing it to the dangers of free roaming. From luxury models to DIY projects, there's a solution for every budget! Read more at www.catsandbirds.ca

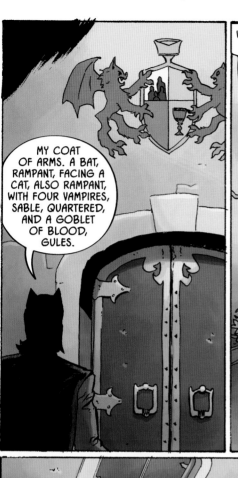

MY COAT OF ARMS. A BAT, RAMPANT, FACING A CAT, ALSO RAMPANT, WITH FOUR VAMPIRES, SABLE, QUARTERED, AND A GOBLET OF BLOOD, GULES.

WHAT'S HE SAYING?

WHO KNOWS?

OH, COUNT! YOU'RE SO... NOBLE! IN ONE OF MY LIVES I KNEW A COUNT, BUT NOT SO HANDSOME AS YOU!

THANK YOU, MY DEAR. I'M SURE HE WAS IN BLISS.

NOW I WILL HOIST THE FLAG, TO SHOW I'M IN RESIDENCE.

OOOO!

THE BAT-CAT *FLIES!* RIPPLING IN AN UNEARTHLY WIND!

AAAH!

SHALL WE ENTER?

CREEEAK

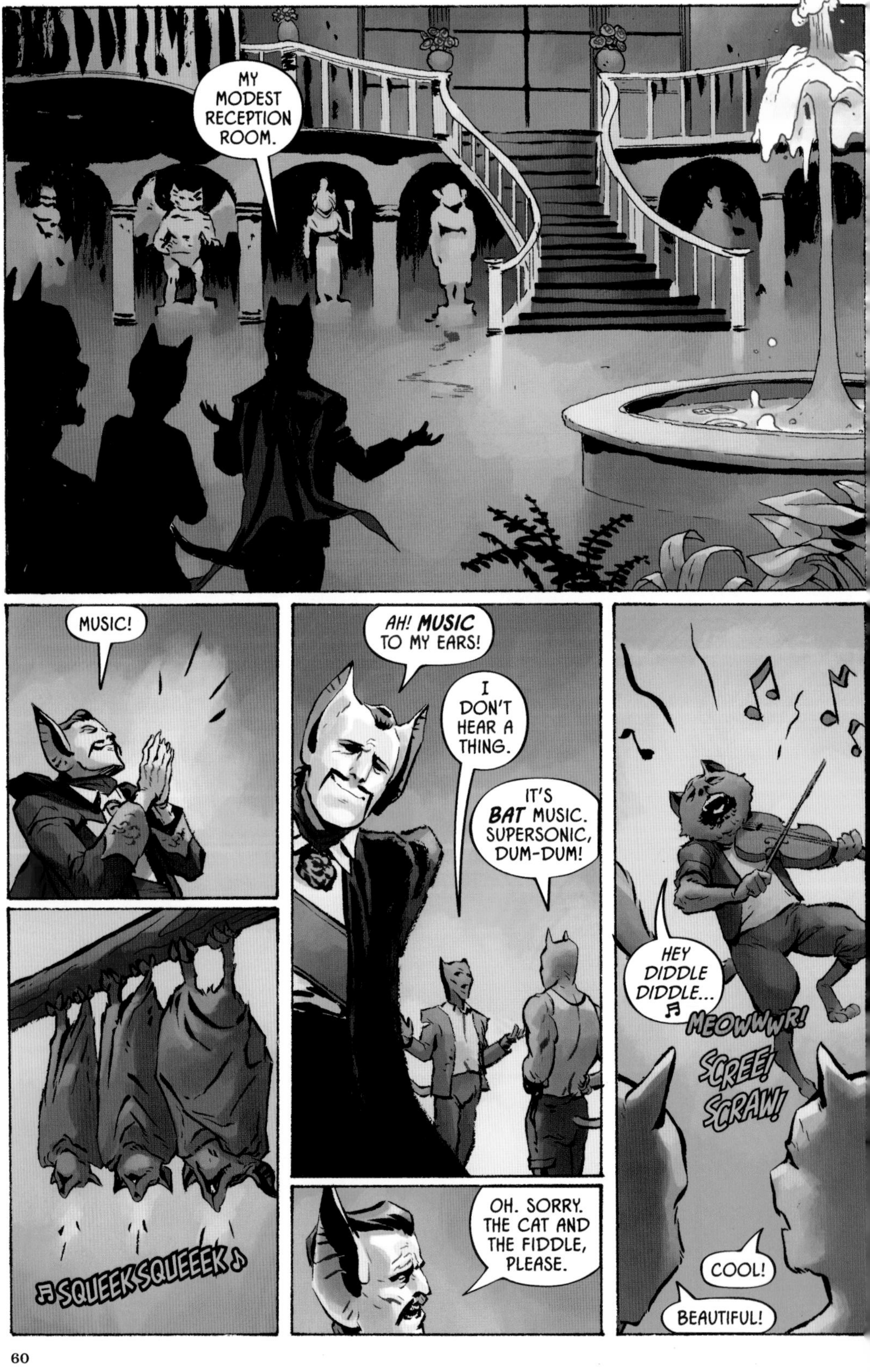

MY MODEST RECEPTION ROOM.
MUSIC!
♫ SQUEEK SQUEEEK ♫
AH! MUSIC TO MY EARS!
I DON'T HEAR A THING.
IT'S BAT MUSIC. SUPERSONIC, DUM-DUM!
OH. SORRY. THE CAT AND THE FIDDLE, PLEASE.
HEY DIDDLE DIDDLE... ♫
MEOWWWR!
SCREE! SCRAW!
COOL!
BEAUTIFUL!

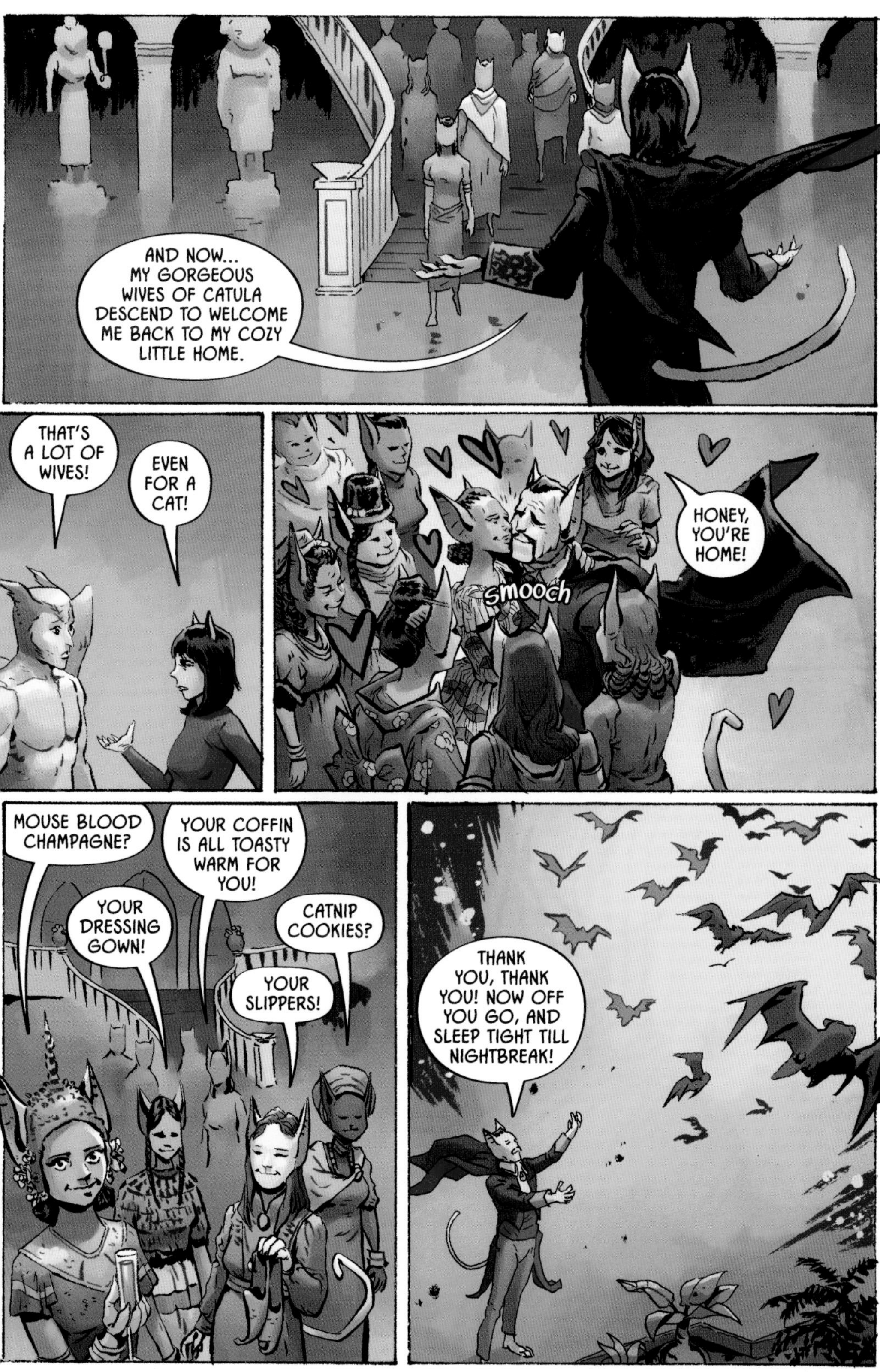
AND NOW... MY GORGEOUS WIVES OF CATULA DESCEND TO WELCOME ME BACK TO MY COZY LITTLE HOME.
THAT'S A LOT OF WIVES!
EVEN FOR A CAT!
HONEY, YOU'RE HOME!
SMOOCH
MOUSE BLOOD CHAMPAGNE?
YOUR DRESSING GOWN!
YOUR COFFIN IS ALL TOASTY WARM FOR YOU!
CATNIP COOKIES?
YOUR SLIPPERS!
THANK YOU, THANK YOU! NOW OFF YOU GO, AND SLEEP TIGHT TILL NIGHTBREAK!

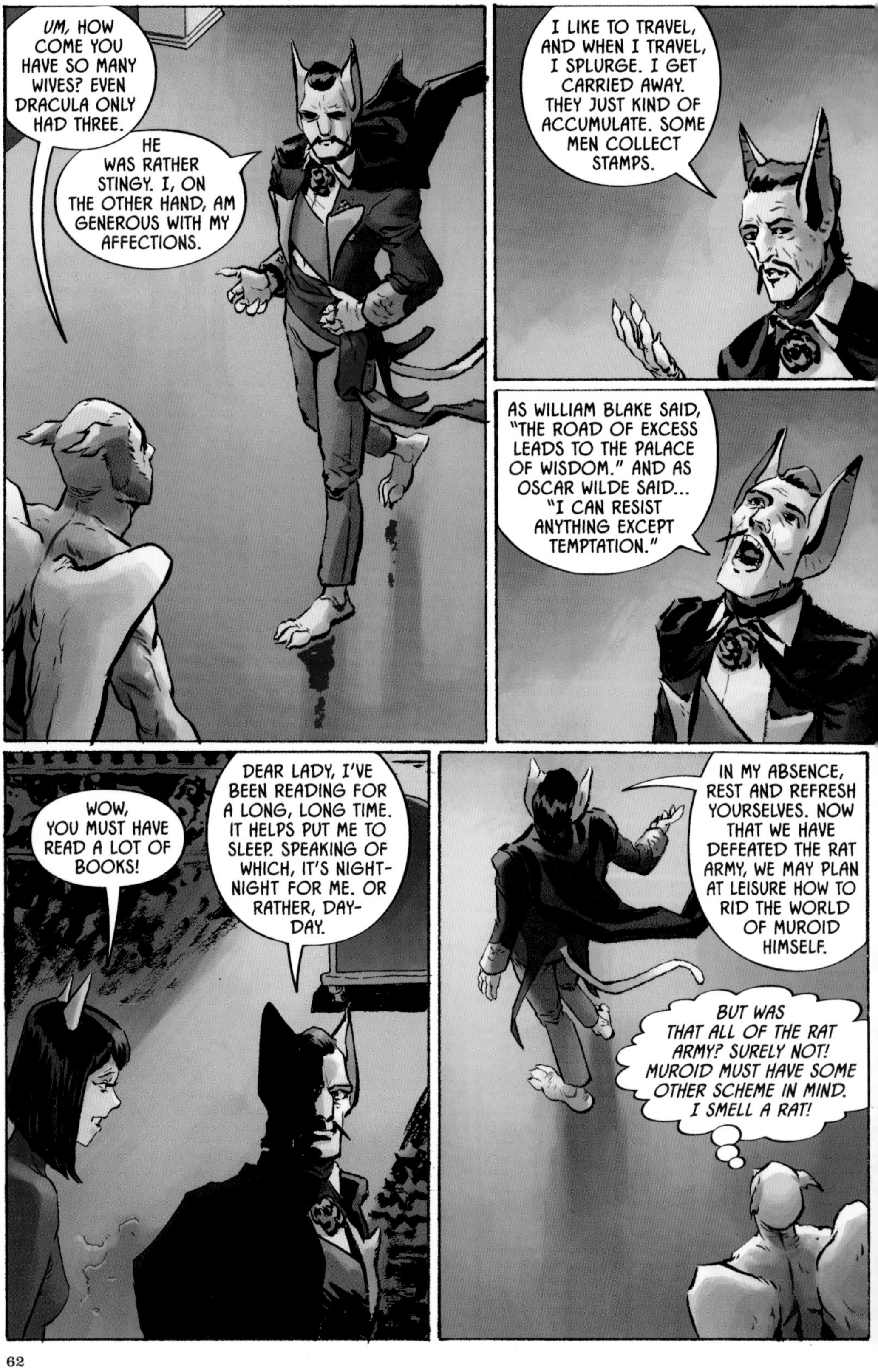

UM, HOW COME YOU HAVE SO MANY WIVES? EVEN DRACULA ONLY HAD THREE.
HE WAS RATHER STINGY. I, ON THE OTHER HAND, AM GENEROUS WITH MY AFFECTIONS.
I LIKE TO TRAVEL, AND WHEN I TRAVEL, I SPLURGE. I GET CARRIED AWAY. THEY JUST KIND OF ACCUMULATE. SOME MEN COLLECT STAMPS.
AS WILLIAM BLAKE SAID, "THE ROAD OF EXCESS LEADS TO THE PALACE OF WISDOM." AND AS OSCAR WILDE SAID... "I CAN RESIST ANYTHING EXCEPT TEMPTATION."
WOW, YOU MUST HAVE READ A LOT OF BOOKS!
DEAR LADY, I'VE BEEN READING FOR A LONG, LONG TIME. IT HELPS PUT ME TO SLEEP. SPEAKING OF WHICH, IT'S NIGHT-NIGHT FOR ME. OR RATHER, DAY-DAY.
IN MY ABSENCE, REST AND REFRESH YOURSELVES. NOW THAT WE HAVE DEFEATED THE RAT ARMY, WE MAY PLAN AT LEISURE HOW TO RID THE WORLD OF MUROID HIMSELF.
BUT WAS THAT ALL OF THE RAT ARMY? SURELY NOT! MUROID MUST HAVE SOME OTHER SCHEME IN MIND. I SMELL A RAT!

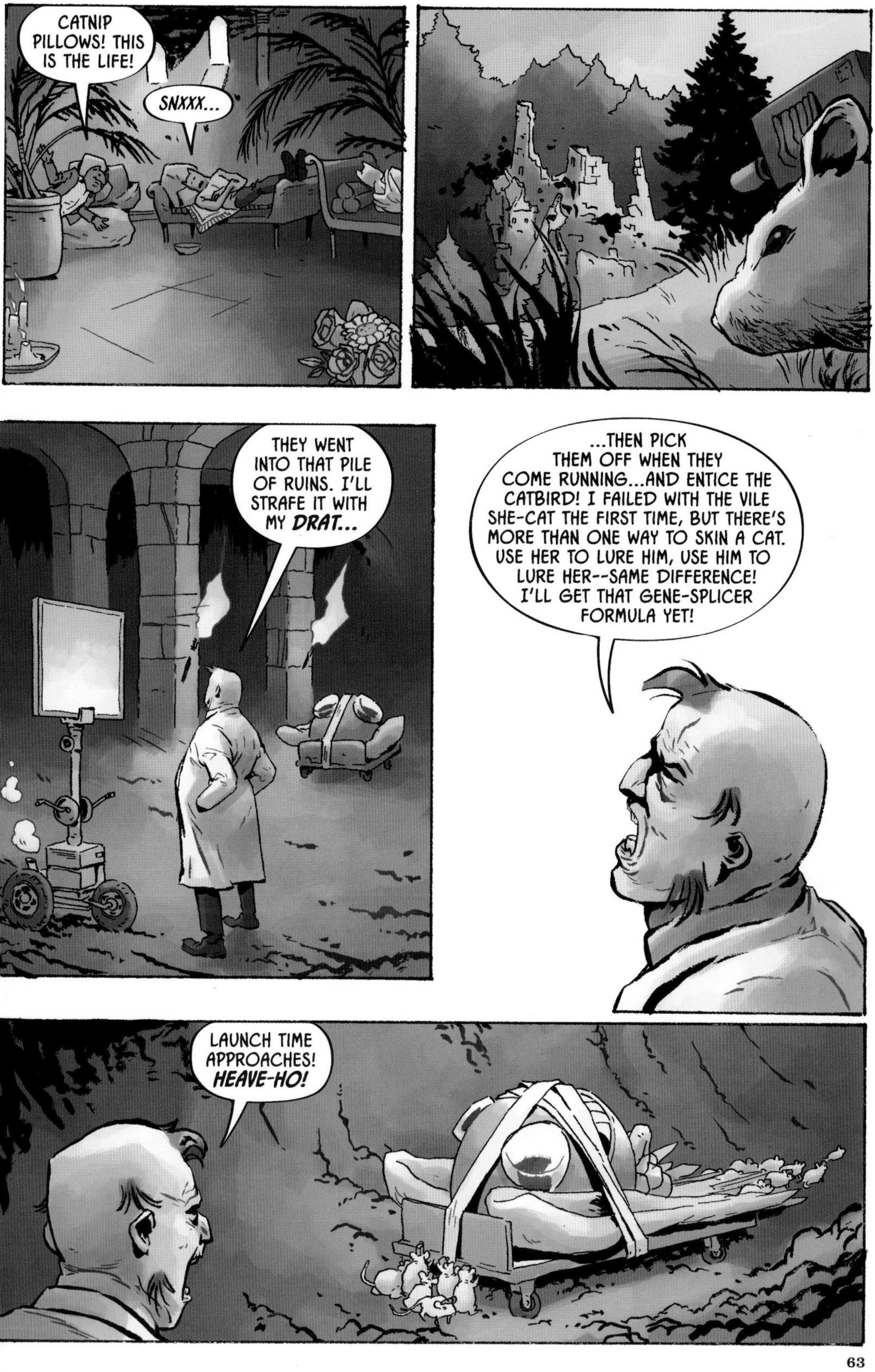
CATNIP PILLOWS! THIS IS THE LIFE!
SNXXX...
THEY WENT INTO THAT PILE OF RUINS. I'LL STRAFE IT WITH MY DRAT...
...THEN PICK THEM OFF WHEN THEY COME RUNNING...AND ENTICE THE CATBIRD! I FAILED WITH THE VILE SHE-CAT THE FIRST TIME, BUT THERE'S MORE THAN ONE WAY TO SKIN A CAT. USE HER TO LURE HIM, USE HIM TO LURE HER--SAME DIFFERENCE! I'LL GET THAT GENE-SPLICER FORMULA YET!
LAUNCH TIME APPROACHES! HEAVE-HO!

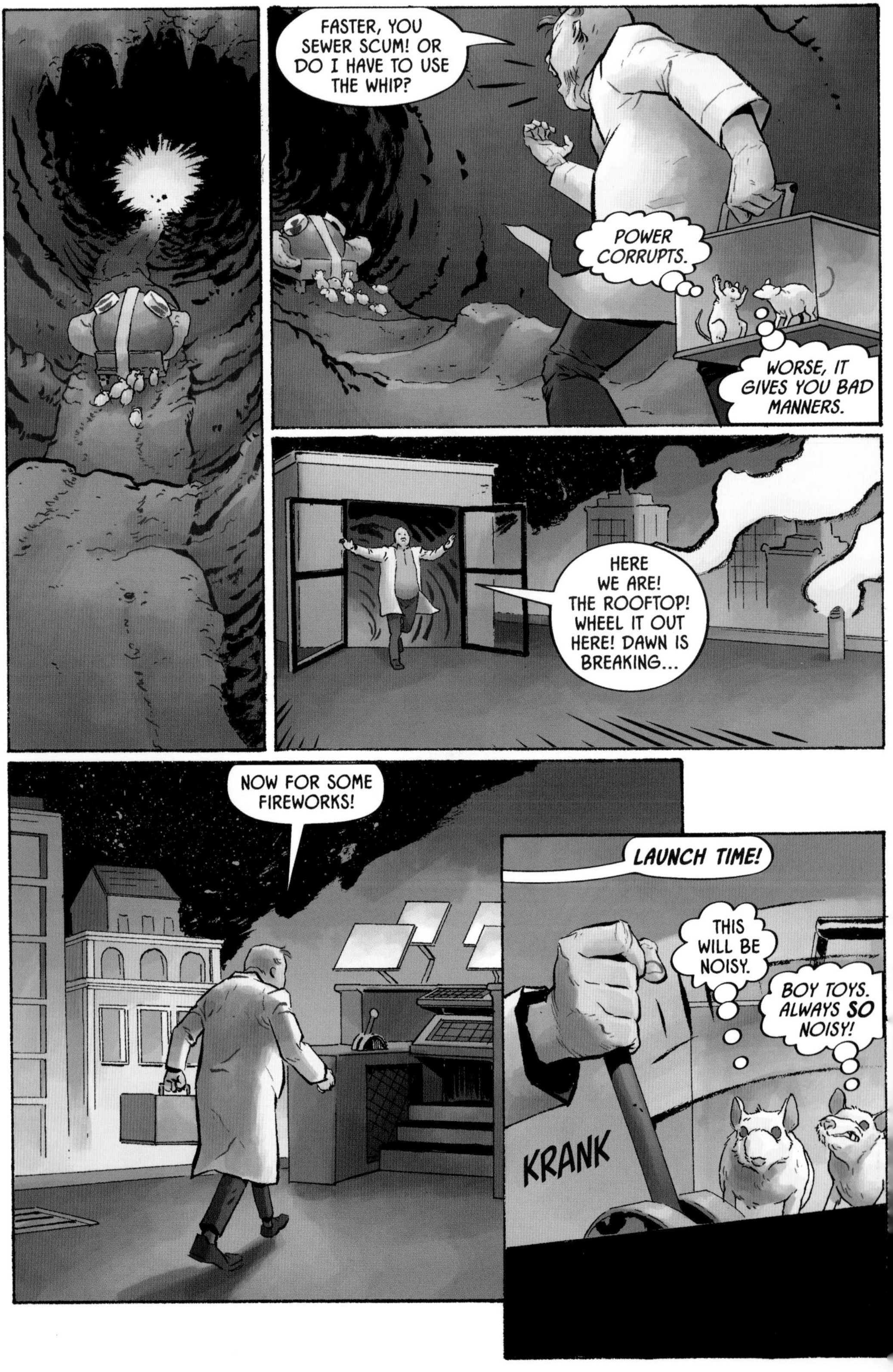
FASTER, YOU SEWER SCUM! OR DO I HAVE TO USE THE WHIP?
POWER CORRUPTS.
WORSE, IT GIVES YOU BAD MANNERS.
HERE WE ARE! THE ROOFTOP! WHEEL IT OUT HERE! DAWN IS BREAKING...
NOW FOR SOME FIREWORKS!
LAUNCH TIME!
THIS WILL BE NOISY.
BOY TOYS. ALWAYS SO NOISY!
KRANK

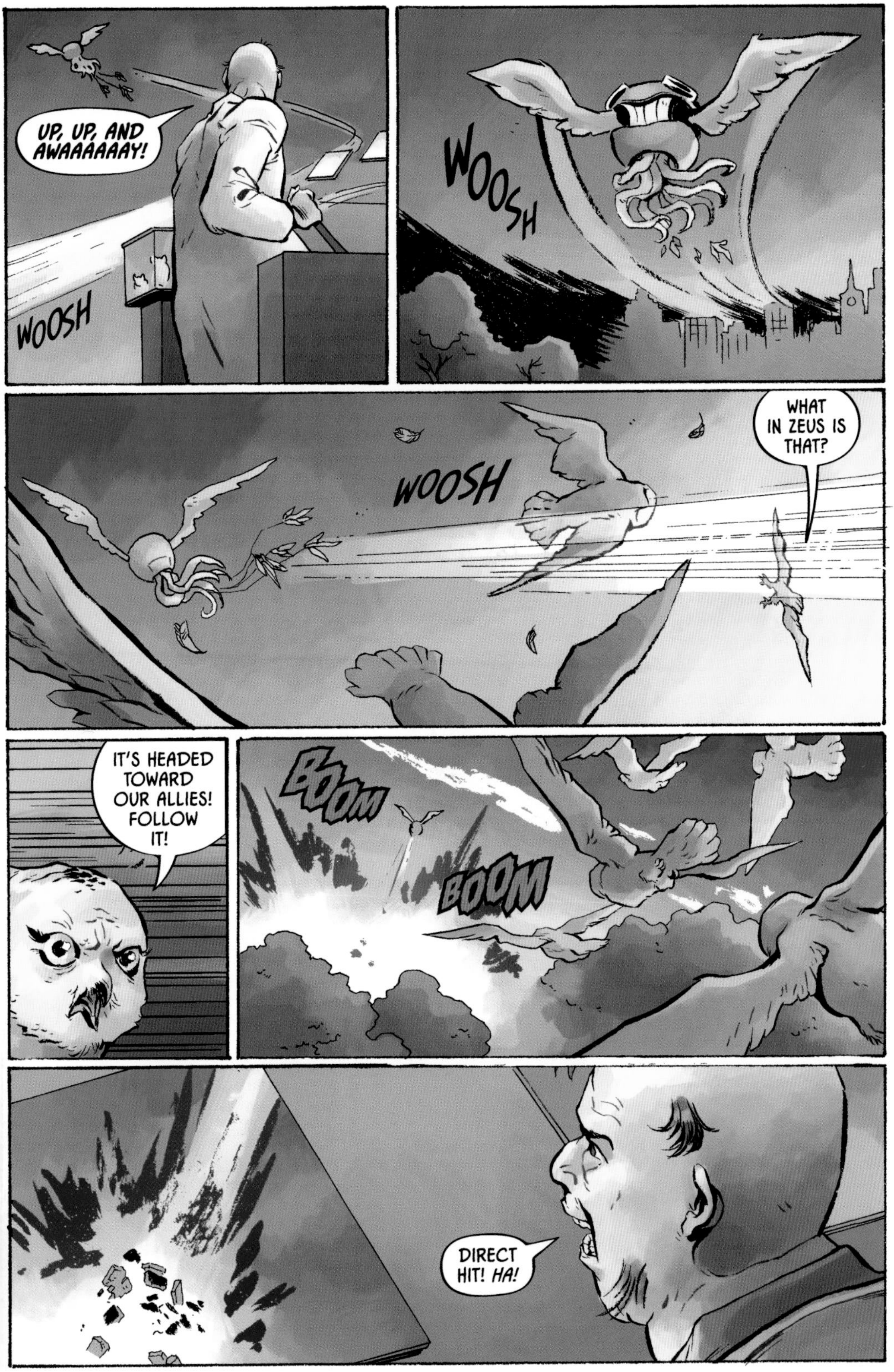
UP, UP, AND AWAAAAAAY!
WOOSH
WOOSH
WHAT IN ZEUS IS THAT?
WOOSH
IT'S HEADED TOWARD OUR ALLIES! FOLLOW IT!
BOOM
BOOM
DIRECT HIT! HA!

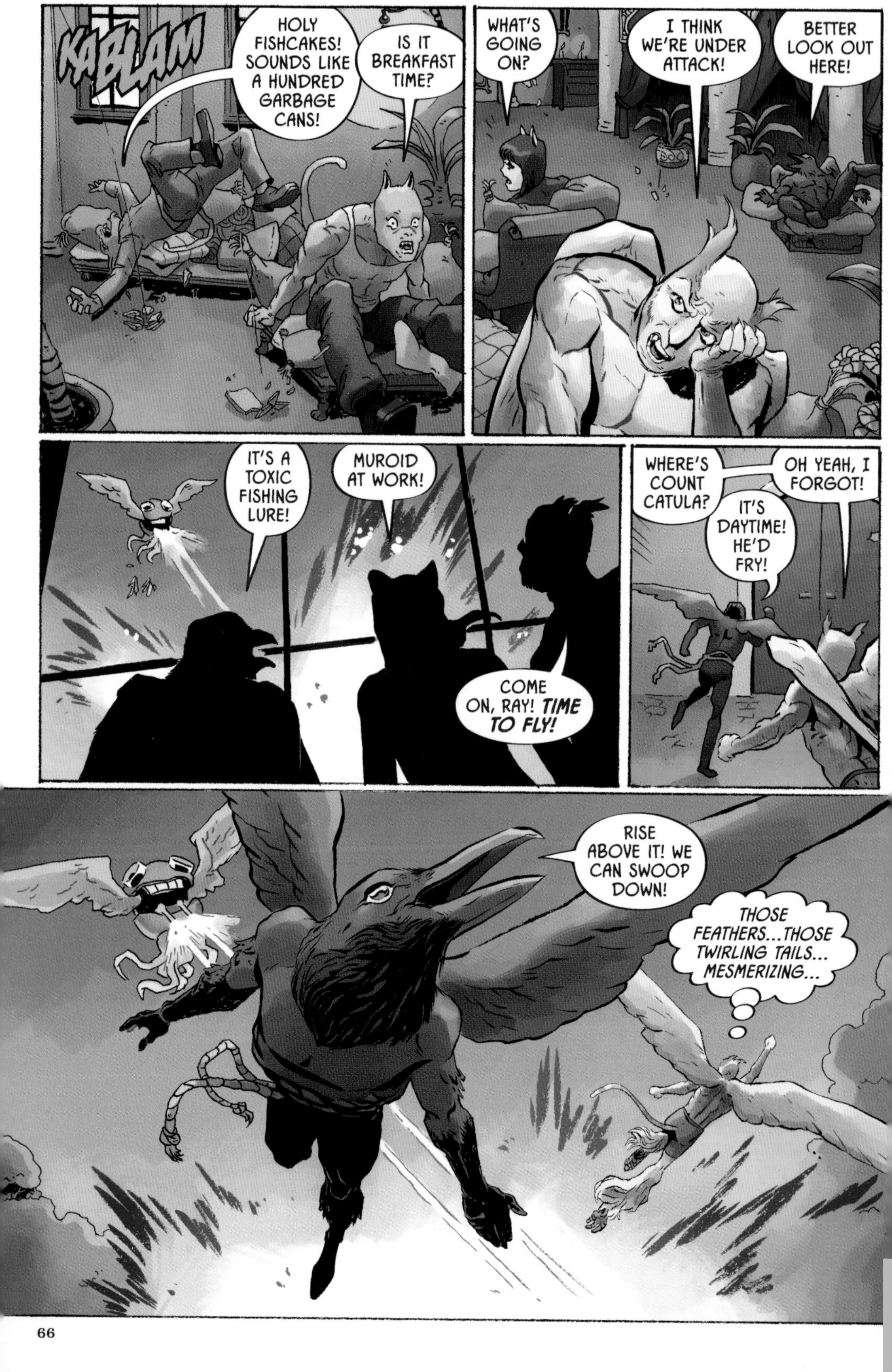
KABLAM
HOLY FISHCAKES! SOUNDS LIKE A HUNDRED GARBAGE CANS!
IS IT BREAKFAST TIME?
WHAT'S GOING ON?
I THINK WE'RE UNDER ATTACK!
BETTER LOOK OUT HERE!
IT'S A TOXIC FISHING LURE!
MUROID AT WORK!
COME ON, RAY! TIME TO FLY!
WHERE'S COUNT CATULA?
OH YEAH, I FORGOT!
IT'S DAYTIME! HE'D FRY!
RISE ABOVE IT! WE CAN SWOOP DOWN!
THOSE FEATHERS...THOSE TWIRLING TAILS... MESMERIZING...

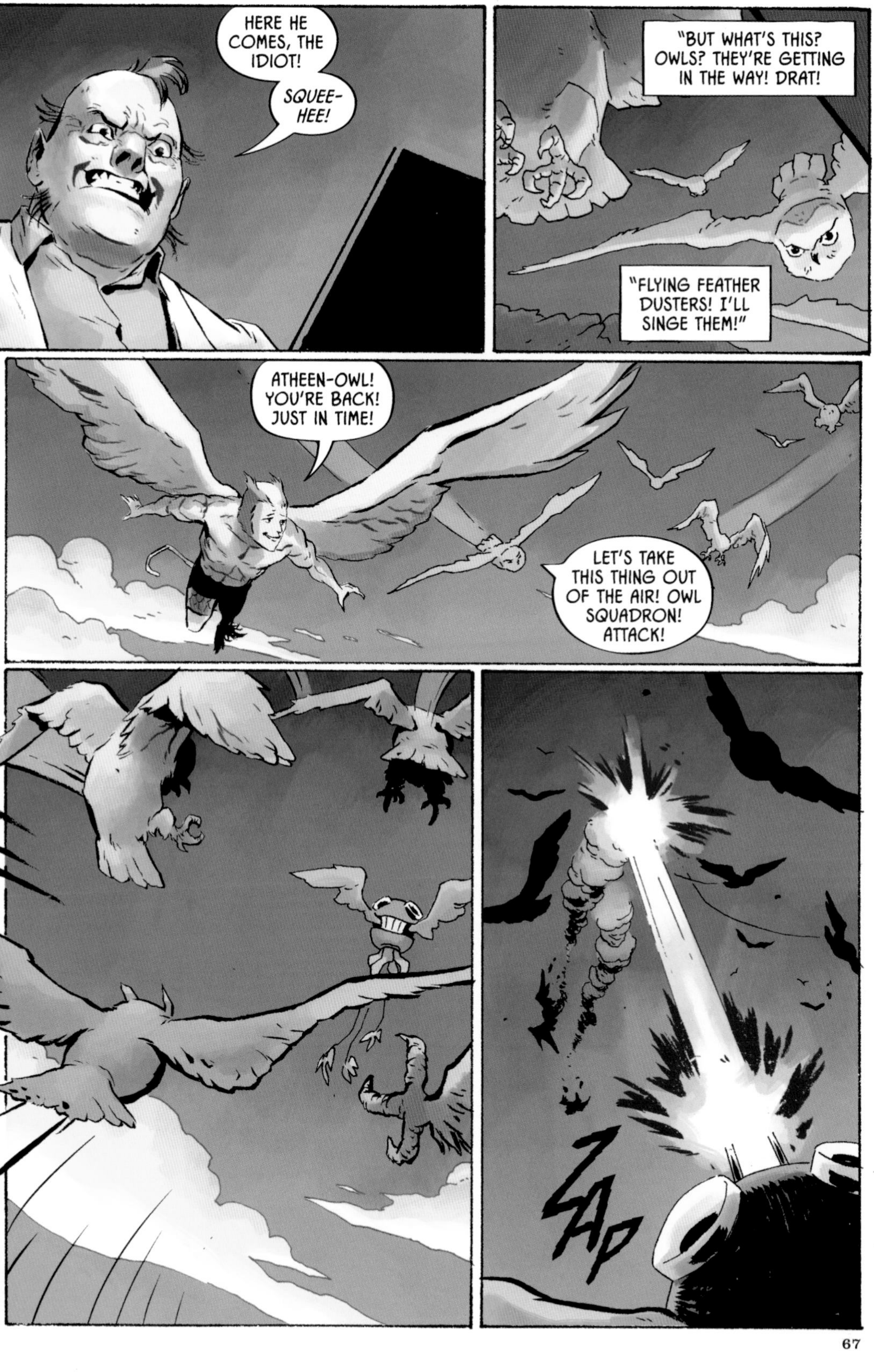
HERE HE COMES, THE IDIOT!
SQUEE-HEE!
"BUT WHAT'S THIS? OWLS? THEY'RE GETTING IN THE WAY! DRAT!
"FLYING FEATHER DUSTERS! I'LL SINGE THEM!"
ATHEEN-OWL! YOU'RE BACK! JUST IN TIME!
LET'S TAKE THIS THING OUT OF THE AIR! OWL SQUADRON! ATTACK!
ZAP

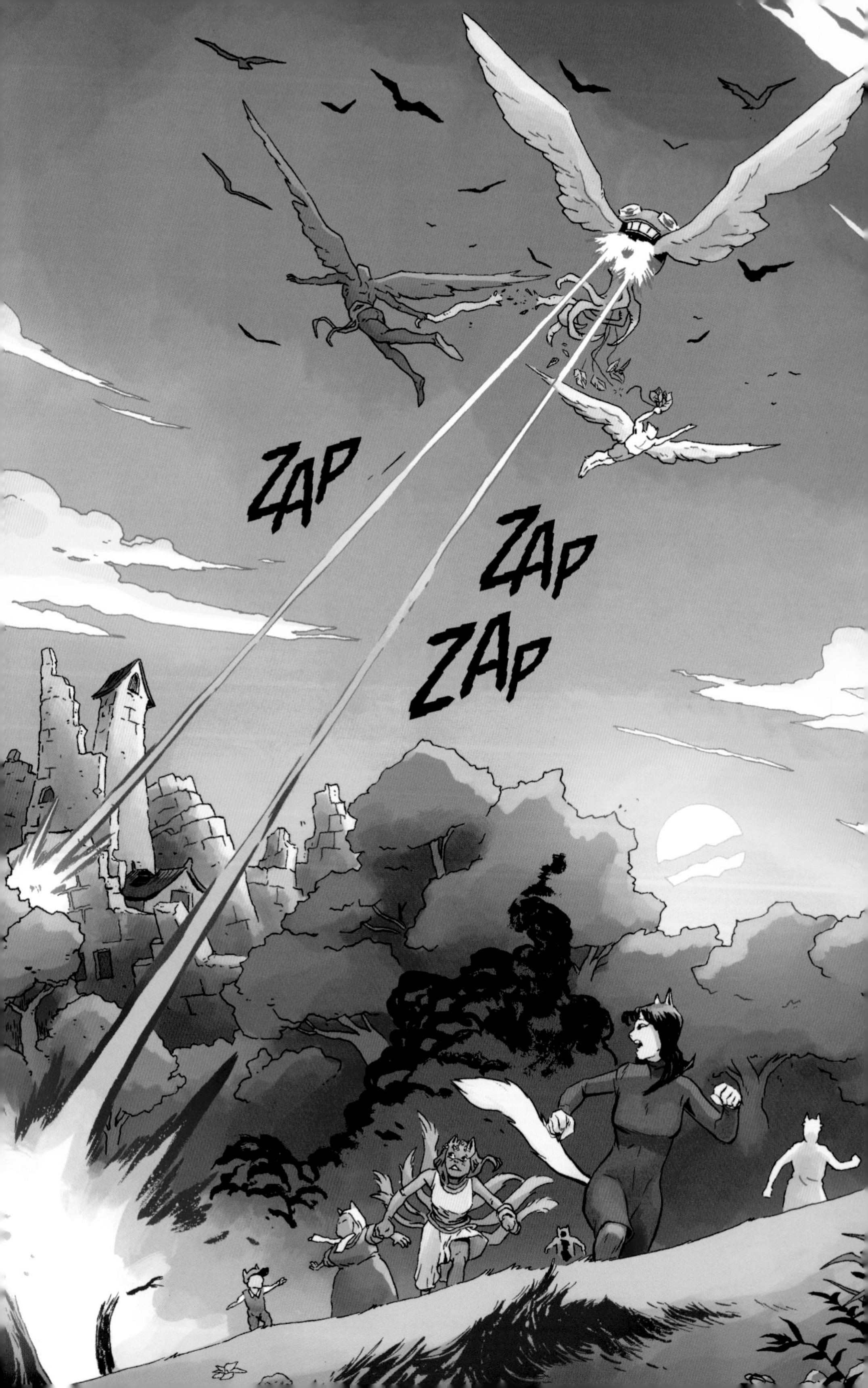
ZAP
ZAP
ZAP

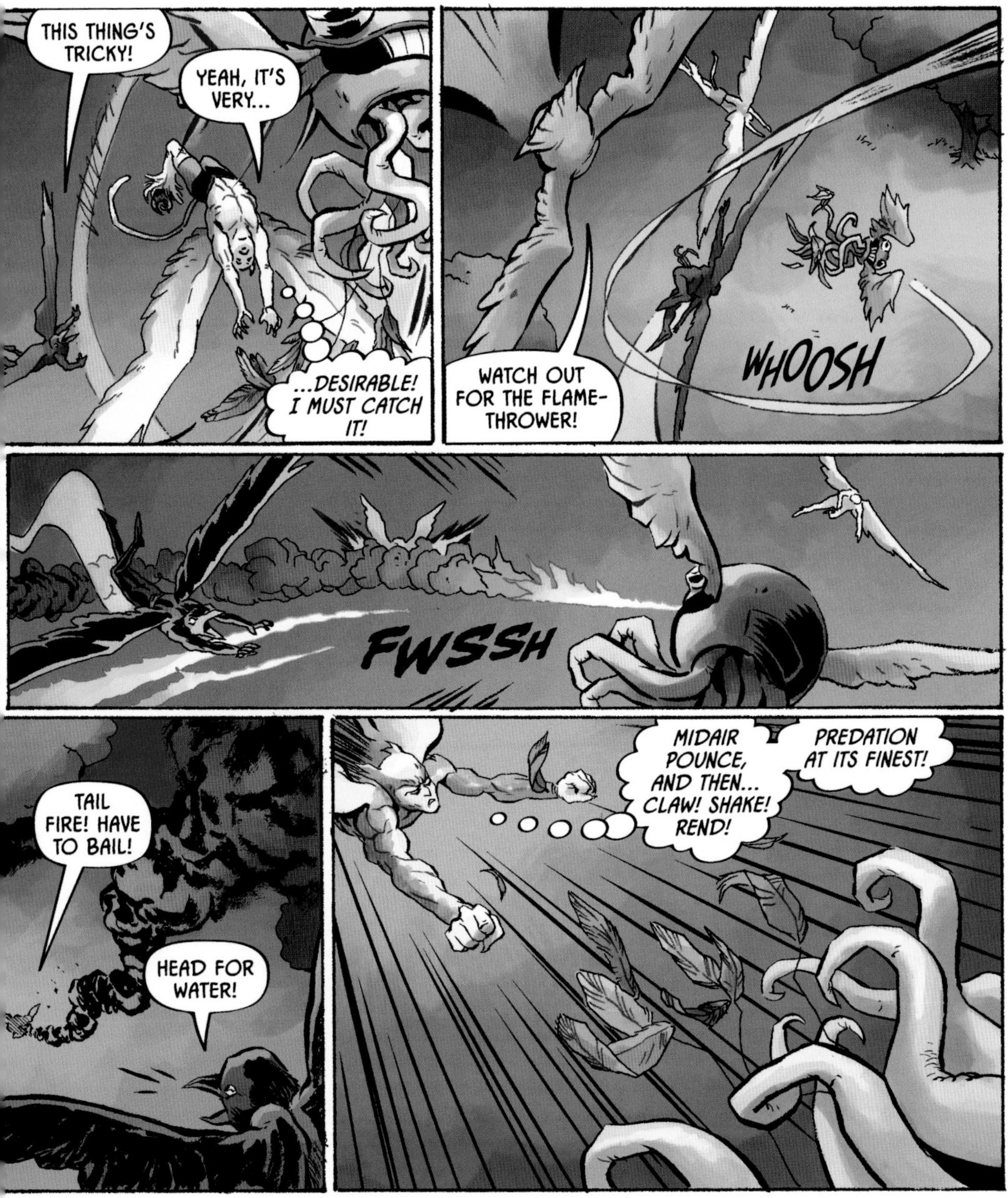
THIS THING'S TRICKY!
YEAH, IT'S VERY...
...DESIRABLE! I MUST CATCH IT!
WATCH OUT FOR THE FLAME-THROWER!
WHOOSH
FWSSH
TAIL FIRE! HAVE TO BAIL!
HEAD FOR WATER!
MIDAIR POUNCE, AND THEN... CLAW! SHAKE! REND!
PREDATION AT ITS FINEST!

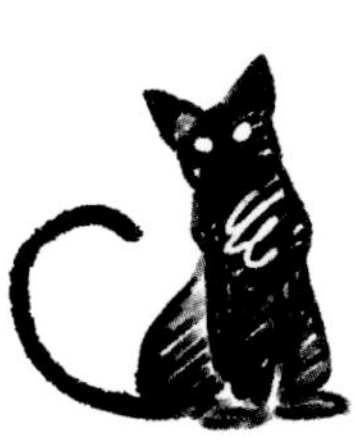

PLAY WITH FOOD . . . OR FOOD FOR PLAY?

Pet cats hunt for stimulation, not food. Get them toys that imitate their favorite prey and you can keep them safely entertained without the risk to local birds and wildlife! Read more at www.catsandbirds.ca

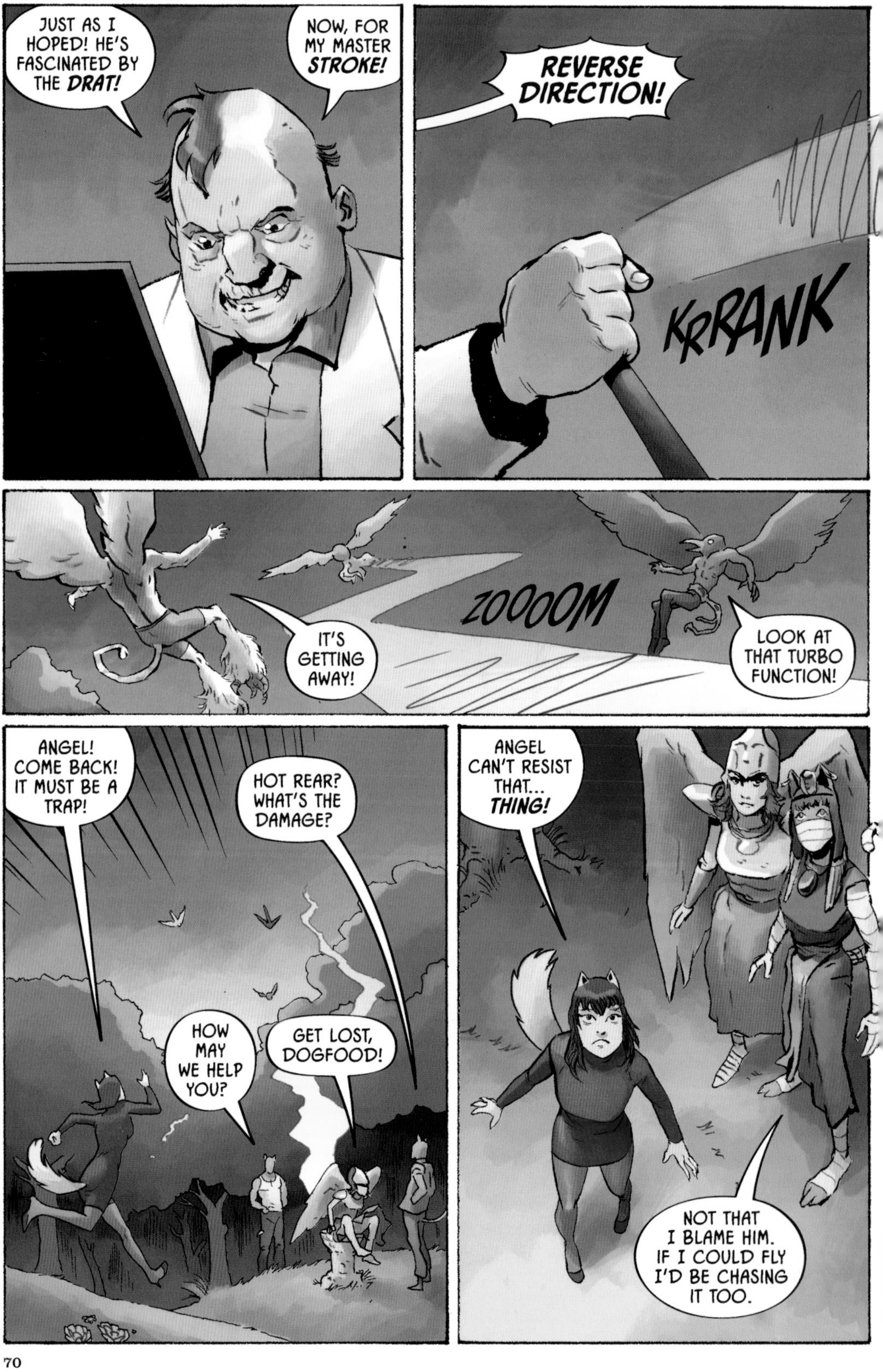
JUST AS I HOPED! HE'S FASCINATED BY THE *DRAT!*
NOW, FOR MY MASTER *STROKE!*
REVERSE DIRECTION!
KRRANK
ZOOOOM
IT'S GETTING AWAY!
LOOK AT THAT TURBO FUNCTION!
ANGEL! COME BACK! IT MUST BE A TRAP!
HOT REAR? WHAT'S THE DAMAGE?
HOW MAY WE HELP YOU?
GET LOST, DOGFOOD!
ANGEL CAN'T RESIST THAT... *THING!*
NOT THAT I BLAME HIM. IF I COULD FLY I'D BE CHASING IT TOO.

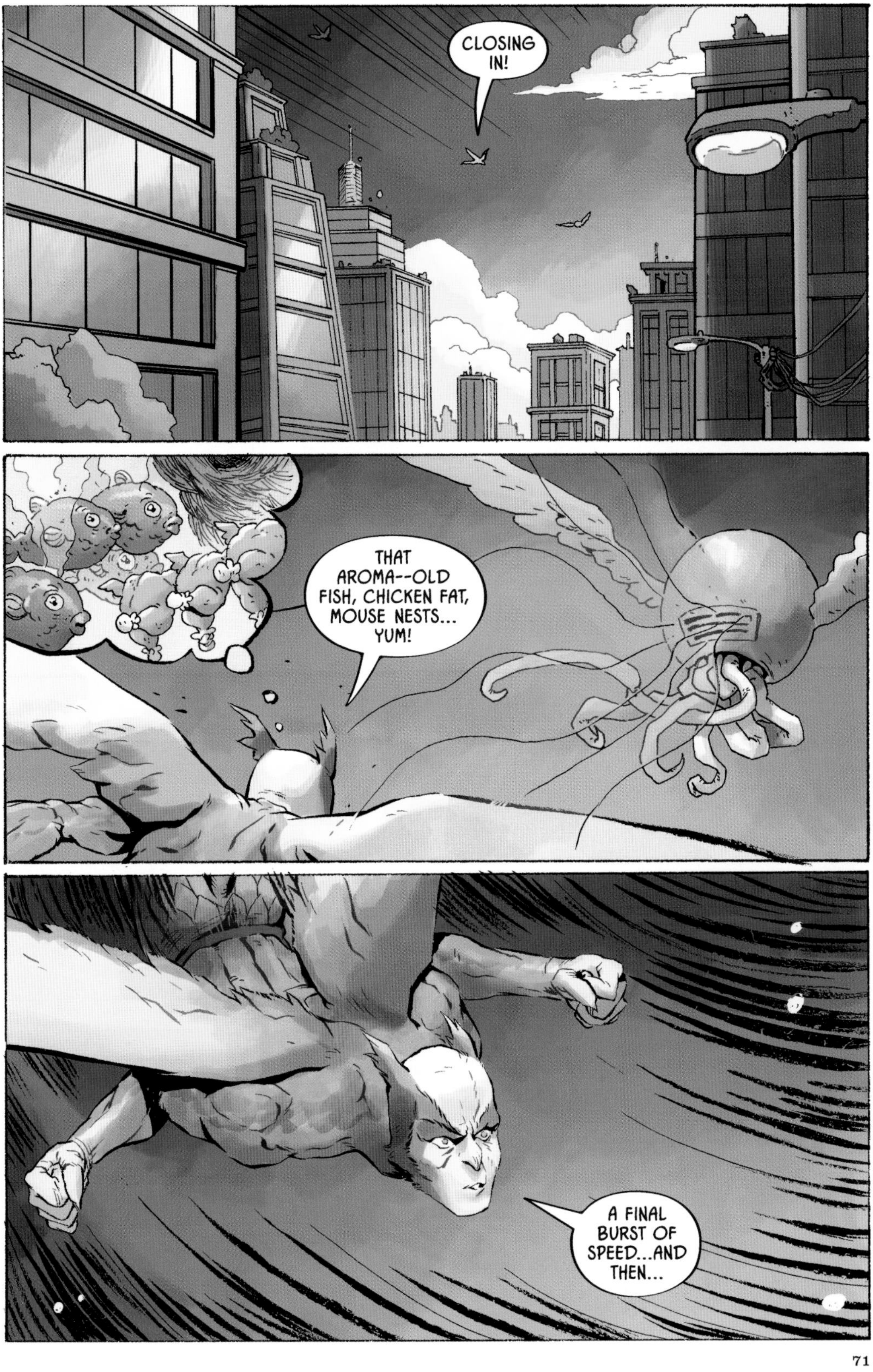
CLOSING IN!
THAT AROMA--OLD FISH, CHICKEN FAT, MOUSE NESTS... YUM!
A FINAL BURST OF SPEED...AND THEN...

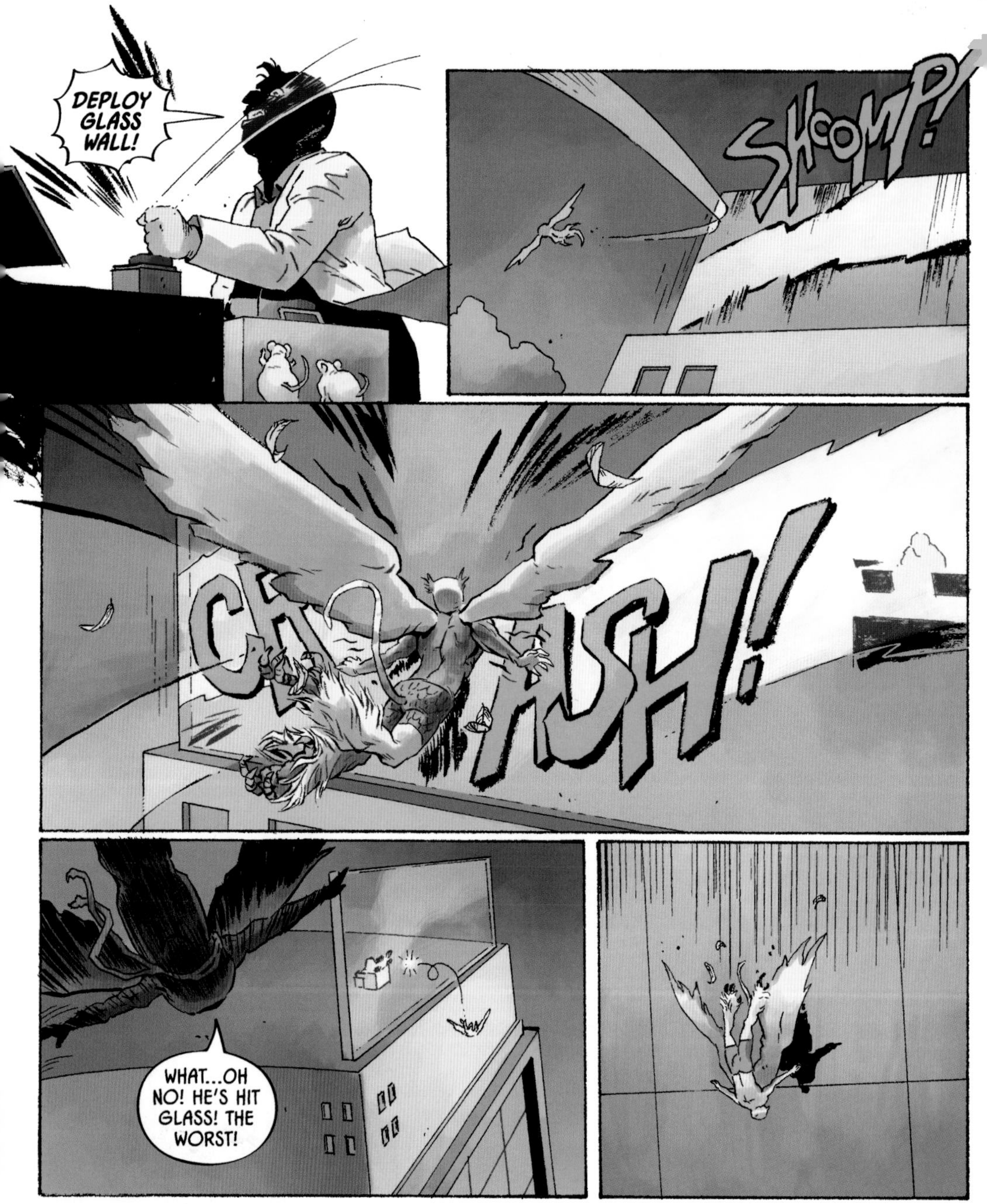
DEPLOY GLASS WALL!
SHOOMP!
CRASH!
WHAT...OH NO! HE'S HIT GLASS! THE WORST!

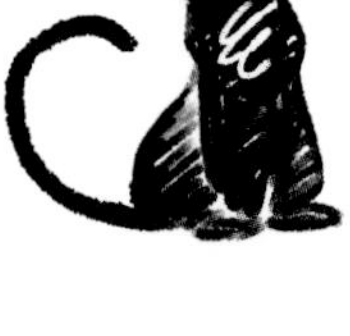

GLASS, INVISIBLE GLASS

After habitat loss, climate change, and cats, window collisions are the biggest problem people cause for birds. There are simple, low-cost solutions to make your home bird friendly!
Read more at www.naturecanada.ca

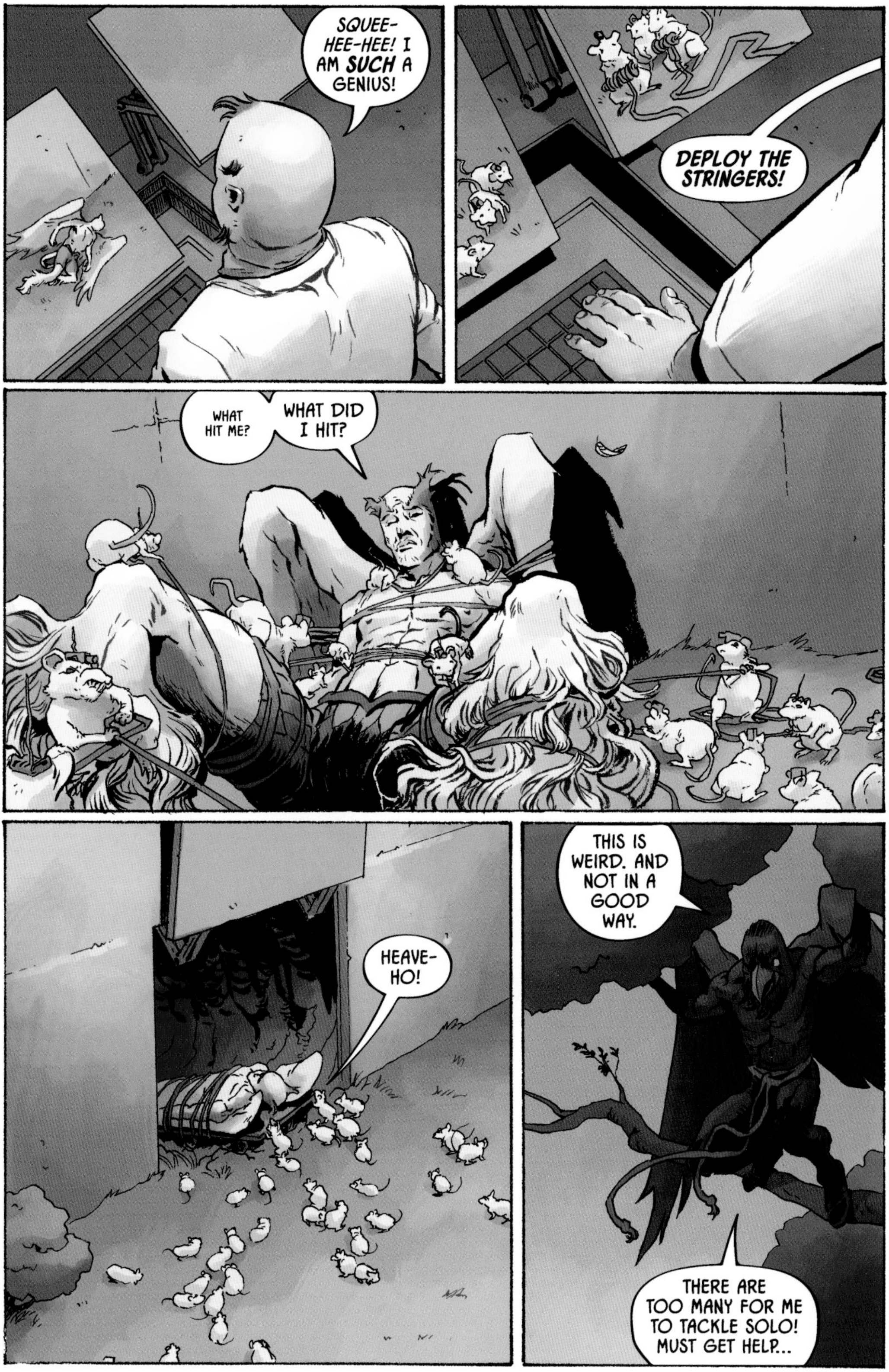
SQUEE-HEE-HEE! I AM SUCH A GENIUS!
DEPLOY THE STRINGERS!
WHAT HIT ME?
WHAT DID I HIT?
HEAVE-HO!
THIS IS WEIRD. AND NOT IN A GOOD WAY.
THERE ARE TOO MANY FOR ME TO TACKLE SOLO! MUST GET HELP...

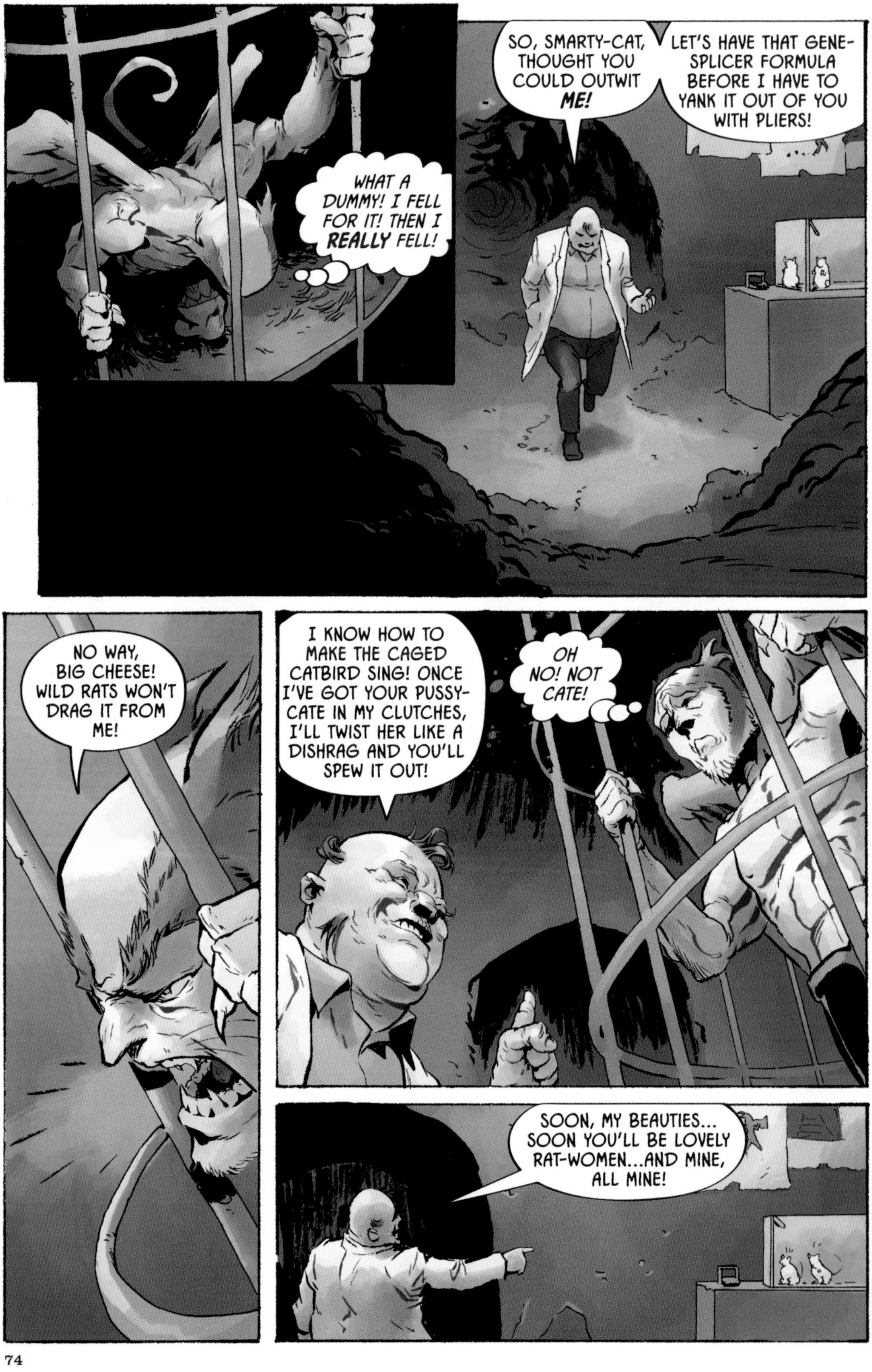
WHAT A DUMMY! I FELL FOR IT! THEN I REALLY FELL!
SO, SMARTY-CAT, THOUGHT YOU COULD OUTWIT ME!
LET'S HAVE THAT GENE-SPLICER FORMULA BEFORE I HAVE TO YANK IT OUT OF YOU WITH PLIERS!
NO WAY, BIG CHEESE! WILD RATS WON'T DRAG IT FROM ME!
I KNOW HOW TO MAKE THE CAGED CATBIRD SING! ONCE I'VE GOT YOUR PUSSY-CATE IN MY CLUTCHES, I'LL TWIST HER LIKE A DISHRAG AND YOU'LL SPEW IT OUT!
OH NO! NOT CATE!
SOON, MY BEAUTIES... SOON YOU'LL BE LOVELY RAT-WOMEN...AND MINE, ALL MINE!

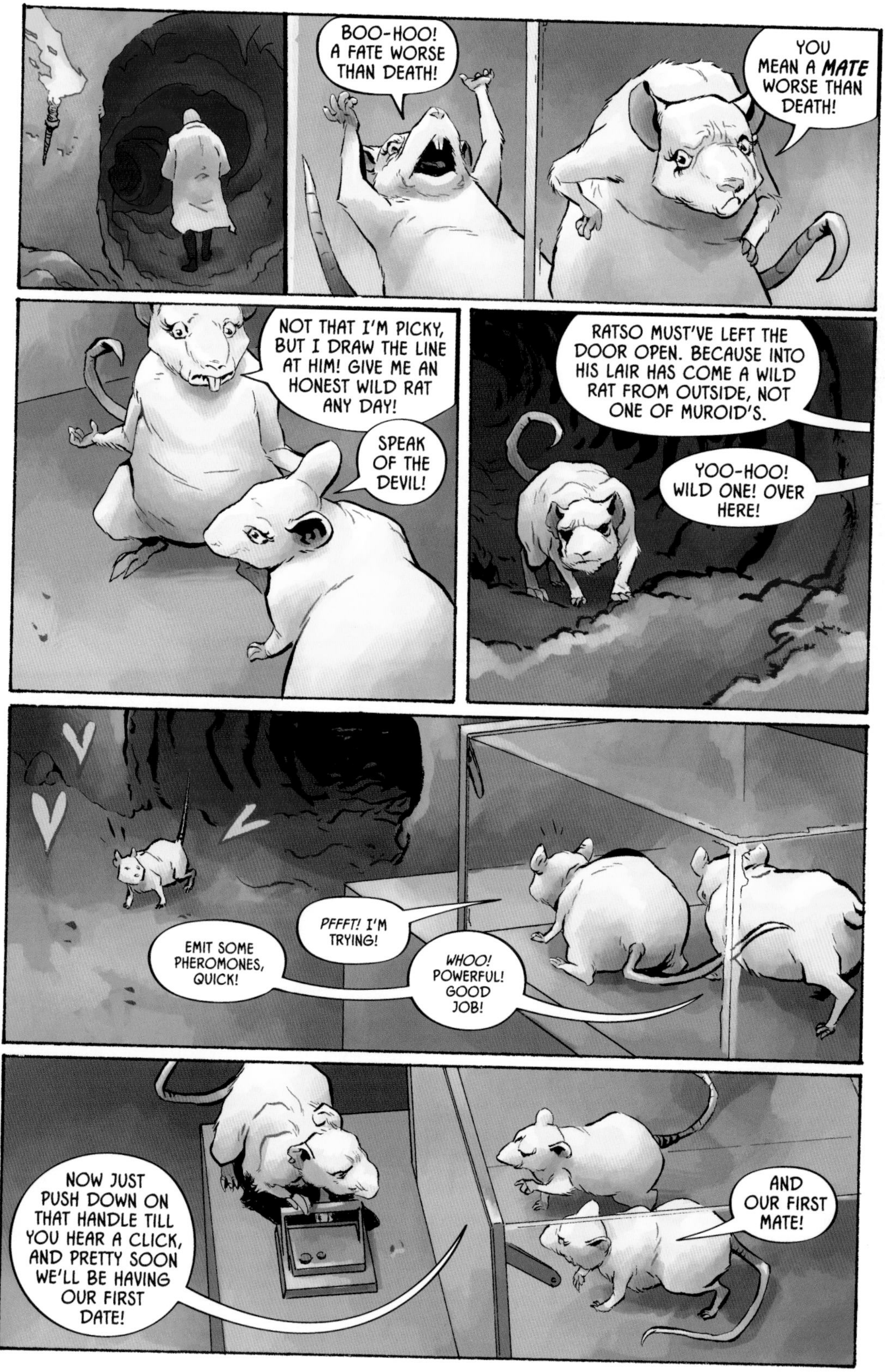
BOO-HOO! A FATE WORSE THAN DEATH!
YOU MEAN A ***MATE*** WORSE THAN DEATH!
NOT THAT I'M PICKY, BUT I DRAW THE LINE AT HIM! GIVE ME AN HONEST WILD RAT ANY DAY!
SPEAK OF THE DEVIL!
RATSO MUST'VE LEFT THE DOOR OPEN. BECAUSE INTO HIS LAIR HAS COME A WILD RAT FROM OUTSIDE, NOT ONE OF MUROID'S.
YOO-HOO! WILD ONE! OVER HERE!
EMIT SOME PHEROMONES, QUICK!
PFFFT! I'M TRYING!
WHOO! POWERFUL! GOOD JOB!
NOW JUST PUSH DOWN ON THAT HANDLE TILL YOU HEAR A CLICK, AND PRETTY SOON WE'LL BE HAVING OUR FIRST DATE!
AND OUR FIRST MATE!

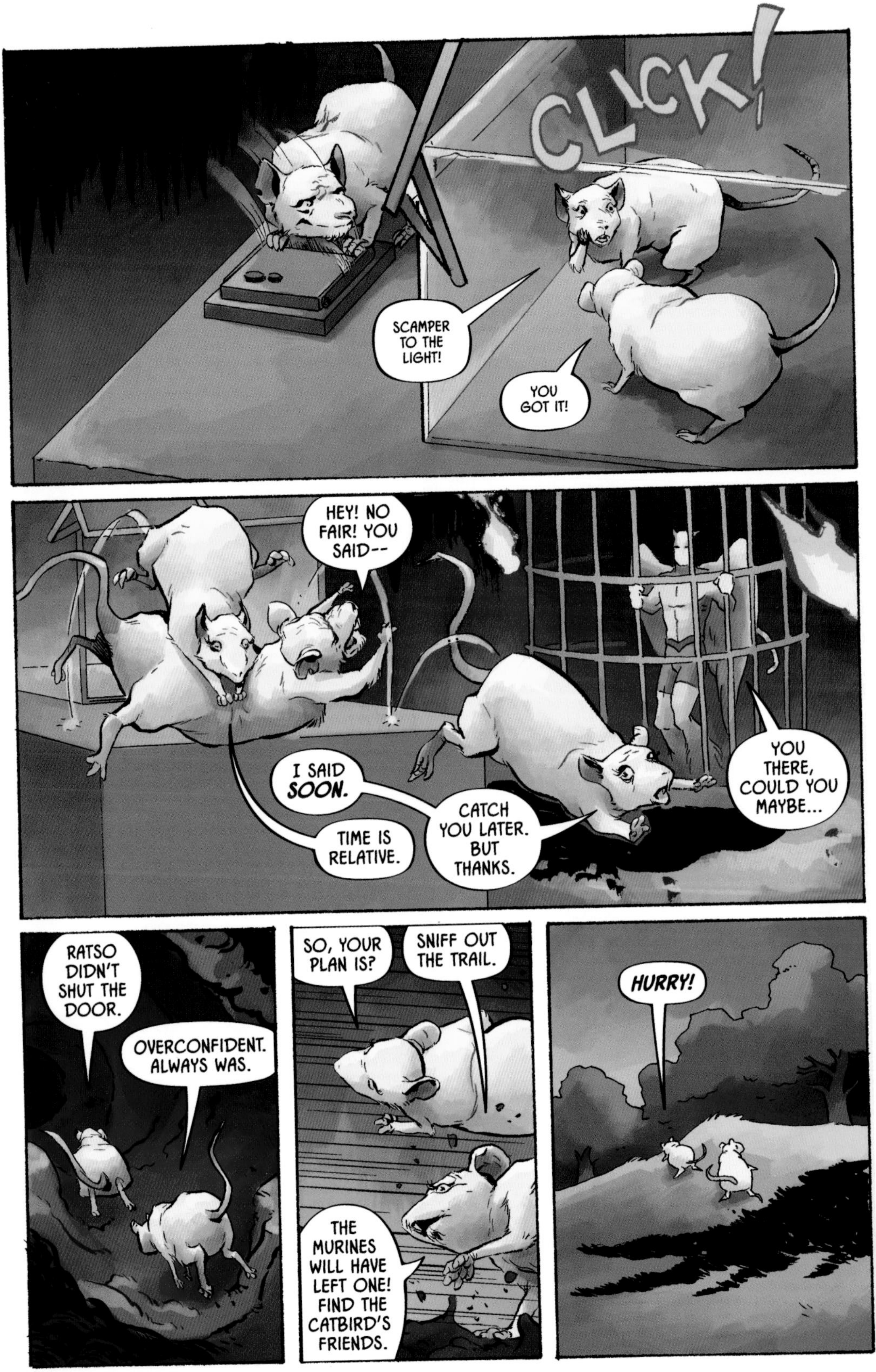
CLICK!
SCAMPER TO THE LIGHT!
YOU GOT IT!
HEY! NO FAIR! YOU SAID--
I SAID **SOON.**
TIME IS RELATIVE.
CATCH YOU LATER. BUT THANKS.
YOU THERE, COULD YOU MAYBE...
RATSO DIDN'T SHUT THE DOOR.
OVERCONFIDENT. ALWAYS WAS.
SO, YOUR PLAN IS?
SNIFF OUT THE TRAIL.
THE MURINES WILL HAVE LEFT ONE! FIND THE CATBIRD'S FRIENDS.
HURRY!

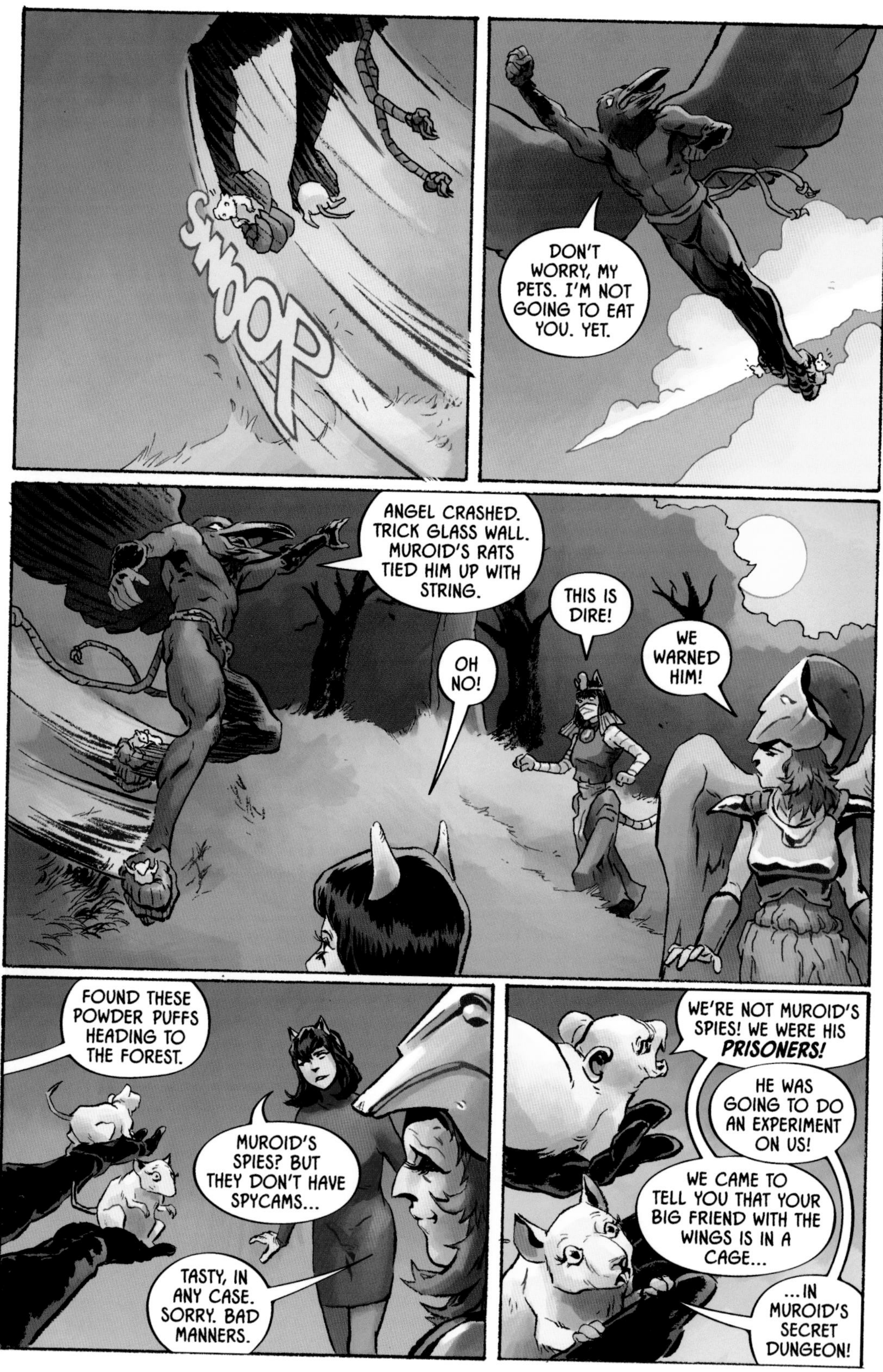
SWOOP
DON'T WORRY, MY PETS. I'M NOT GOING TO EAT YOU. YET.
ANGEL CRASHED. TRICK GLASS WALL. MUROID'S RATS TIED HIM UP WITH STRING.
THIS IS DIRE!
WE WARNED HIM!
OH NO!
FOUND THESE POWDER PUFFS HEADING TO THE FOREST.
MUROID'S SPIES? BUT THEY DON'T HAVE SPYCAMS...
TASTY, IN ANY CASE. SORRY. BAD MANNERS.
WE'RE NOT MUROID'S SPIES! WE WERE HIS ***PRISONERS!***
HE WAS GOING TO DO AN EXPERIMENT ON US!
WE CAME TO TELL YOU THAT YOUR BIG FRIEND WITH THE WINGS IS IN A CAGE...
...IN MUROID'S SECRET DUNGEON!

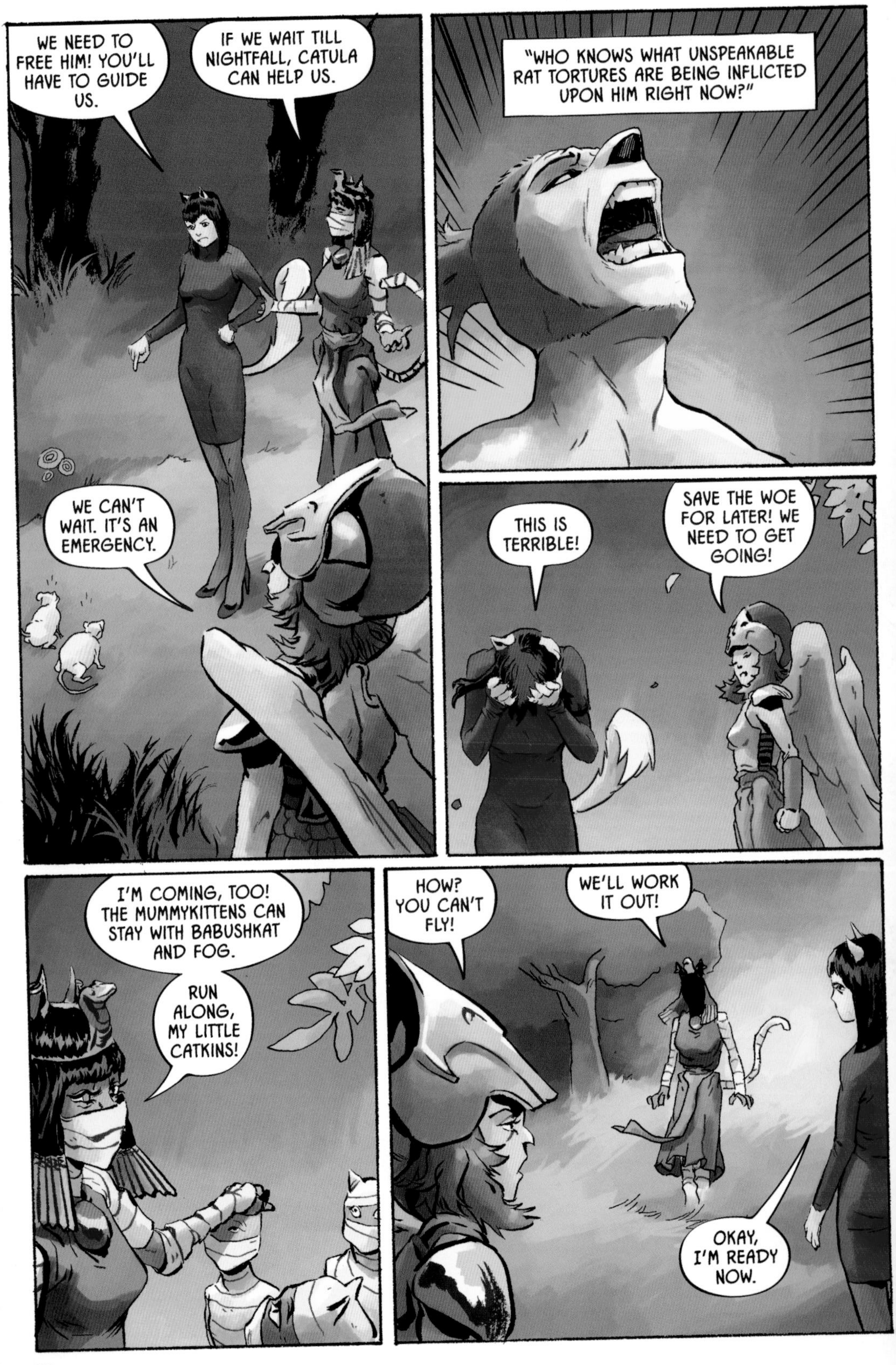
WE NEED TO FREE HIM! YOU'LL HAVE TO GUIDE US.
IF WE WAIT TILL NIGHTFALL, CATULA CAN HELP US.
WE CAN'T WAIT. IT'S AN EMERGENCY.
"WHO KNOWS WHAT UNSPEAKABLE RAT TORTURES ARE BEING INFLICTED UPON HIM RIGHT NOW?"
THIS IS TERRIBLE!
SAVE THE WOE FOR LATER! WE NEED TO GET GOING!
I'M COMING, TOO! THE MUMMYKITTENS CAN STAY WITH BABUSHKAT AND FOG.
RUN ALONG, MY LITTLE CATKINS!
HOW? YOU CAN'T FLY!
WE'LL WORK IT OUT!
OKAY, I'M READY NOW.

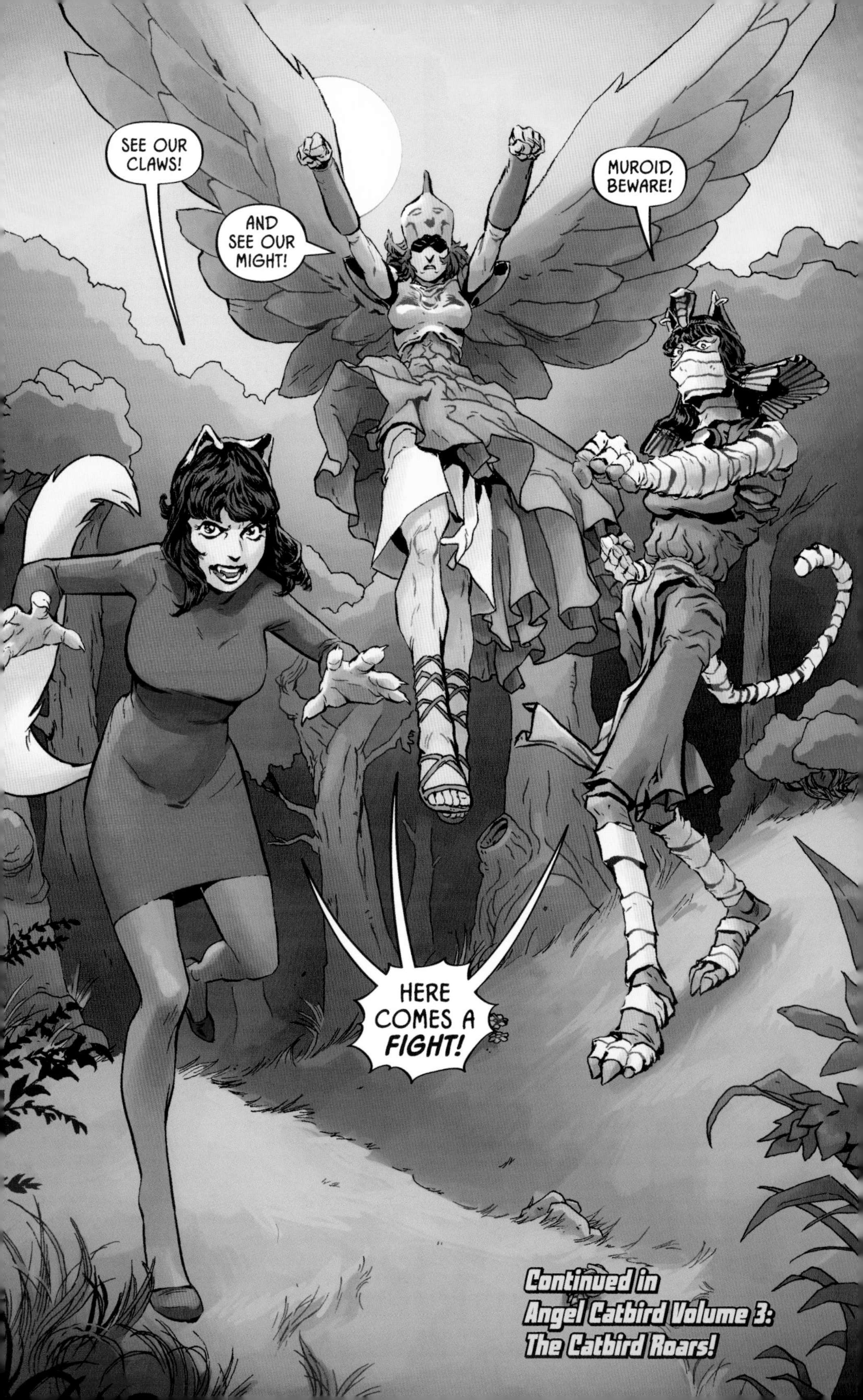
SEE OUR CLAWS!
AND SEE OUR MIGHT!
MUROID, BEWARE!
HERE COMES A FIGHT!
Continued in Angel Catbird Volume 3: The Catbird Roars!

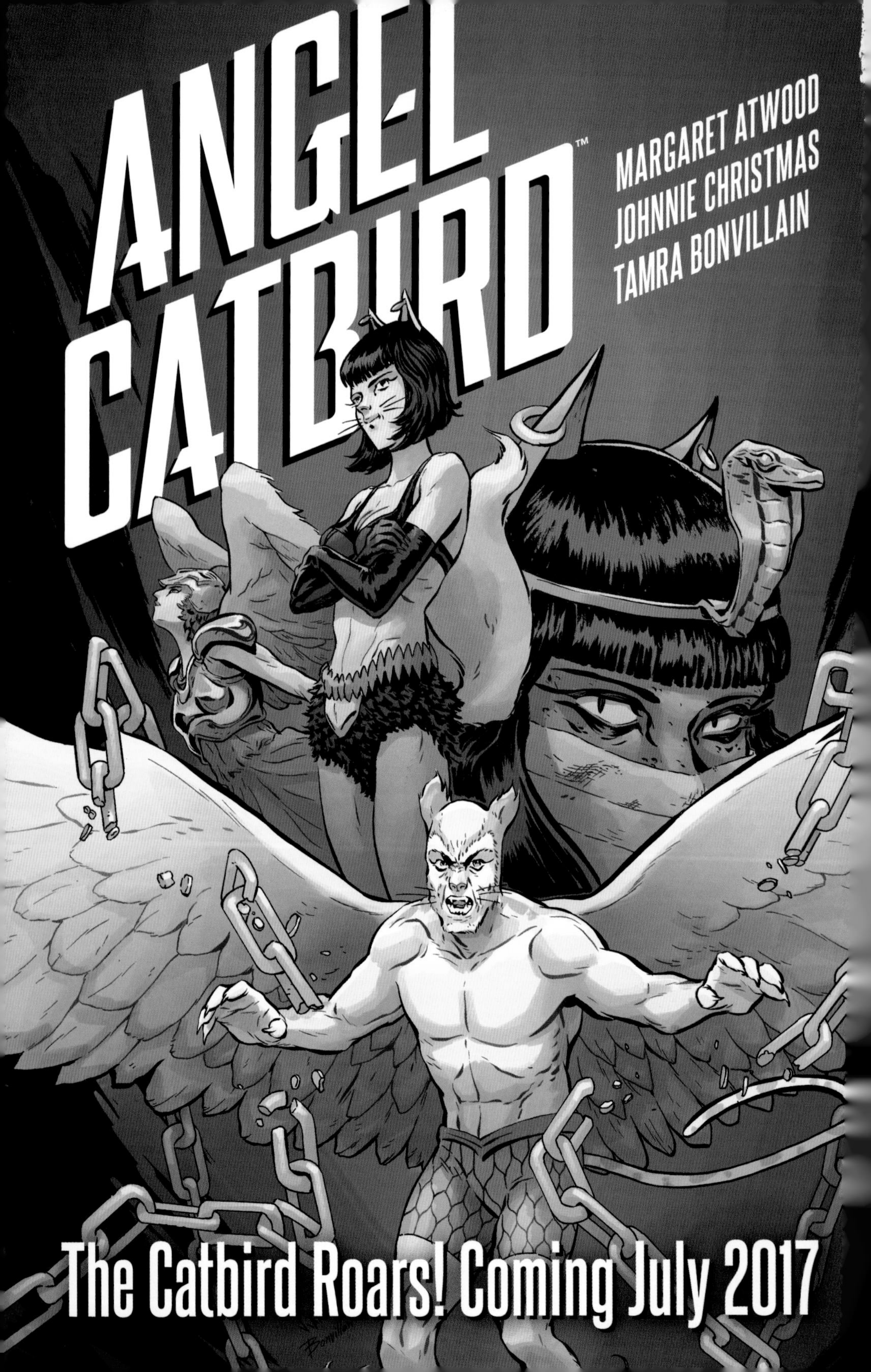

ANGEL CATBIRD™
MARGARET ATWOOD
JOHNNIE CHRISTMAS
TAMRA BONVILLAIN
The Catbird Roars! Coming July 2017

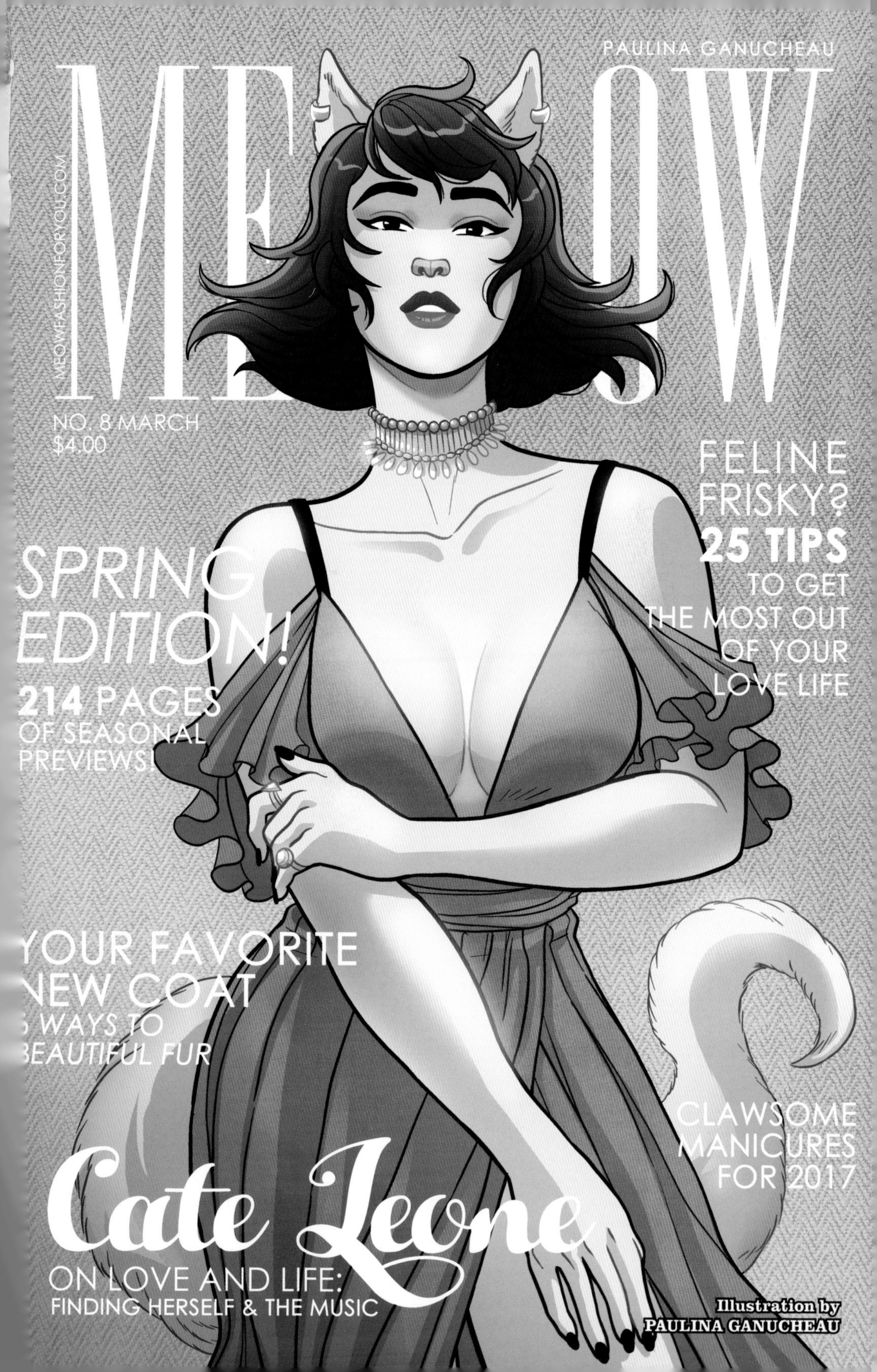
PAULINA GANUCHEAU
MEOWFASHIONFORYOU.COM
NO. 8 MARCH
$4.00
FELINE
FRISKY?
25 TIPS
TO GET
THE MOST OUT
OF YOUR
LOVE LIFE
SPRING
EDITION!
214 PAGES
OF SEASONAL
PREVIEWS!
YOUR FAVORITE
NEW COAT
WAYS TO
BEAUTIFUL FUR
CLAWSOME
MANICURES
FOR 2017
Cate Leone
ON LOVE AND LIFE:
FINDING HERSELF & THE MUSIC
Illustration by
PAULINA GANUCHEAU

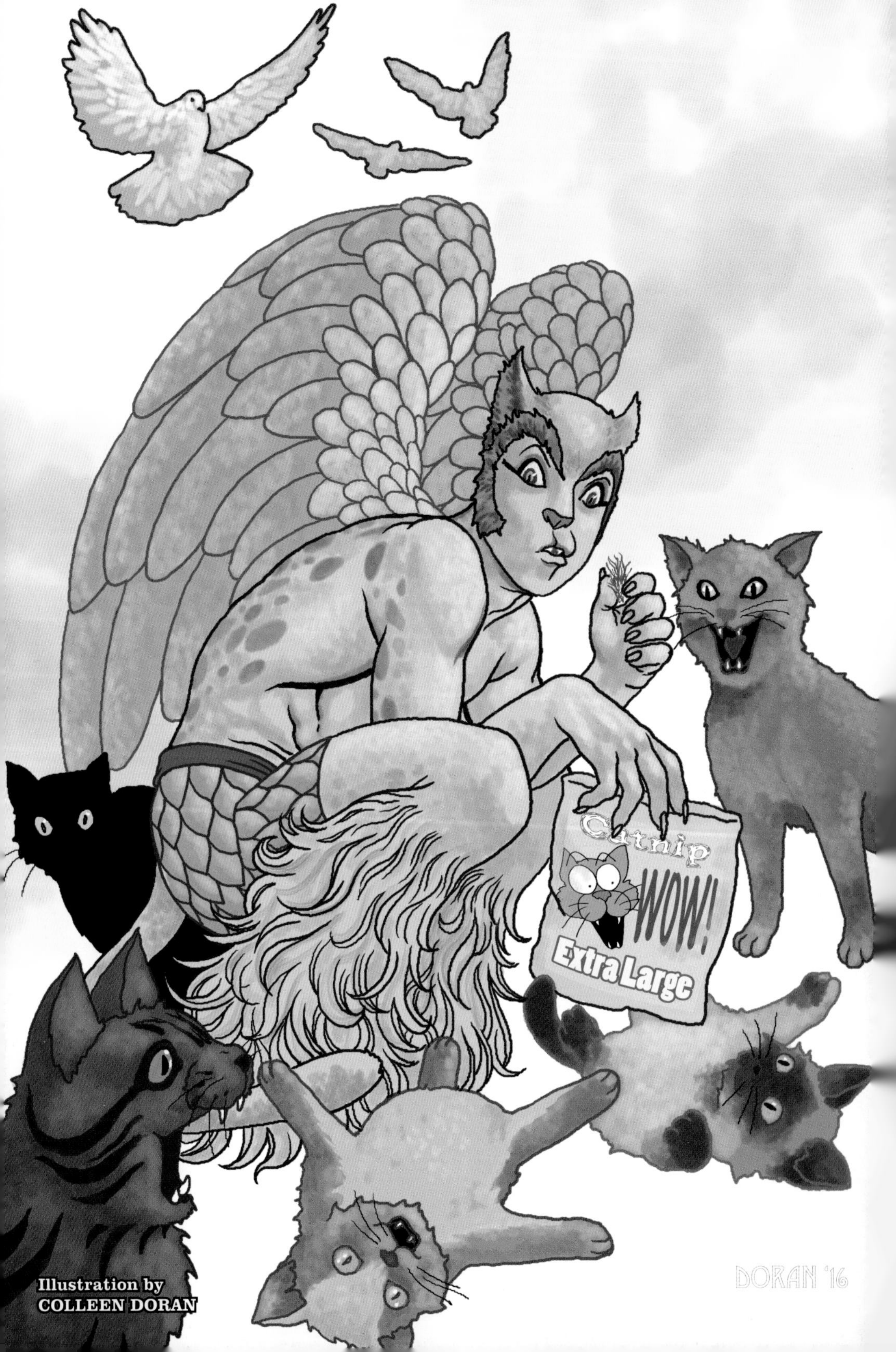
Catnip
WOW!
Extra Large
DORAN '16

Illustration by
COLLEEN DORAN

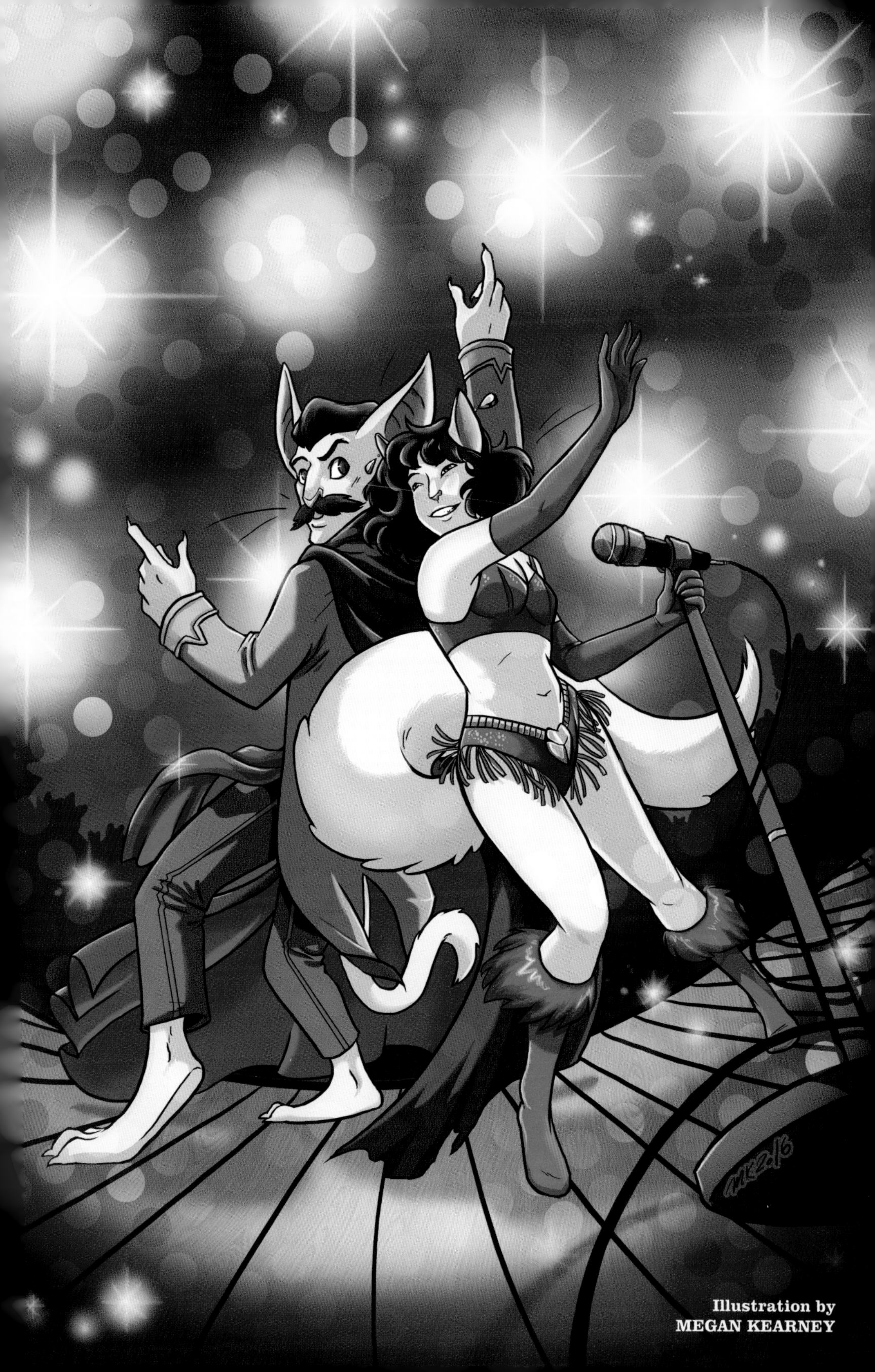

Illustration by
MEGAN KEARNEY

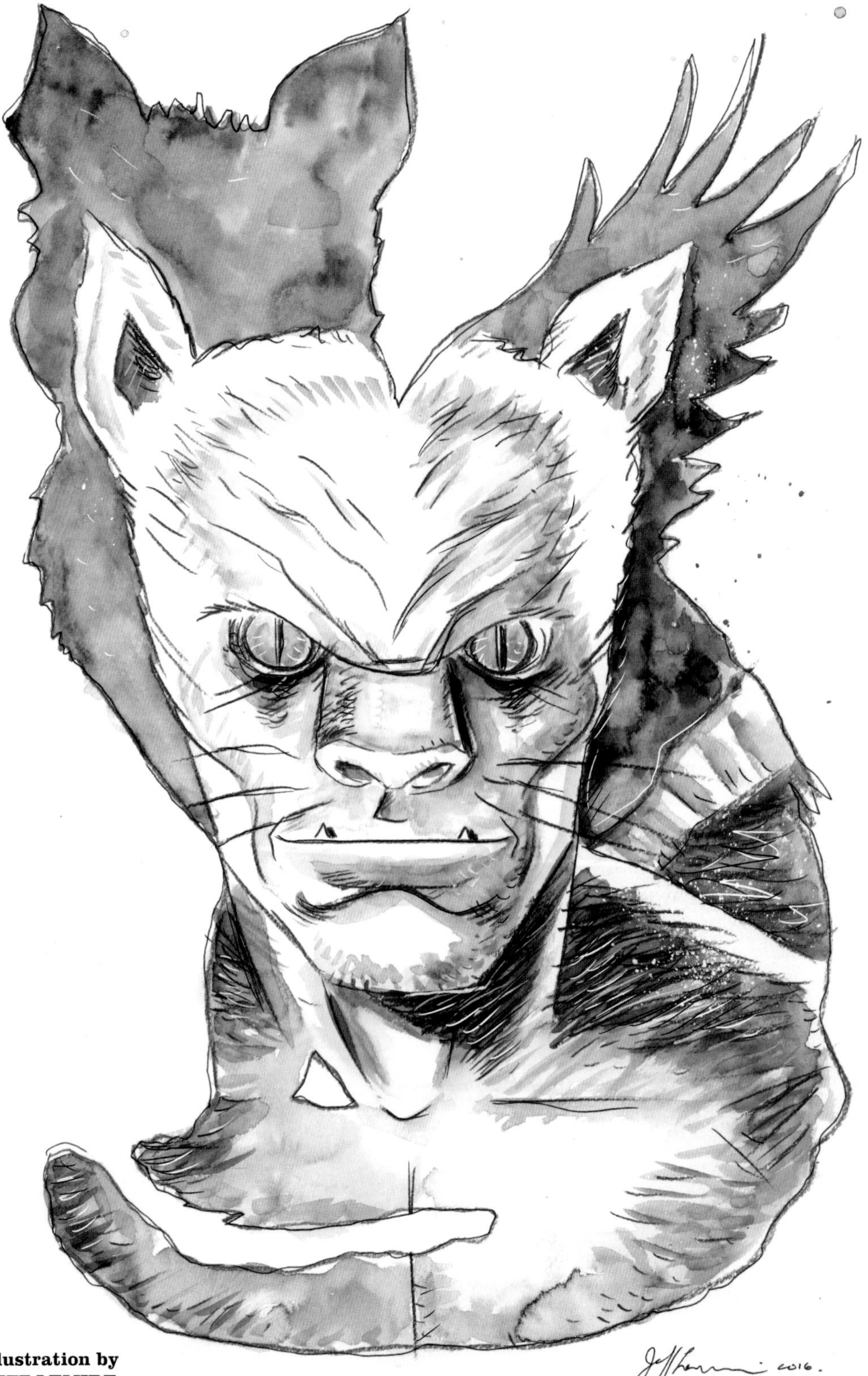

Illustration by
JEFF LEMIRE

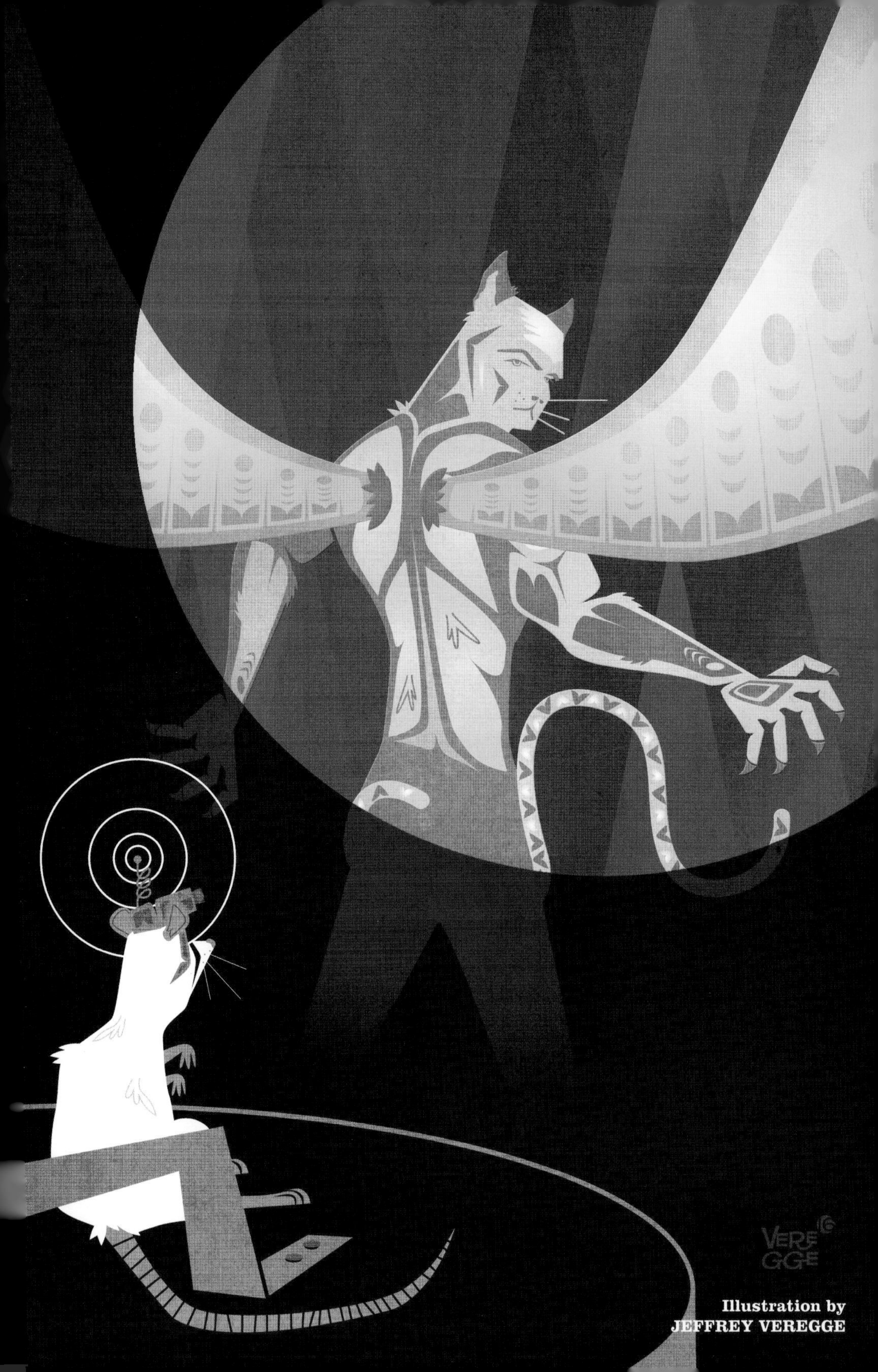
VEREGGE

Illustration by
JEFFREY VEREGGE

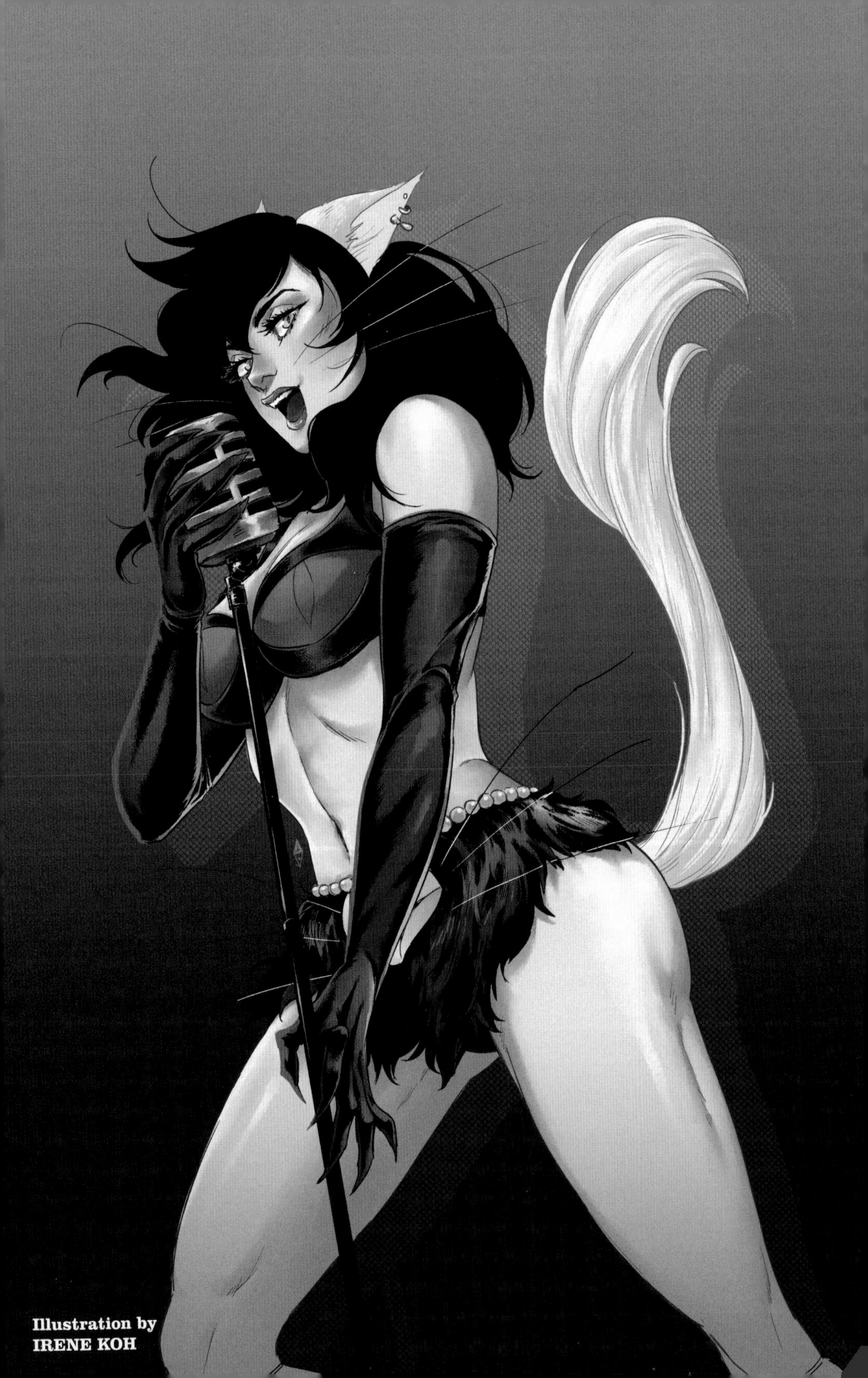

Illustration by
IRENE KOH

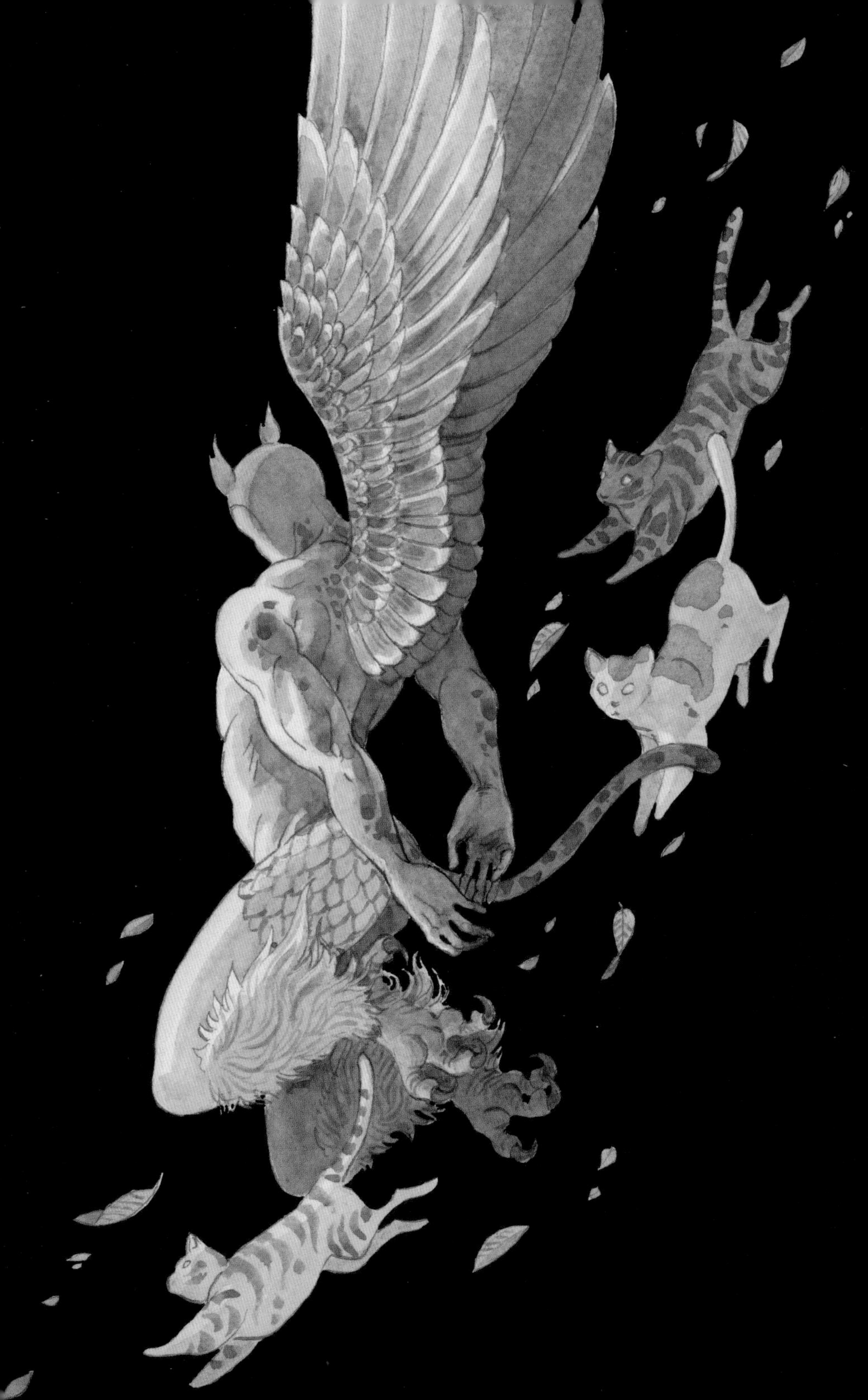

Illustration by
RENEE NAULT

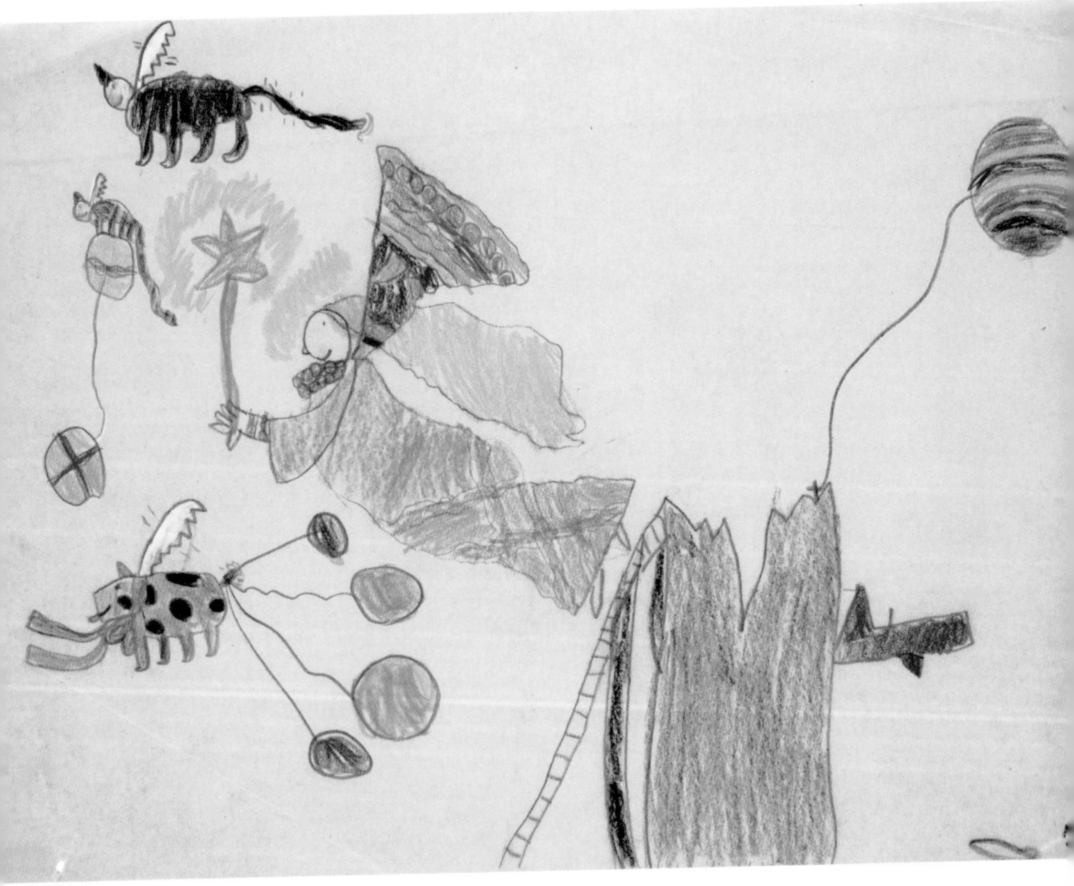

Margaret Atwood: The deep origins of Angel Catbird: Here is a drawing I did when I was six or seven, and drawing cats with wings.

SKETCHBOOK

Notes by
Johnnie Christmas

Character design for this volume's fierce
new warrior, Atheen-Owl.

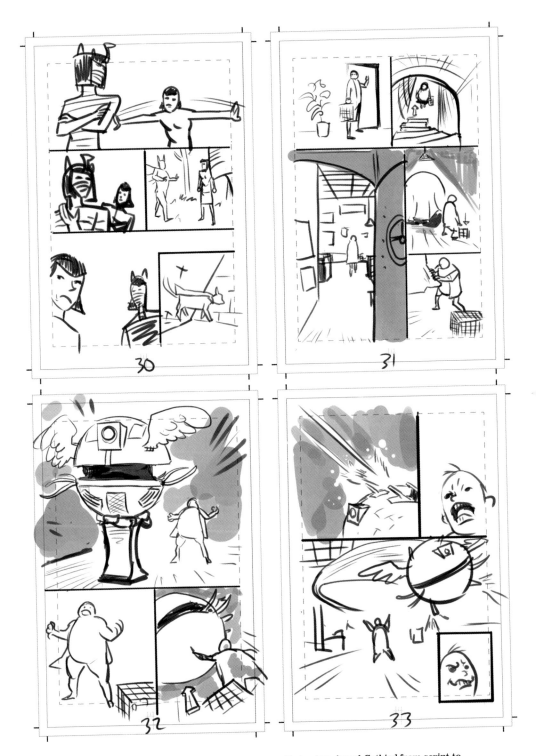

Here is a look into my part of the process of bringing *Angel Catbird* from script to page. I start with thumbnail drawings that show placement and page composition. I send these over to Margaret and our editors, Daniel and Hope, for feedback.

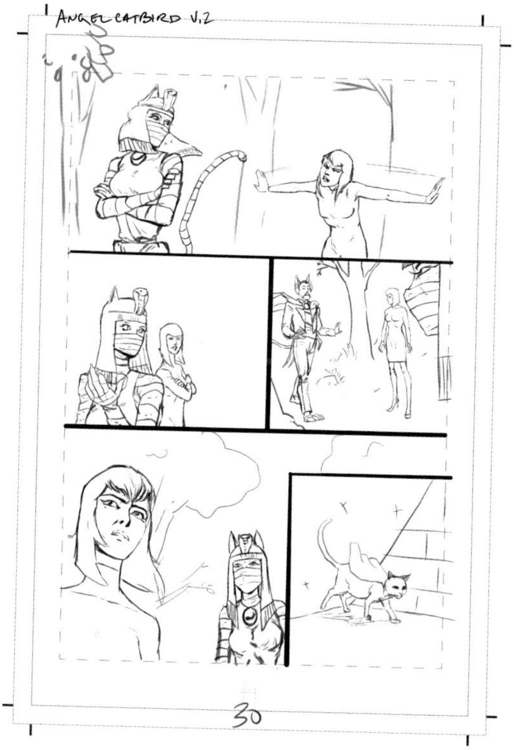
ANGEL CATBIRD V.2
30

Pencils are then drawn digitally and . . .

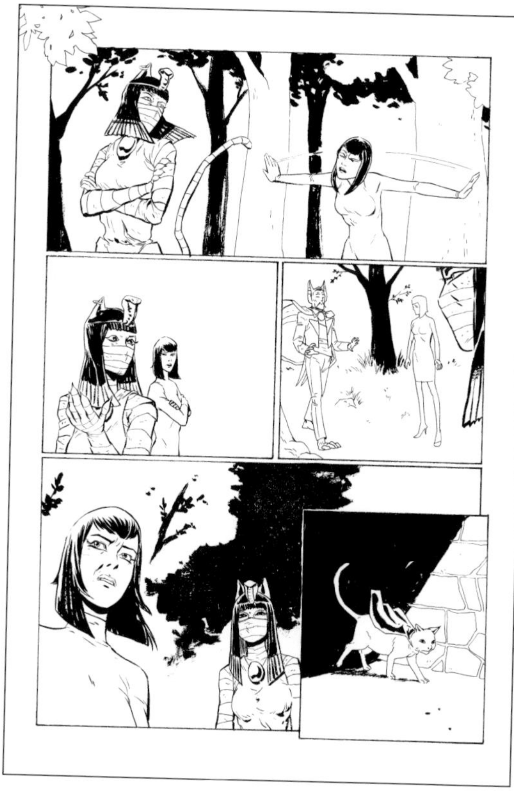

. . . final drawings are done in ink, with a watercolor brush. Details are added, and the drawings are clarified.

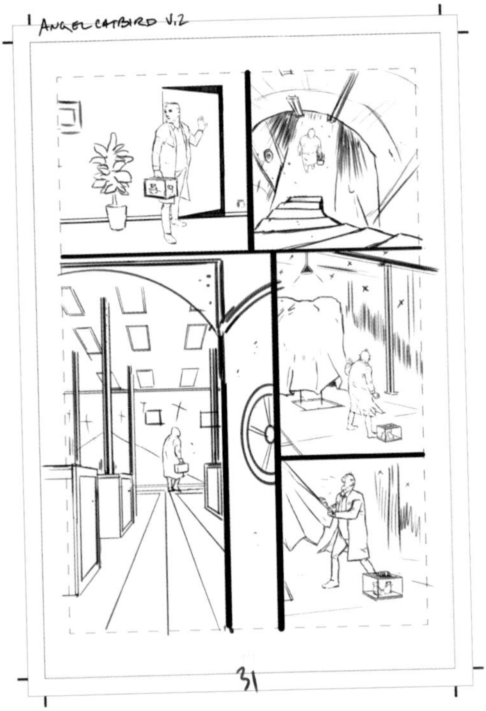
ANGEL CATBIRD V.2
31

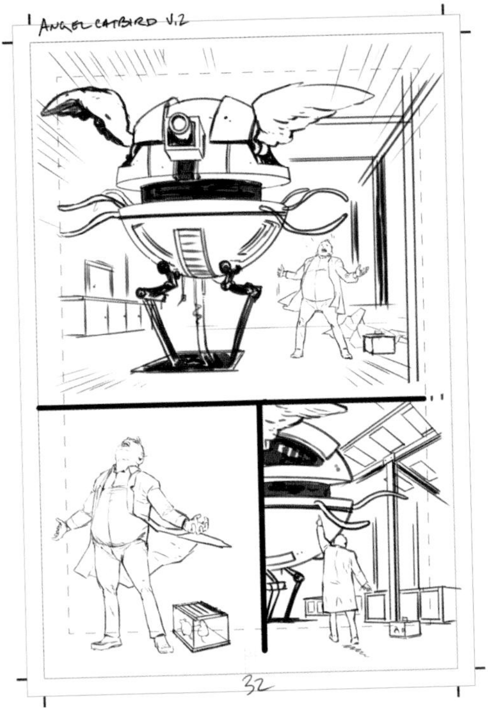
ANGEL CATBIRD V.2
32

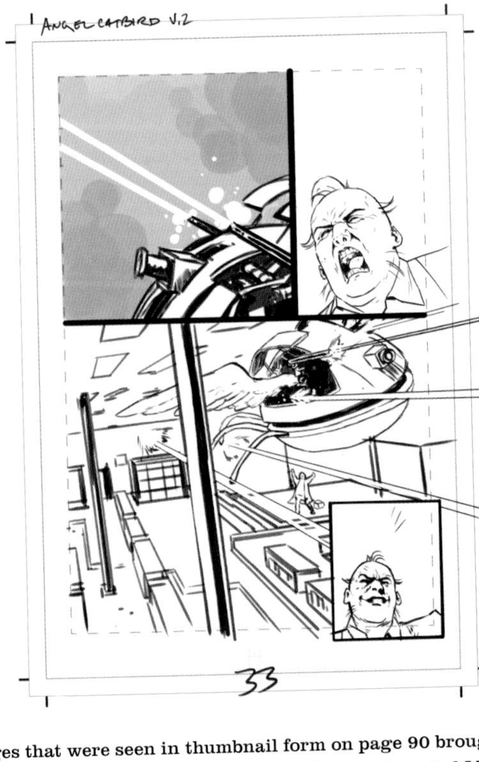
ANGEL CATBIRD V.2
33

Here we see the pages that were seen in thumbnail form on page 90 brought to the pencils stage. These pages didn't make it into the book in this form. Margaret wanted Muroid's lair to look more like a rat's underground nest than a science lab—a great idea. Also, the DRAT in this version is more sleek and mean. Margaret wanted it to look more like an actual cat toy . . . with laser beams!

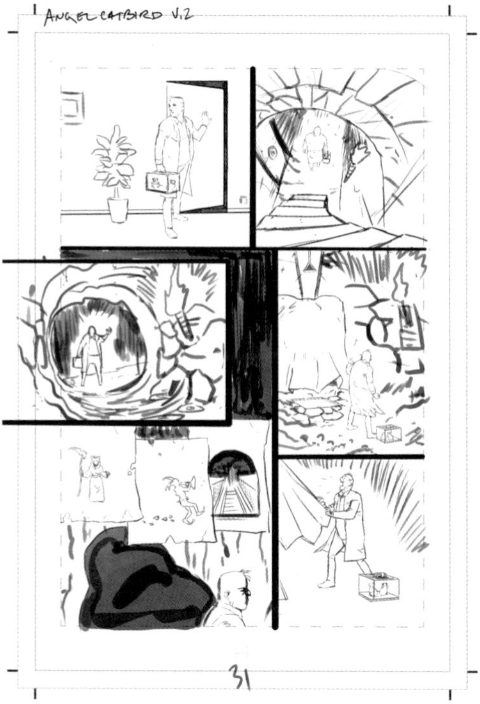
ANGEL CATBIRD V.2
31

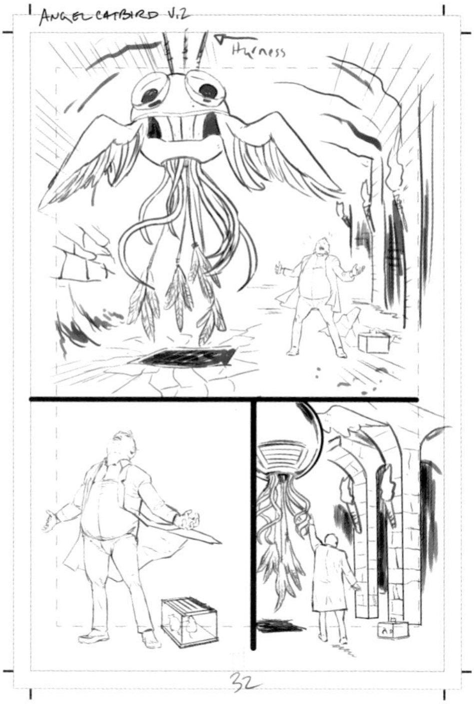
ANGEL CATBIRD V.2
Harness
32

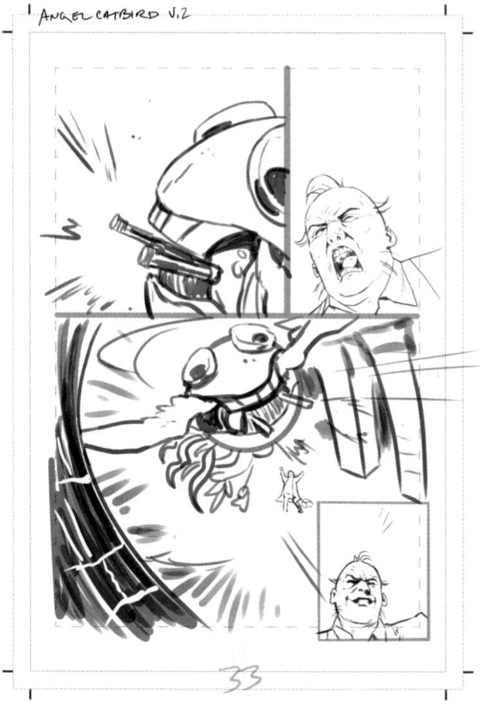
ANGEL CATBIRD V.2
33

Revised pencils for lair and DRAT.

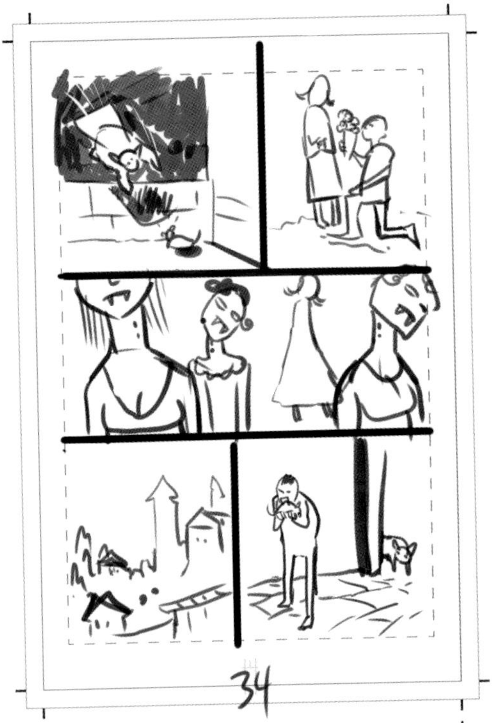
34

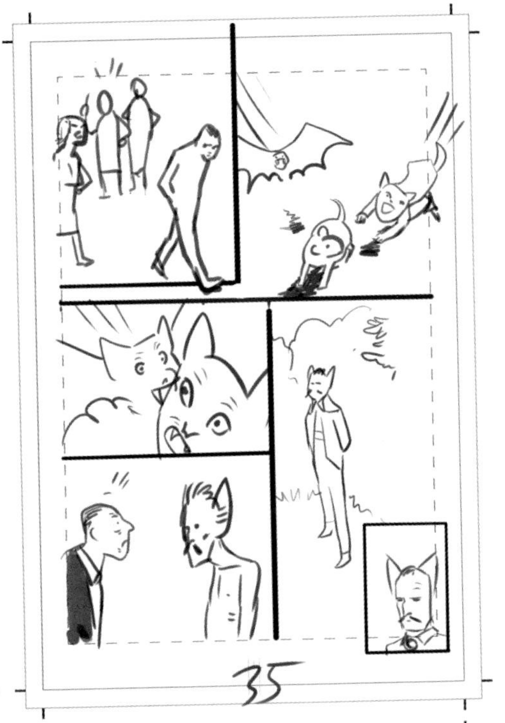
35

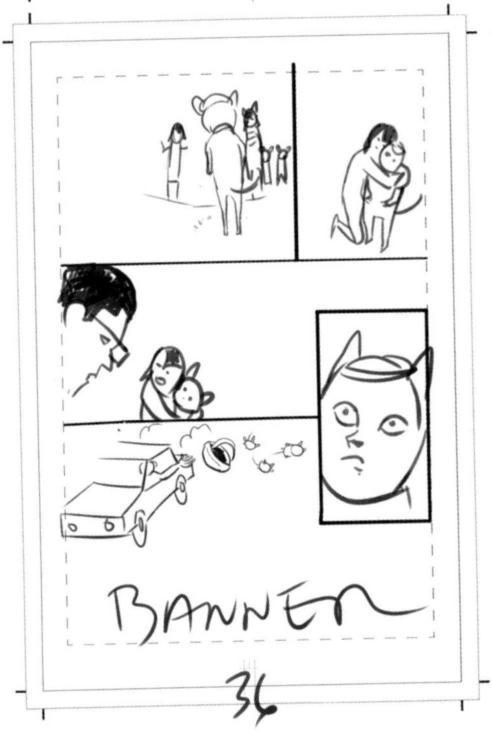
BANNER
36

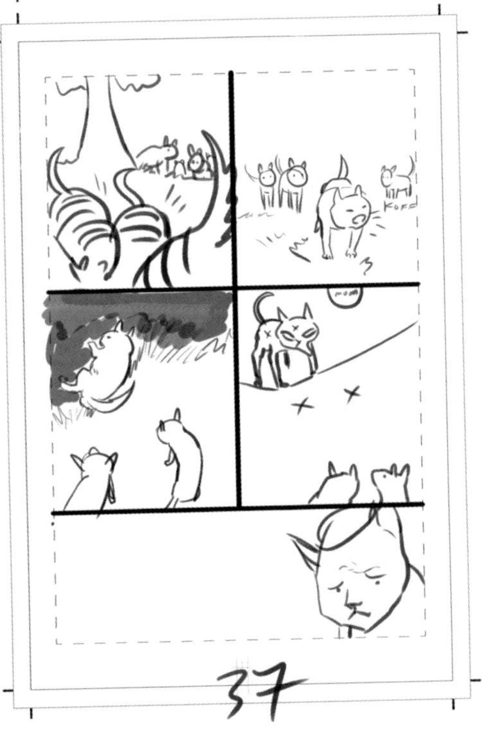
37

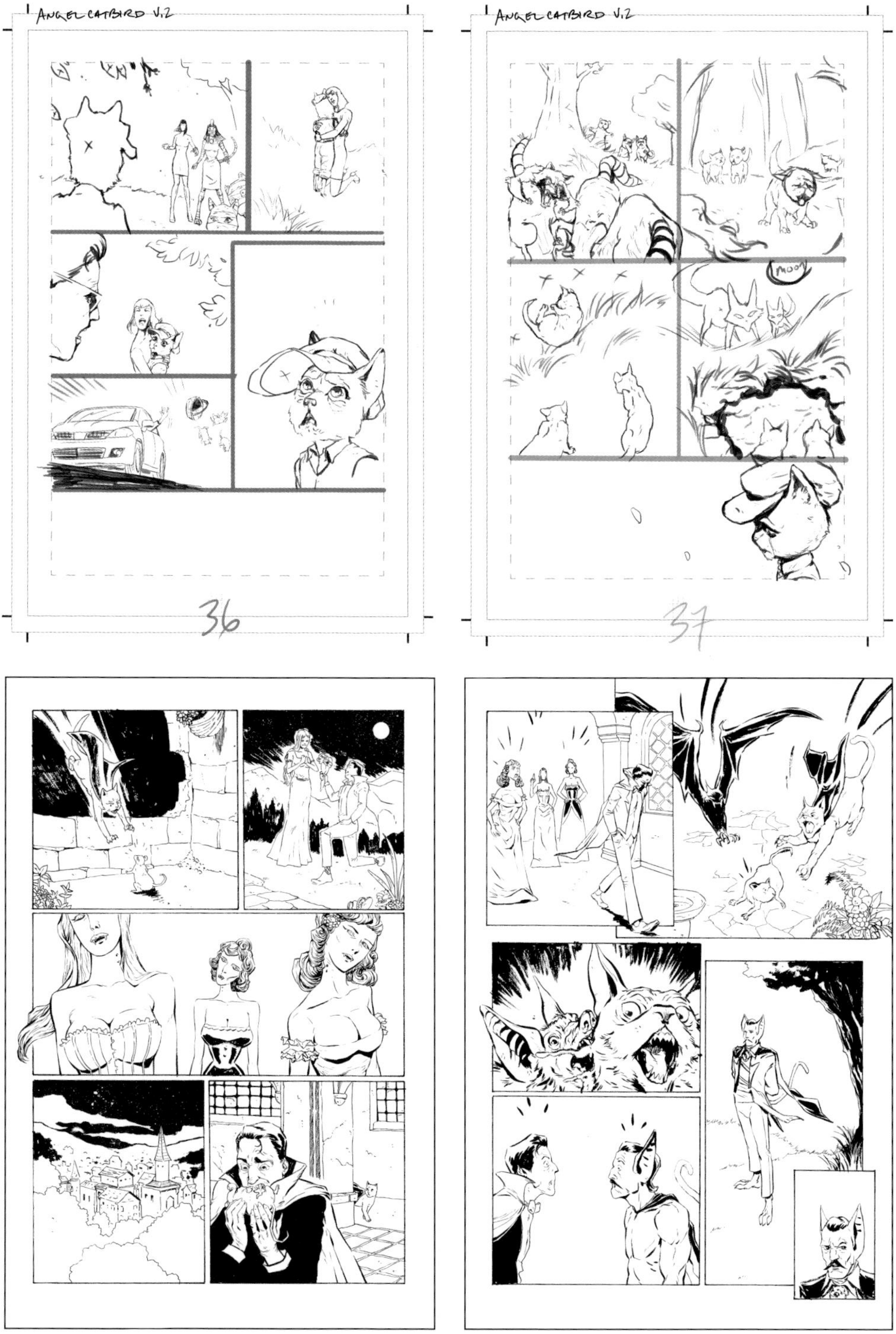
ANGEL CATBIRD V.2
36
ANGEL CATBIRD V.2
37

The origin of Count Catula, from thumbs to inks. I really enjoyed this sequence. Dracula seems so hapless.

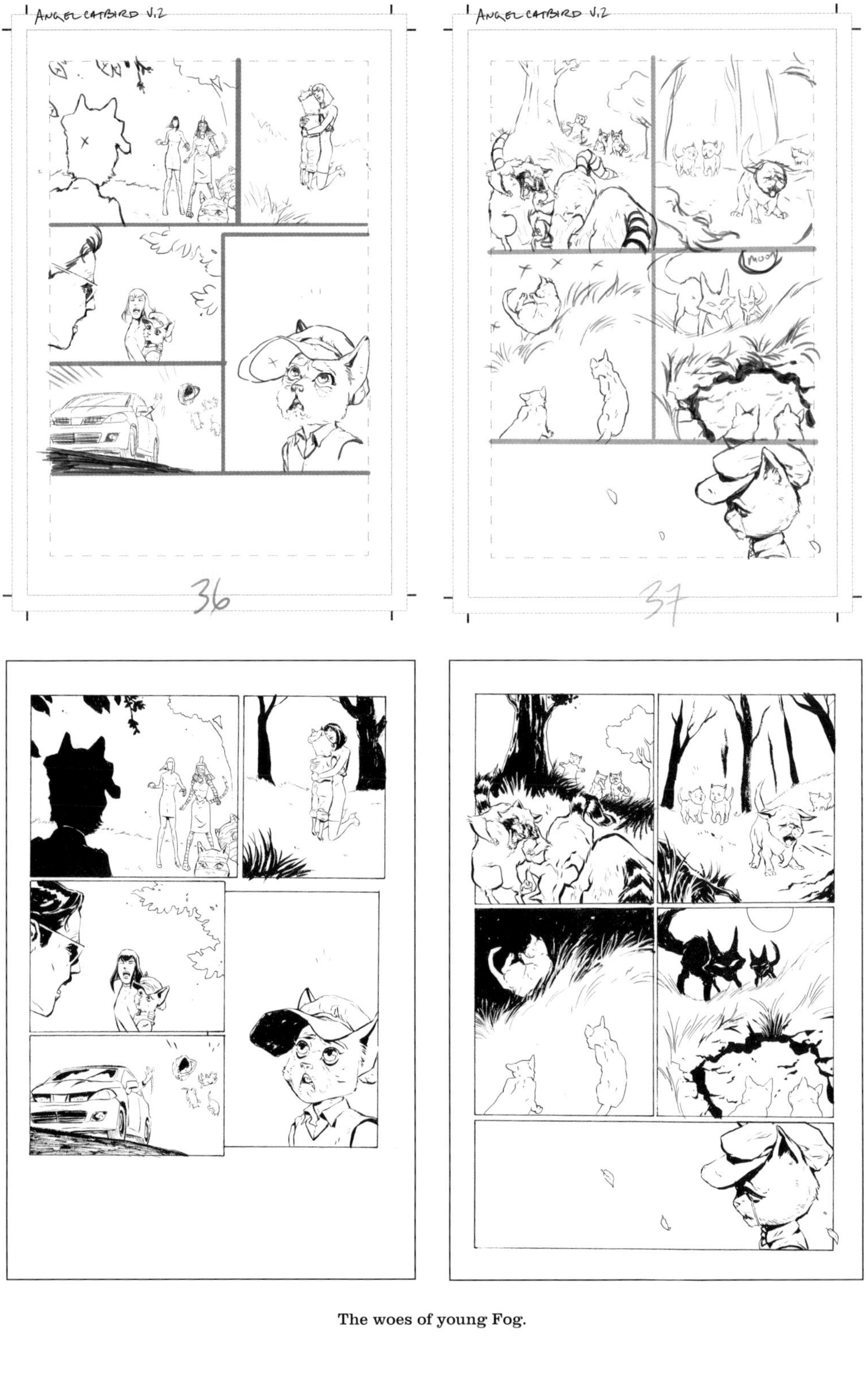
ANGEL CATBIRD V.2
36
ANGEL CATBIRD V.2
37

The woes of young Fog.

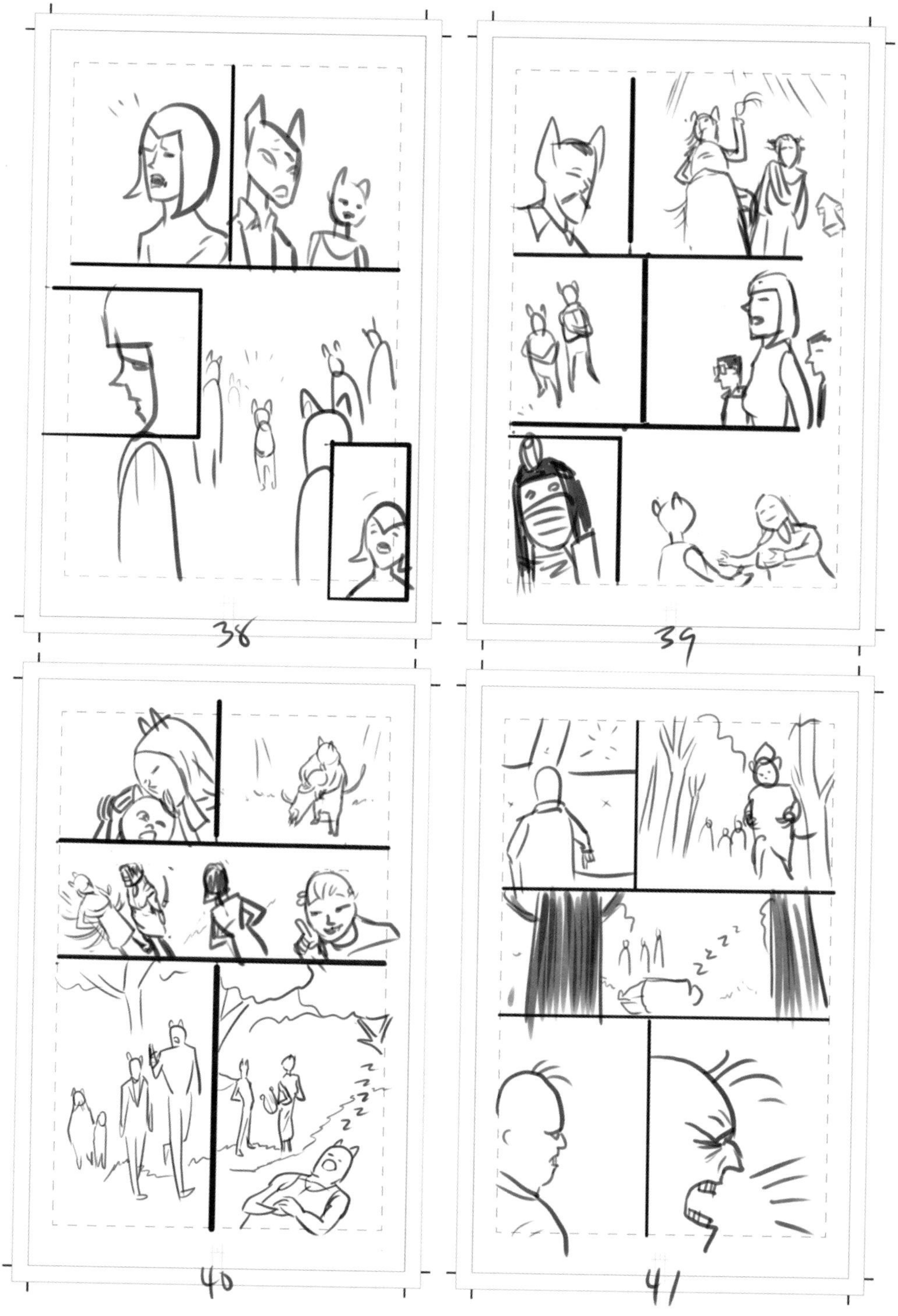
38
39
40
41

More thumbs.

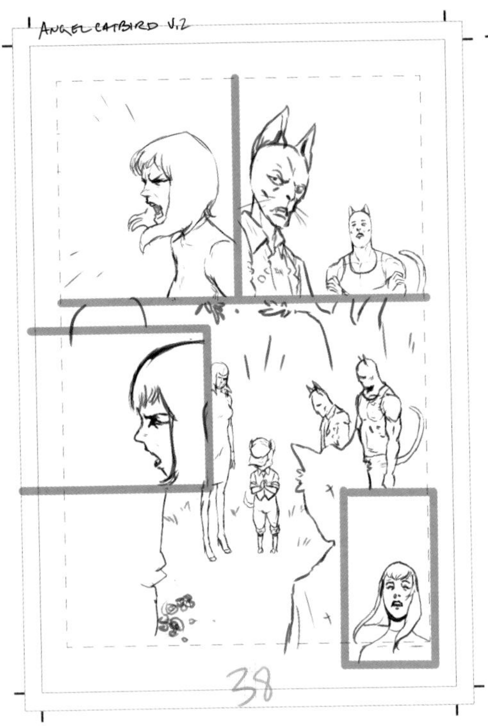
ANGEL CATBIRD V.2
38

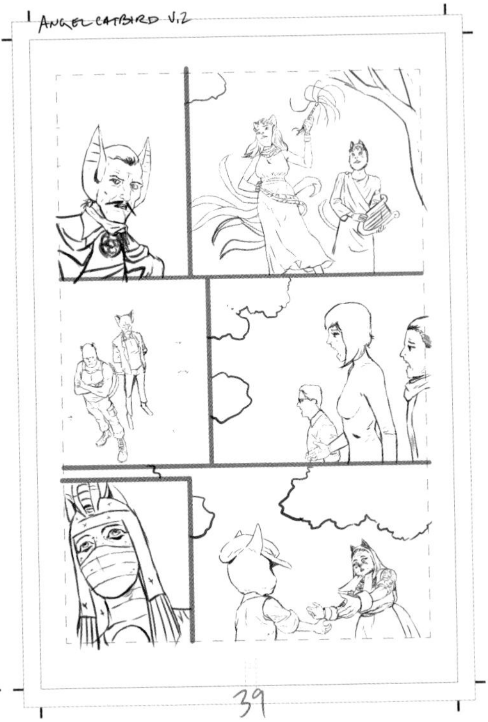
ANGEL CATBIRD V.2
39

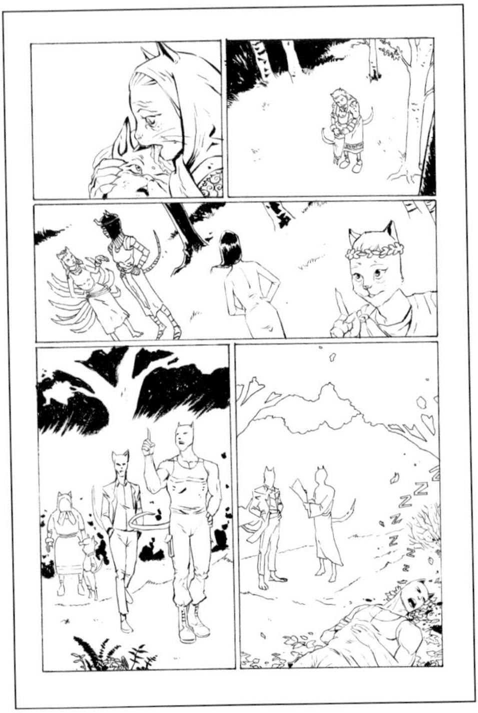

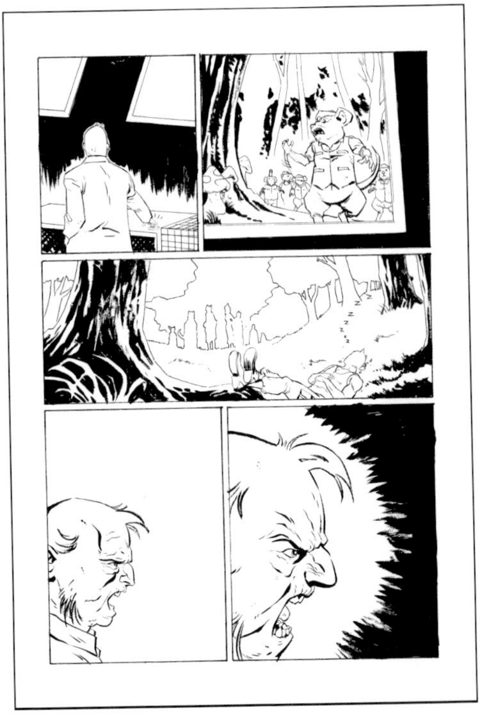

One of the unique challenges of drawing *Angel Catbird* is the many speaking roles on a given page. I need to find ways to position the characters in respect to their speaking order—in comics that are read from left to right, the person who speaks first is preferably on the left side of the panel.

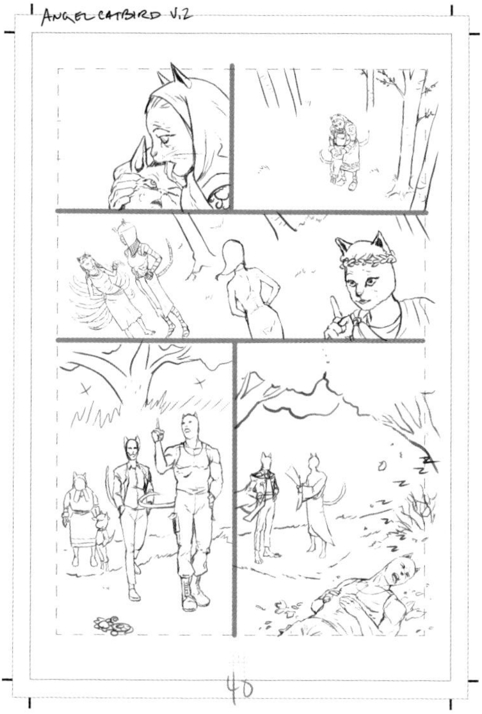
ANGEL CATBIRD V.2
40
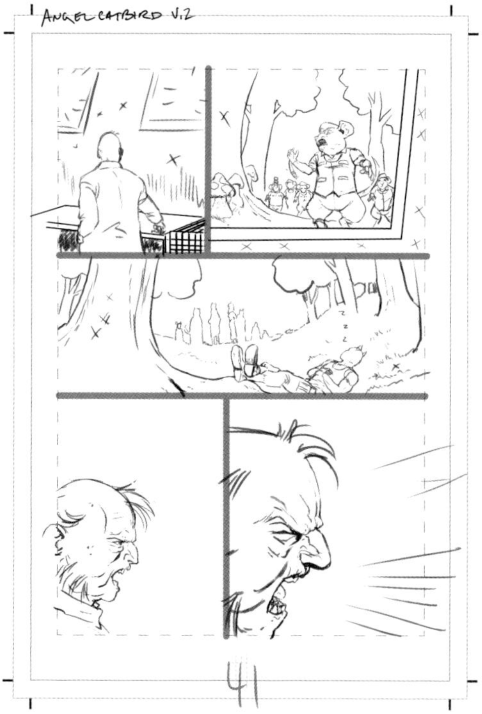
ANGEL CATBIRD V.2
41
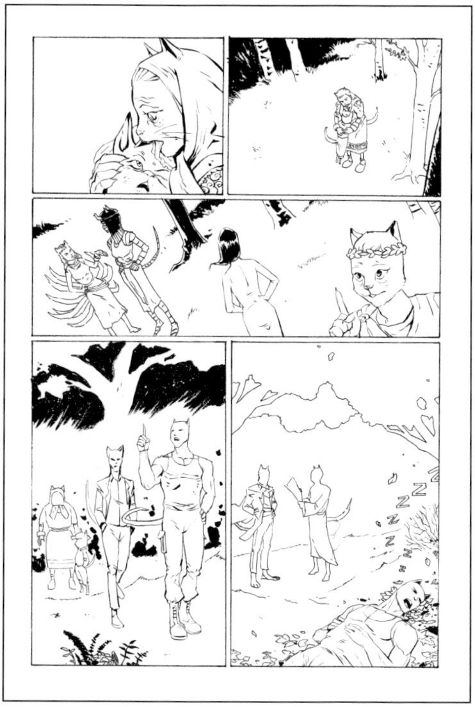
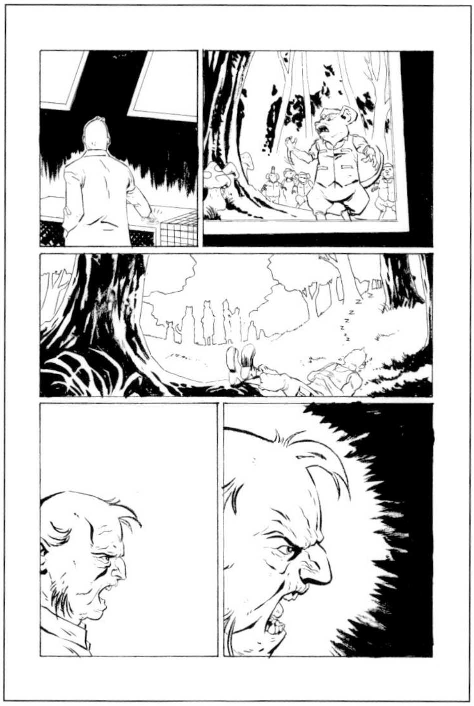

One of my favorite things to draw is Muroid emoting. He's always wound up. That makes for fun villainy.

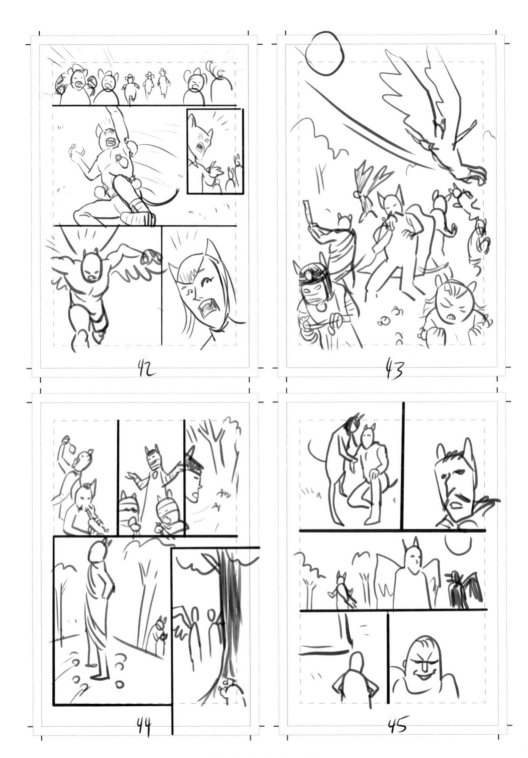

Thumbs for the big battle.

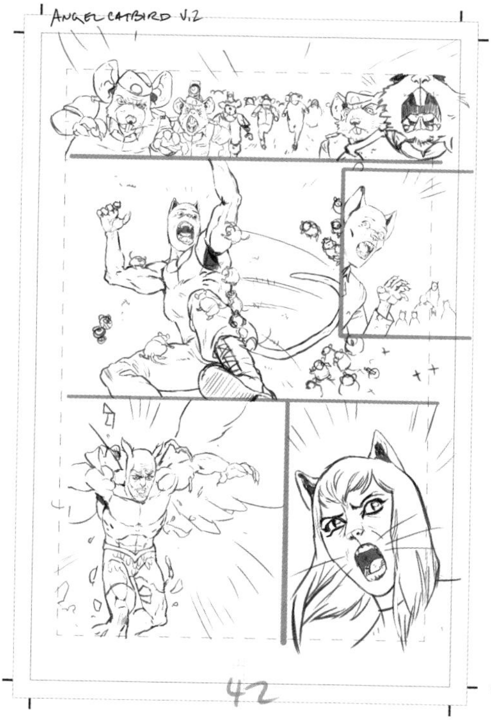
ANGEL CATBIRD V.2
42

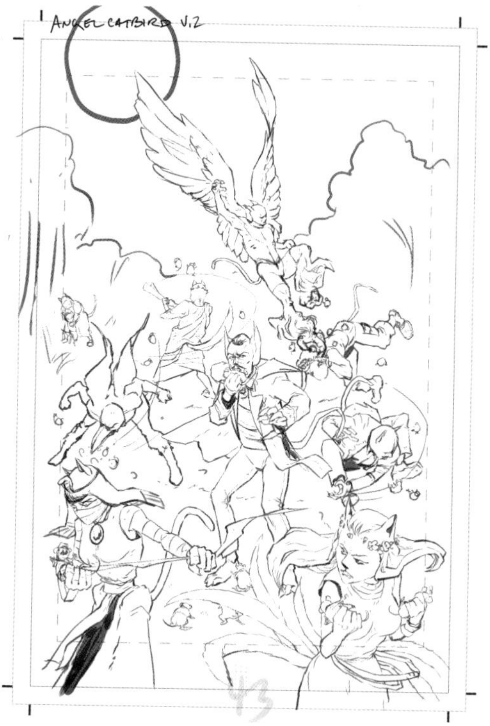
ANGEL CATBIRD V.2
43

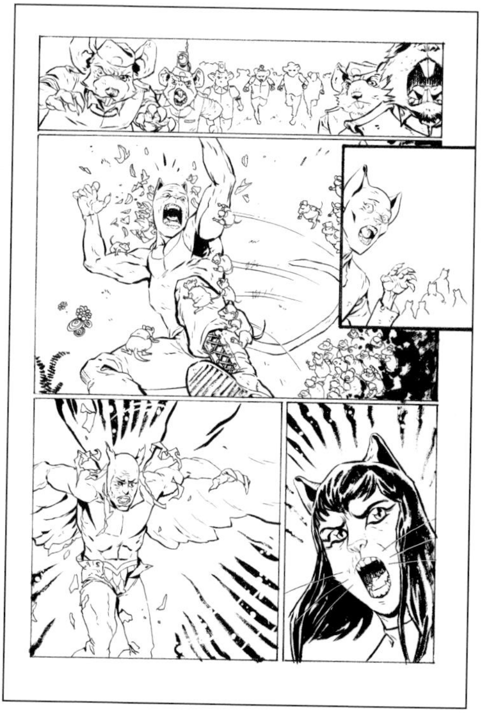

This fight scene was a favorite. Our heroes springing into action and giving the Murines what for.

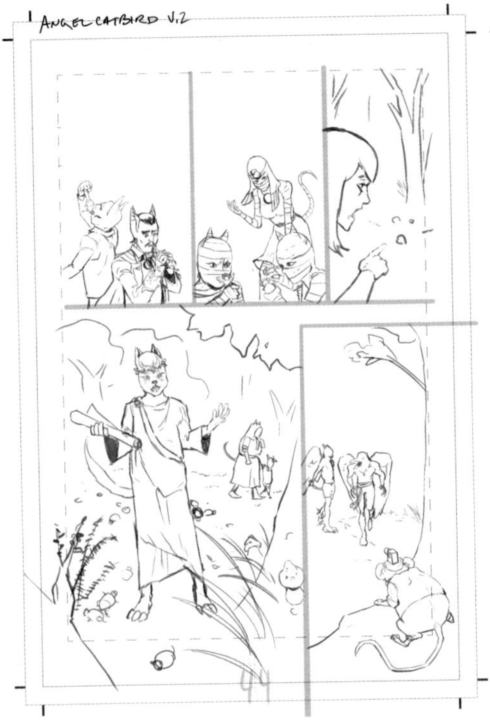
ANGEL CATBIRD V.2
44

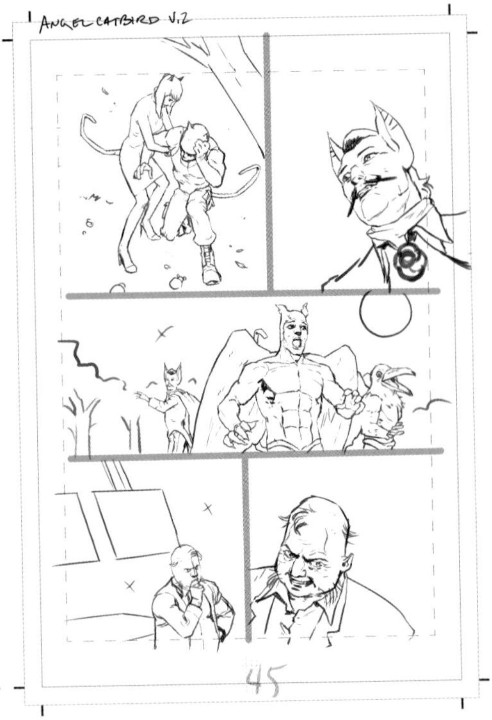
ANGEL CATBIRD V.2
45

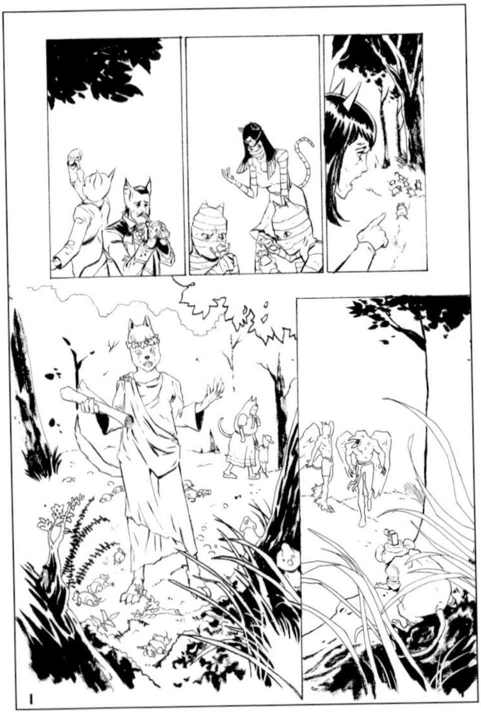

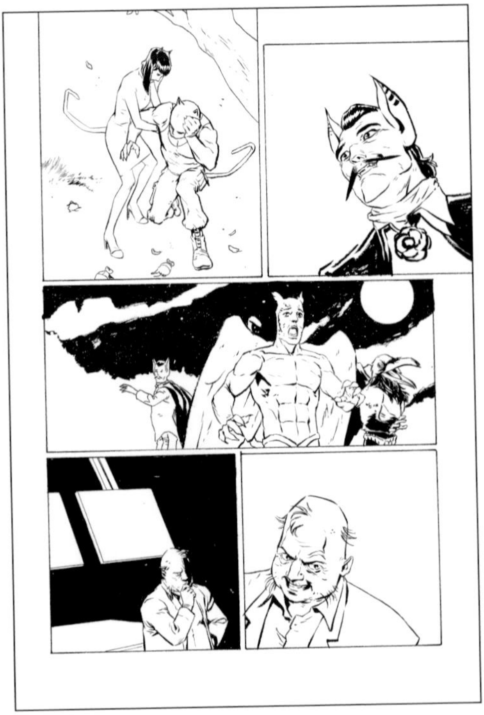

After inks are approved, they're sent off to Tamra. She then adds another dimension to the project with her coloring.

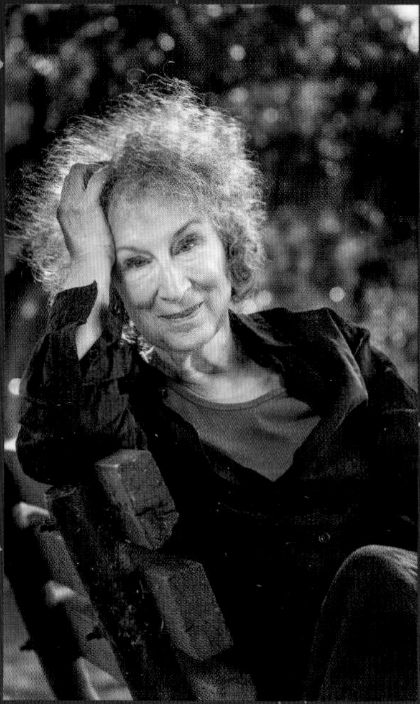
Photograph by LIAM SHARP

MARGARET ATWOOD

Margaret Atwood was born in 1939 in Ottawa and grew up in northern Ontario, Quebec, and Toronto. She received her undergraduate degree from Victoria College at the University of Toronto and her master's degree from Radcliffe College.

Atwood is the author of more than forty volumes of poetry, children's literature, fiction, and nonfiction, but is best known for her novels, which include *The Edible Woman* (1969), *The Handmaid's Tale* (1985), *The Robber Bride* (1993), *Alias Grace* (1996), and *The Blind Assassin*, which won the prestigious Man Booker Prize in 2000. Her latest work is a book of short stories called *Stone Mattress: Nine Tales* (2014). Her newest novel, *MaddAddam* (2013), is the final volume in a three-book series that began with the Man Booker Prize–nominated *Oryx and Crake* (2003) and continued with *The Year of the Flood* (2009). *The Tent* (mini-fictions) and *Moral Disorder* (short fiction) both appeared in 2006. Her most recent volume of poetry, *The Door*, was published in 2007. *In Other Worlds: SF and the Human Imagination*, a collection of nonfiction essays, appeared in 2011. Her nonfiction book *Payback: Debt and the Shadow Side of Wealth* was adapted for the screen in 2012. Ms. Atwood's work has been published in more than forty languages, including Farsi, Japanese, Turkish, Finnish, Korean, Icelandic, and Estonian.

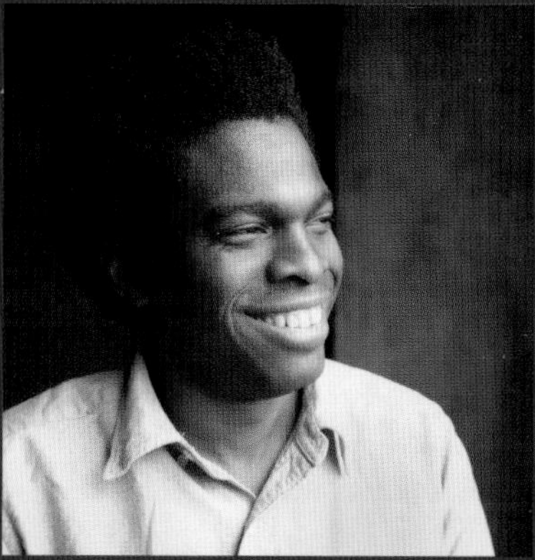
Photograph by AVALON MOTT

JOHNNIE CHRISTMAS

Johnnie Christmas was born in Río Piedras, Puerto Rico, and raised in Miami, Florida. He attended the Center for Media Arts magnet program at South Miami Senior High School and received a BFA from Pratt Institute in Brooklyn, New York, before going on to a career in graphic design and art direction. In 2013 he entered the world of comics as cocreator of the critically acclaimed Image Comics series *Sheltered*. He's also the creator, writer, and artist of *Firebug*, serialized in *Island*, also published by Image Comics. His work has been translated into multiple languages.

Johnnie makes Vancouver, BC, his home.

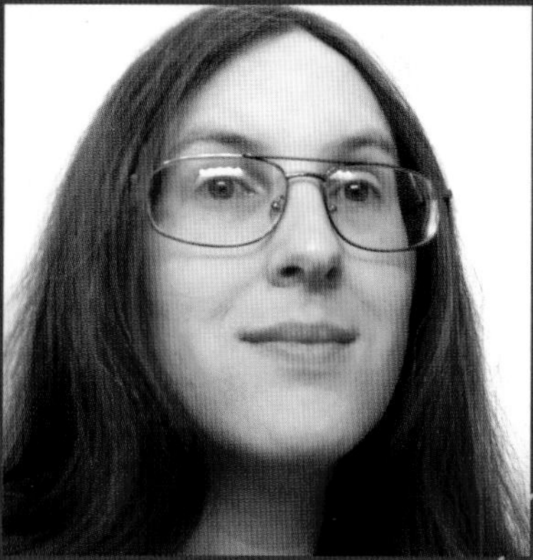

TAMRA BONVILLAIN

Tamra Bonvillain is originally from Augusta, Georgia, and took an interest in art and comics at a young age. After graduating from the local Davidson Fine Arts Magnet School in 2000, she majored in art at Augusta State University. She later attended the Joe Kubert School, and upon graduating in 2009, she began working full time as an assistant and designer for Greg Hildebrandt and Jean Scrocco's company, Spiderwebart. During this time, she also began to take on work as a comics colorist, eventually leaving the company to pursue a career in the comics industry full time. In the years since, she has worked for many major comic publishers, including Dark Horse, Dynamite, Boom, Image, and Marvel. She is currently the colorist for *Rat Queens*, *Wayward*, and several other titles.

AS SEEN ON

A daily dose of fantasy is better than reality.

As cat owners, we can provide our cats with engaging entertainment options that have a positive plot-line. Keeping cats from roaming freely outdoors protects both our cats and the birds they love to watch.

By keeping your cat safe, you've taken an important first step. Celebrate by joining our growing movement.

Learn more & take the pledge at www.catsandbirds.ca

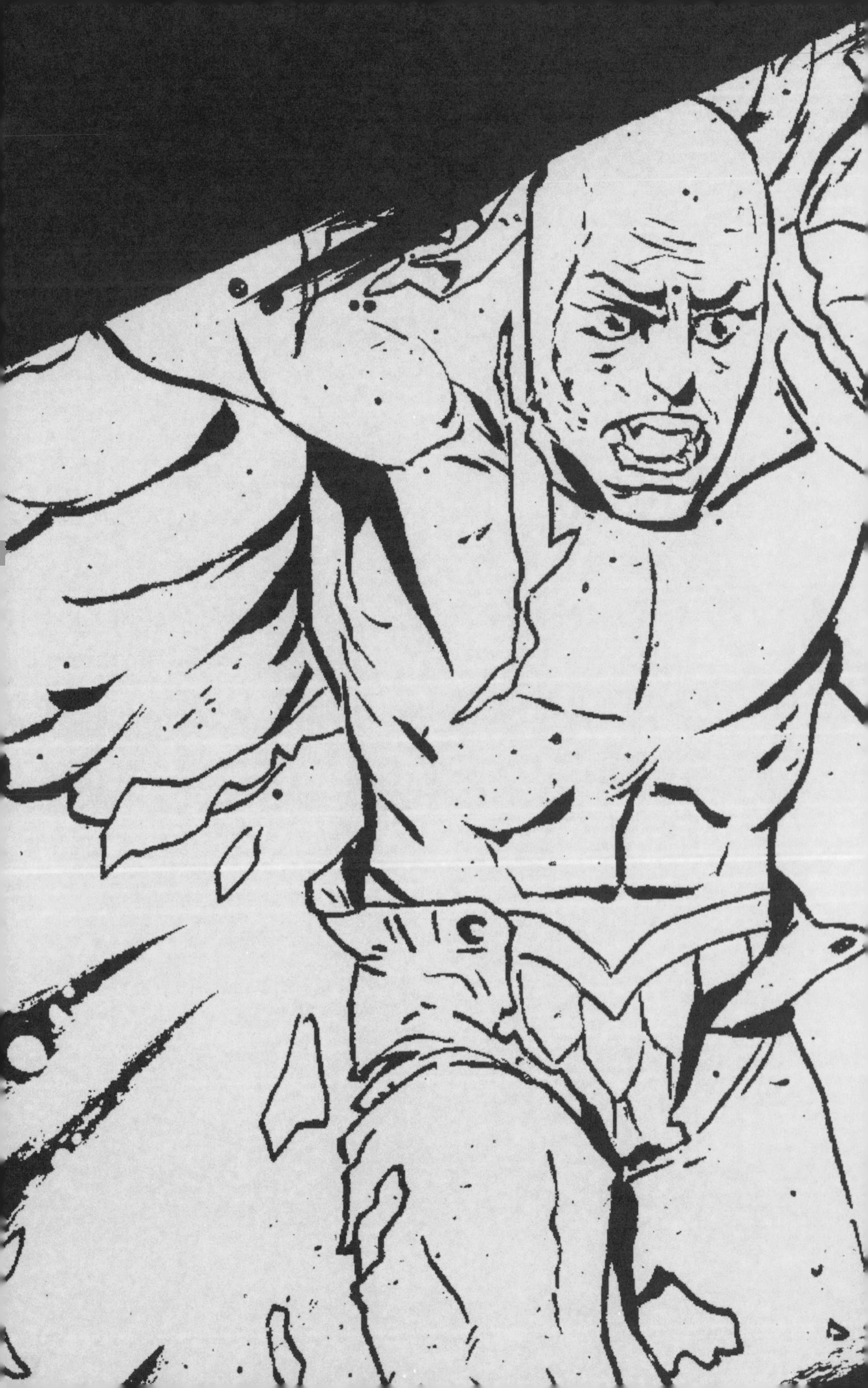